WE'LL MEET AGAIN

Philippa Carr, who died in January 1993, was also known to millions as Victoria Holt and Jean Plaidy, and was one of the world's best-loved writers of romantic fiction. She described her bestselling 'Daughters of England' series as follows:

'Philippa Carr comes between Jean Plaidy and Victoria Holt. Jean Plaidy is writing authentic history in the form of the novel, Victoria Holt writes mystery and suspense with a strong dash of romance; but Philippa Carr, while giving a truly historical background, does not allow the history to overwhelm the story. The main concern of these books is what is happening to the people and to bring in the historical content only to show its effect on their lives.

'But the chief idea behind them all is to give readers those unputdownable stories about characters whom they can love or hate (in other words, characters in whom they can believe), and in which the historical content can be picked up as a bonus. They are first and foremost entertainment.'

PHILIPPA CARR

We'll Meet Again

HarperCollins*Publishers*,
77–85 Fulham Palace Road,
Hammersmith, London W6 8JB

This paperback edition 2008

1 3 5 7 9 8 6 4 2

First published in Great Britain by
HarperCollins*Publishers* 1993

Copyright © Mark Hamilton as Literary Executor
for the Estate of the Late E.A.B. Hibbert

ISBN 978 0 00 784145 5

Set in Linotron Sabon by
Hewer Text Composition Services, Edinburgh

Printed and bound in Great Britain by
Clays Ltd, St Ives plc

All rights reserved. No part of this publication may be reproduced, stored in a retrieval system, or transmitted, in any form or by any means, electronic, mechanical, photocopying, recording or otherwise, without the prior permission of the publishers.

This book is sold subject to the condition that it shall not, by way of trade or otherwise, be lent, re-sold, hired out or otherwise circulated without the publisher's prior consent in any form of binding or cover other than that in which it is published and without a similar condition including this condition being imposed on the subsequent purchaser.

CONTENTS

Violetta

The Night Comers

On that March morning, I arose at dawn. I had slept little during the night. Old Mrs Jermyn had given a dinner party at Jermyn Priory to celebrate my engagement to her grandson – though perhaps it could scarcely be called a celebration in every way as Jowan was to leave for the Front the following day.

I had known he would ask me to marry him from that September day soon after war had been declared and he told me he was going to join the Army.

We had been drawn to each other since our first meeting when, trespassing on Jermyn land, I fell from my horse and he came along to rescue me. One might say that that was the beginning of the end of the feud between the Tregarland and Jermyn families. I was not, however, a Tregarland, my connection with the family being only through my twin sister, Dorabella, who had married into it and whom I was visiting at the time.

Not that Jowan was concerned about the feud. He laughed at it as a piece of nonsense beloved and preserved by the local people. Yet it had kept the families apart for many years – and now here we were, about to be joined in holy matrimony.

As soon as the war was over we were to be married.

'Another six months perhaps,' said Jowan. 'Maybe earlier.'

Sometimes it seemed to me that Jowan went through life taking what was and making it acceptable. Perhaps that was why he had been such a great help to me during the terrifying time through which I had passed.

Jowan had been brought up by his grandmother, for his mother had died when he was very young; he had inherited Jermyn Priory only a few years ago. His somewhat dissolute uncle had neglected the property, and since Jowan came into possession of it he had been attempting to put it in order. This he was doing with great success. He loved the house in which he had spent his early years before joining his father in New Zealand. His father had died before his uncle, and the estate had passed to Jowan.

I admired him for his single-minded purpose. So did his grandmother. She could never speak of him without betraying her pride.

'Jowan always sees what has to be done,' she told me. 'And he never says "can't". He loves this place as I did and it is right and proper that it should be his.'

That was why I was rather taken aback when he immediately decided to leave Jermyn's and go into the Army; but as he saw it, the war had to be won for the prosperity of the entire country and that included Jermyn's. He had an excellent manager who had a good assistant. They were both considerably older than he was and married with families to support. He could be better spared, he said, and he could trust them to look after the place in his absence.

'We'll settle the Germans in no time,' he said.

I had not seen much of him during the last months. There were his leaves, but they were never very long. This was one of the reasons why I stayed in Cornwall – another was that my sister refused to hear of my leaving.

Jowan had joined the Royal Field Artillery, whose training ground was at Lark Hill on Salisbury Plain, which was no great distance from Tregarland's.

How we cherished those leaves! How we planned for

the future! I felt uplifted by them while they lasted, but I was filled with foreboding after he had gone back to camp, knowing that the day of his departure was growing nearer.

Now it had come.

My parents were delighted with the match and Jowan's grandmother and I were already good friends. Everything should have been perfect, but how could it be with the menace of war hanging over us?

On that morning, when I was washed and dressed, it was still very early and I felt a need to be out in the fresh morning air so I put on a coat and went out to my favourite seat in the garden.

Tregarland's had been built on the top of a cliff, like a fortress overlooking the sea. The gardens stretched down to a beach which was originally a private one, but it had been necessary for there to be a right of way through it, otherwise people walking along the beach would have to scale the cliff to get round, and, as I had once discovered, when caught by the tide, this was almost an impossibility.

I sat down on a bench which had been placed conveniently among the flowering shrubs and looked across the sea. Very soon Jowan would be somewhere on the other side of that strip of water. Destination unknown. It was no use trying to delude myself that he was not going into danger.

I heard a footstep and, looking up, saw my sister, Dorabella, coming towards me. She was smiling.

'I heard you,' she said. 'I looked out of my window and there you were. So I followed.'

'It's very early,' I said.

'The best part of the day, I've heard. What's the matter, Vee?'

She occasionally used the shortened version of my name, which was Violetta; and this morning there was a note of tenderness in her voice. She knew what I was feeling.

Dorabella and I were not identical twins, but there was a firm bond between us. She had once called it 'the Gossamer Cord'.

It was strong, she had said. She believed it was unbreakable, but so fine that no one knew it was there except us. But it always had been and it always would be. I think she was right in that.

She was rather frivolous and charming; I was reckoned to be the sensible, practical one. There was about her a misguiding air of fragility which had always appealed to the opposite sex. I had always been conscious of her superior attractions but never – or possibly rarely – jealous.

When I considered where her impulsive actions had led her, I was fearful for her and I felt sure that the most recent one must have had a lasting effect on her. She had rashly married Dermot Tregarland, and so set in motion consequences which had affected us all deeply. In fact, but for that marriage, I should never have met Jowan. I should not have been sitting in this place at that moment.

I glanced at her. Yes, what had happened had had a sobering effect even on her. I was afraid for her, but whatever she did, I would never stop loving her. Nothing could change that.

She took my hand and said: 'Don't worry. He'll be all right. I know it in my bones. He's a survivor. I'm one myself and I recognize a kindred spirit.'

'You're certainly right about yourself,' I said.

She looked at me ruefully, telling me with her eyes that she was sorry for all the anxiety she had caused us. I had forgiven her, as our parents had.

'Of course I am,' she said. 'The war will soon be over. He'll be back . . . a hero. There will be wedding bells. The gathering of the clans. That stupid feud between Tregarland

and Jermyn at an end for ever. It was all rather ridiculous, wasn't it?'

'And you, Dorabella, what shall you do? Shall you stay at Tregarland's?'

She was thoughtful, so I knew the idea of getting away had occurred to her.

'It will be different,' she said. 'You'll be the Lady of Jermyn Priory.'

'That is old Mrs Jermyn.'

'Oh, she will graciously step aside. She is so pleased that you are going to marry her bonny boy. When this miserable war is over, I think I shall be able to bear it if you are not far away. We're all living in a sort of limbo now, aren't we? Nobody can make any plans. We don't know what will happen from one minute to the next. This war . . . how long do you really think it's going on?'

'I don't know. We're constantly hearing that we are doing well, but the Germans seem to be very strong. It is difficult to know whether we are hearing everything and if things are being kept from us.'

'You are getting morbid, Vee.'

'I like to know the truth.'

'Ignorance is bliss, remember.'

'Less so when the truth is forced upon us, as it could be in some circumstances.'

'Snap out of it! I know Jowan's going and you are naturally worried, but we are here together. I can't tell you how pleased I am about that. The best thing for me is that you and I will be neighbours. Think of that.'

'And you have Tristan.'

'Auntie Violetta has a proprietary interest and Nanny Crabtree believes, I am sure, that he is more hers than mine. I wonder if that child realizes how many lay claim to him. I pick him up and Nanny Crabtree thinks I am going to drop him.' She was sober suddenly. 'After what happened, she probably feels I'm not to be trusted. It was she – and you – who saved him from Mad Matilda when I was not there . . . as I should have been.'

'It's all in the past.'

'Is it? Don't you think the things we do . . . the really important things . . . never really go away? They leave their effect behind for ever after.'

'You have to stop thinking like that.'

'I do most of the time, but it comes back and haunts me. I went off with a lover. I left my husband and child . . . and now I'm back. My husband died, my child might have been murdered but for you and Nanny Crabtree. You see how it feels sometimes.'

'As long as you have learned your lesson . . .'

Her mood changed and she burst out laughing.

'I can't help it,' she said. 'Always the same old Violetta. Preaching the truth, grappling heroically with the problems of the wayward twin – and never forgetting to point to the moral.'

'Someone has to do it with people like you around!'

'And you do. You always have. Don't think I forget. I don't ever. That's why I have to have you near me and if you are not there I get a bit panicky. I shall never forget how you told the tale for me. And I know how you hate to lie. I had run away with my lover. I had staged my departure to look like a drowning . . . as though I had gone down to swim, leaving my wrap and slippers there on the beach . . . and all the time I was crossing the Channel on my way to Paris. And what did you do? You worked out a tale for me. I had gone swimming, lost consciousness, been picked up by a yacht. Oh . . . it was wonderful!'

'It was quite implausible and we should never have got away with it if war had not been declared just at that time, and if people had not had other things to think about than the wayward, wanton conduct of a frivolous young woman.'

'You are right, dear sister, as always. You see why I can't live without you? Even Tregarland's is tolerable because you will be my neighbour when you marry your Jowan. Your name Jermyn, mine Tregarland. It worked out quite neatly in the end, didn't it?'

'We can't know that yet.'

'You are determined to be morbid. Surely one of your maxims tells you that is not very helpful.'

'I just want to face facts.'

'I know. But sometimes I feel the past will never go away. It's here in this house. Matilda Lewyth with her madness. She seems to be still here. And there is Gordon. How does he feel? His own mother a murderess . . . living out her life in an asylum . . .'

'Gordon is one of the most sensible men I know. He will see everything clearly as it really is. His mother wanted Tregarland's for him and she allowed that desire to become an obsession. The old man teased her. He was mischievous. He wanted to see how she would act. Well, he saw, and he wishes now that it was something he had never seen. He blames himself in a way – and he certainly did play a part in the drama. But it is over. Thank God Matilda was prevented from harming Tristan. Matilda is now in safe care and Tristan has Nanny Crabtree and the whole household to dote on him. Even old Mr Tregarland thinks his grandson is the most wonderful child that ever was. Tristan is safe. We have to go on from there.'

'But I can't rid myself of guilt. I should have been there. Dermot should be alive.'

'Dermot was badly injured. He knew he would never recover. So he took his life. It's all in the past.'

'What do people think about me? They must suspect.'

'They don't think much about you. They are concerned

with more important matters. What is happening on the Continent, for instance. Where will Hitler turn next? We are at war. The actions of Mrs Dermot Tregarland with a French artist are trivial compared with the affairs of Europe. They are prepared to accept your story of loss of memory, implausible as it is, because they are not really greatly concerned.'

'You are right,' she said. 'You are always right. And, best of all, you are here. You are going to marry Jowan Jermyn and the star-crossed lover of a hundred years ago can rest in peace. My dear sister Violetta came to Tregarland and set it all right.'

We laughed and sat in silence for a while. I drew comfort from her and I know she did from me. It is wonderful to have another human being who is so close to you as to be almost a part of yourself. It had been so from the beginning of our lives and would remain so.

She knew what I was thinking, as often happened. There had been few periods in our lives when we had been apart – the longest being when she had eloped with the French artist and had staged an 'accident' to cover up the truth.

I was convinced that she would never do anything so foolish again; but all through that time I had never believed that she was dead. I think it had taught her that she should never allow us to be parted again. It was one of those moments when there was no need for words.

'Let's go in to breakfast,' she said at length.

Breakfast at Tregarland's was a meal which extended over two hours so that we could take it according to our plans for the day. James Tregarland rarely appeared for meals nowadays. He had been greatly shaken by the death of his son and what had happened to his mistress-housekeeper. He was well aware that he shared some blame for that bizarre affair. It had affected us all, though it appeared least of all to have affected Matilda's son, Gordon. He was practical in the extreme and on him depended the prosperity of the Tregarland estate. He carried on as though little had changed. I had always known he was a remarkable man.

However, we rarely saw him at breakfast, and on that morning Dorabella and I were alone.

The post was brought in by one of the maids. There were letters from my mother – one for each of us. She always wrote to both, even though the contents were similar.

We opened them and I read:

My dearest Violetta,

Life is uncertain here and I am a little anxious about Gretchen. It is a miserable time for her. She is so anxious for her family in Germany. Goodness knows what is happening to them, and with Edward going overseas soon . . . Well, imagine, he will be fighting her fellow countrymen. Poor Gretchen, she is most unsettled and unhappy. You can imagine how it is with her. Of course, she has little Hildegarde. I am so pleased about that. The child is such a comfort to her.

She has been staying with us. It is not easy being in a country which is at war with her own.

I was wondering whether you would ask her down to Cornwall for a spell. I am writing of this to Dorabella, as it will be for her to give the invitation. Gretchen was always so fond of you two, and it would be good for her to be with people of her own age. Of course, it is difficult travelling in these days of blackouts and all that – especially with children – but if you could have her and little Hildegarde for a while, I am sure that would cheer her up.

Hildegarde would be company for Tristan, of

course, and I am sure Nanny Crabtree would be delighted to cope.

Poor Gretchen! People know she is German. Her accent, of course, and with Edward away . . . well, you can see how difficult it is.

Talk it over with Dorabella. I do hope you will have her.

I was sorry, and so was your father, that we could not be there for the engagement party. We are so happy about it. Both of us are so fond of Jowan. Your father thinks he is an excellent manager and we both know that you and he will be happy together. It will be so nice for you to be near Dorabella.

With lots of love from Daddy and me,

Mummy

Dorabella looked up from her letter.

'Gretchen,' she said.

I nodded.

'Of course she must come,' she said.

'Of course,' I echoed.

Gretchen arrived about two weeks later. Dorabella drove to the station to meet her and I went with her.

I could see that Gretchen was a little distraught. She was as anxious for Edward as I was for Jowan, and neither of us could get any news of what was happening on the Front. Moreover, she had the additional anxiety of her family in Bavaria, of whom she had heard nothing for a very long time.

Little Hildegarde was an enchanting child. Tristan would be three years old in November and Hildegarde was about five months younger. She was an only child, dark like her mother, and had none of Edward's fairness.

Nanny Crabtree pounced on her with glee, and, as for Tristan, he was obviously glad to have her company.

Nanny Crabtree was at this time in a state of mild rebellion because of what she referred to as 'them imps upstairs'.

Because it was feared that the enemy would attack from the air, throughout the country children had been evacuated from the big towns and billeted in country houses. Two of these children had been assigned to us, and they were Nanny Crabtree's 'imps'.

Above the nursery were the attics, some of which were occupied by servants. They were large rambling rooms, oddly shaped with sloping roofs. Two of these were used as bedrooms for the young evacuees, who were two brothers from London's East End, Charley and Bert Trimmell, aged eleven and eight. Nanny Crabtree kept an eye on them, supervising their meals, making sure that they washed regularly and went to school in East Poldown with the others who had been billeted in the Poldowns or the surrounding neighbourhood. As the school in Poldown was not big enough to accommodate all the children, some rooms in the town hall had been given over to the schoolmasters and -mistresses who had accompanied their pupils; and all the newcomers could go to school with their friends.

We were sorry for these children, who looked very forlorn when they arrived with labels bearing their names and gas masks over their shoulders.

Gordon had gone down to the town hall where they were all assembled and come back with the Trimmells.

Nanny Crabtree's rebellion was only on the surface. Where children were concerned, she would be the first to care for them; but she always disliked change, so it was only a natural reaction.

'Poor little mites,' she said of the evacuees. 'It's no picnic for them being taken away from their homes. Still, they've got to learn the way we do things here and the sooner the better. I could murder that Hitler.'

When Charley came home with bruises on his face and a torn jacket, she was most displeased – particularly when he stubbornly refused to tell her how he had come to be in such a state.

'We don't have that sort of goings-on down here, you know. You have to behave. You're not in the back streets now.'

Charley remained silent, giving her that look of veiled contempt which she had seen before and which was the easiest way to irritate Nanny Crabtree because she could not complain of insolence when the boy had said nothing.

She told me about it afterwards.

'"Charley Trimmell," I said, "you'll have to learn, that's what you'll have to do." And there he stood, defying me . . . without saying a word.'

'It must be dreadful for those children,' I said. 'Just imagine, being taken away from your home and family and sent to strangers.'

Nanny nodded. 'Poor mites, but they've got to learn life's not all beer and skittles.'

I think she was rather contrite when she heard the way in which Charley had acquired his scars.

She heard it through Bert, with whom it was easier to communicate. He told her how the boys in East Poldown had set on him, teasing him. They were going to throw him into the river because he couldn't swim like they could, and he talked in a funny way. They were all round Bert, who shouted for his brother, and then Charley appeared – stalwart Charley – who dashed into the crowd of jeering boys and, according to Bert, gave them such a going-over that they all ran away, but only after inflicting some battle scars on the noble defender.

'Why didn't he tell me what it was all about,' demanded Nanny Crabtree, 'instead of just giving me that look of his?'

'Children don't always act reasonably,' I said.

After that there was a truce between Nanny and Charley. No. There was more than that. They were both Londoners; they shared a knowledge of the metropolis and they both had that special shrewdness and the unshakeable belief that, because they were citizens of the greatest city in the world, they could only feel a certain pity for those who did not share that privilege.

In due course, Charley talked to Nanny about his home. He would sit in her room with his brother Bert, for Bert never liked to be far away from Charley, and Nanny discovered that the boys' father was at sea. He had been a sailor before the war and had been away from home most of the time, a fact which had given the boys little cause for regret; their mother worked as a barmaid and, as she was out late at night, Charley had to look after Bert.

'They're not a bad pair,' said Nanny. 'There's a lot of good in Charley, and of course Bert thinks the sun, moon and stars shine out of his eyes. I'm not sorry we got them two. Could have done a lot worse.'

So, with Tristan and Hildegarde in the main nursery and the Trimmells in their attic rooms above, Nanny Crabtree, as she said, 'had her work cut out', and we all knew that her occasional murmurings against her lot were not to be taken seriously.

Meanwhile, the weeks were passing. The campaign in Norway was not going well and there was no news of Jowan. One day was very like another. Dorabella, Gretchen and I would take the children on to the beach and watch them building sandcastles. They liked to build close to the water and watch the incoming tide make moats in the channels round the edge of the piles of sand. It was pleasant to hear their shrieks of laughter.

When we went into Poldown the streets seemed crowded. We had a much greater population now. It was amusing to hear the mingling of the Cockney and Cornish accents. At first the children had some difficulty in understanding each other, but the original antagonism and suspicion of strangers, I fancied, had disappeared to some extent.

There was change and I often thought of the days when I had first come here before Dorabella's marriage, how quaint it had all seemed, and how my mother and I had laughed at the old Cornish superstitions. Then there had been my meeting with Jowan . . . I always came back to Jowan.

Sometimes Dorabella did not come to the beach and Gretchen and I would take the children. We could talk to each other freely. There was no need to hide our fears because we shared them.

Often I would catch her looking across the sea with that look of sadness in her eyes. Gretchen had suffered so much in her life that she expected disaster. It had been different with me. I had been brought up by doting parents in an atmosphere of love and tenderness. Life had gone smoothly until that visit to Bavaria. That had been the key that had opened the door leading to the drama.

How different everything might have been if we had never gone there! I might have known Gretchen, because Edward had already met her and been attracted to her; but Dorabella and I would never have met Dermot Tregarland. I should never have seen this place. I had to remember, too, that I should never have known Jowan.

It was hard to believe that it was only five years ago that we had sat in the café near the schloss and Dermot had sauntered by. An Englishman in a foreign land meets fellow countrywomen – and, of course, he stops to talk. That might have been the end of it. But then there was that fearful night when the Hitler Youth had invaded the schloss and tried to wreck it and insult its owners because they were of the Jewish race.

I should never forget it as long as I lived. Dorabella would remember it, too. It was horror such as I could not have believed existed. It was my first experience of mindless cruelty and bestiality. Never, never would I forget it.

Gretchen put her hand over mine suddenly.

'I know what you are thinking,' she said.

I turned to her and said: 'I wish we could get some news. What do you think is happening over there?'

She shook her head. 'I cannot guess. I just hope they will be all right. Perhaps we shall soon hear something.'

'I was thinking, if they fall into the hands of those people . . . those who were in the schloss that night.'

'They would be prisoners of war. But my family are Jewish. That was what that was all about. Dear Violetta, you can never forget it, can you?'

'No,' I said. 'Never.'

'I fear I shall never see my family again.'

'You have Edward now, Gretchen – Edward and Hildegarde.'

She nodded.

But the sadness stayed with her and I realized afresh that, because so much tragedy had touched her, she would always be fearful that she would lose the happiness she had gained.

We both sat for some time looking at the sea, thinking of our loved ones, until Tristan came up. He was near to tears because the handle had come off his bucket.

'Auntie Vee make well,' he said.

I took the bucket and saw that all that was needed was to slip the wire back into the loop. I did it with ease and Tristan smiled broadly, accepting my cleverness as something he had never doubted.

If only our problems could be so easily solved!

May had come. The weather was perfect. The Cornish countryside was at its best at this time of the year. The sea, calm and benign, seemed to caress the rocks as it crept up the beach at high tide.

The peaceful scene was in contrast to the apprehension in our minds. There was no disguising the fact that the war was not going well. There was no more talk of its being over in the next few weeks.

We had been driven out of Norway and it was clear that the storm was about to break over Western Europe. The Prime Minister, Mr Neville Chamberlain, had resigned and Mr Winston Churchill had taken his place. The retiring Prime Minister made a stirring speech in which he asked us to rally round our new leader. But when our newly-appointed Prime Minister spoke, he told us that he had nothing to offer, but blood, toil, tears and sweat, and that we had a grievous task before us and months of struggle and suffering.

I remember well listening to that speech. It did not contain lists of our triumphs. It came over as stark reality, and I think it was what we needed at the time. I still remembered parts of it through the years to come.

'*You say, what is our policy? It is to make war by sea, land and air with all the might and strength that God can give us; to wage war against a monstrous tyranny never surpassed in the dark, lamentable catalogue of human crime.*'

Then I was transplanted to that room in the schloss, and I remembered the look on the face of the young man who had led in his band of ruffians. It was dark, it was lamentable; it had never been surpassed in the catalogue of human crime.

'*And what is our true aim?*' went on the Prime Minister. '*It is victory . . . victory at all cost. Come, let us go forward in our united strength.*'

It was a taste of that inspiration which was to hold us up and give us courage through the dark years to come.

But at least now we were prepared for bad tidings which might come. And we needed to be. The news went from bad to worse. The Germans were advancing through Flanders while the sun shone brilliantly and the countryside seemed more beautiful than ever before.

In the first six months the war had taken on a meaning for us which we would never have believed to be possible. We ourselves were in acute danger and we could not evade the possibility that our precious island might be threatened.

And Jowan and Edward, all those who were in the thick of the fight, what of them?

Each day increased our gloom.

I felt an urge to be alone. I often took out Starlight, the mare I had ridden in those days when I used to go out and meet Jowan.

That was a May morning. In a week or two it would be June – and the perfect weather persisted.

I wanted to escape from the present. I liked to ride to those places I had visited with Jowan. I remembered our first meeting so well, when I had trespassed on Jermyn land. I rode to the field where I had fallen. There we had walked to an inn called The Smithy's into which Jowan had insisted on taking me for a brandy to steady me. The inn was so called because it was next to the blacksmith's shop.

How I longed to be back in those days!

As I was about to ride past, Gordon Lewyth came out of the blacksmith's shop.

'Good morning,' he said. 'What are you doing in this part of the world? No trouble with Starlight, I hope?'

'No,' I replied. 'I was just riding past.'

'I've taken Samson in. He's cast a shoe.'

'Are you going back now?' I asked.

'I thought I might have a light lunch and wait for him. Why not join me?'

I was poignantly reminded of that other occasion, only it was Gordon who sat opposite me now in place of Jowan. Mrs Brodie, the wife of the landlord, came to us just as she had on that other occasion. I remembered how interested she had been. The visitor who was the sister of the new Mrs Tregarland and Jowan Jermyn! A meeting of the enemy families! She would know now, of course, of my engagement to Jowan. Such matters would be frequently discussed in this place.

She said: 'Good day to you, Miss Denver, and Mr Lewyth. There's meat loaf. I can recommend it. They tell me it is one of my best. The best you can hope for these days, I'm afraid.'

'Would you like wine or cider?' asked Gordon.

I asked for cider.

'Any news of Mr Jermyn, Miss Denver?'

'I'm afraid not.'

'Well, they'll have their hands full over there, I reckon. They've got to send them Germans back where they belong to be. It won't be long now, you mark my words.'

I smiled at her. Gordon's eyes met mine and I was aware of his sympathy.

'She must notice the changes these days,' I said when Mrs Brodie had gone.

'As we all do.'

I could see the sadness in his eyes and for the moment I was back to that night in the nursery when Nanny Crabtree and I had prevented his mother from carrying out her obvious intention to murder Tristan. I remembered how, when we had called him in, he had stood there, stunned by the revelation.

I felt a deep sympathy for him, and I remembered with admiration how he had recovered from the shock and quickly taken charge of the situation, how stoically he had done what had to be done, how tender he had been towards his poor demented mother.

I heard myself saying: 'And how was she when you visited her?' before I realized we had not been speaking of her; but he showed no surprise. I suppose she was rarely out of his thoughts.

He replied: 'Her condition does not change much, though there are times when she knows me and at others . . .'

'I am sorry. I should not have spoken of it. It is very upsetting for you.'

'It does no good to keep silent,' he went on. 'It is something which is on our minds whether we talk of it or not.' He smiled at me. 'I can talk to you, Violetta. In fact, it helps in a way.'

I was a little taken aback. I had not thought of his needing help. He always seemed so self-sufficient. But how upsetting it must be, even to the most self-reliant person, to discover that his mother is a murderess.

'It is hard to see her so,' he went on. 'Her poor lost mind wandering, trying to grasp reality. And, Violetta, I can only hope that she never does. It is better for her to go on like this than remember the truth.'

I nodded. 'And she did it all for you, Gordon. All that plotting . . . all that obsession grew out of her love for you.'

'I do not forget it,' he replied. 'I never shall. If only she had confided in me. I hoped, with her, that my father would recognize me. It was true that I had improved the estate, that I was the one who cared for it. But my mother was not his wife, and there was Dermot . . . and then Tristan. I wanted a place of my own. I could have found something, I suppose. It would not have been an estate like Jermyn's or Tregarland's, of course. But there is something about a place of one's own, however small.'

'You are part of Tregarland's, Gordon. You love it. It has been your life.'

'If only . . .'

I touched his hand lightly.

'It is no use looking back. We have to go on, and we are in the midst of this dreadful war. None of us knows from one day to the next what is going to happen. It isn't going very well, is it?'

'Grim,' he said. 'The Germans are flooding into Holland and Belgium. Next it will be France.'

'They seem to be succeeding all along the line.'

'They were prepared. We were not. All during that decade when the Labour and Liberal parties and some Conservatives were preaching disarmament, Hitler was laughing at our blind folly and building up his weapons, waiting for the moment to attack. It came. They were ready and we were not.'

'But we are preparing now.'

'Ever heard of shutting the stable door after the horse has run away?'

'Yes. But we are going to fight now.'

'We shall succeed in the end, and I believe that, now we realize the danger, we are of one mind. But we have to suffer for the blindness of people in the past. But for them, there might not have been a war at all. If only we could go back and do it all again! What we can do is face the facts. If only I had been wiser, I might have seen what was happening to my mother. Alas, the power to see into the future is not given us. I think we should always be ready to look at the truth and not delude ourselves to gain a little comfort temporarily.'

'Is it really very bad, do you think?'

'As bad as it could be, short of defeat, I imagine. But there is a fine spirit in the country – no doubt of that, and when we have our backs to the wall we can stand up as well as any. But let's face it. The Germans have trumped up a story that Britain and France intend to invade Holland and Belgium, and Germany is going to "protect" them. The Dutch and Belgians have different ideas and are standing out against them, but, of course, they are small and unprepared and the Germans are well equipped and disciplined, preparing as they have been over the last decade. One can have no doubt that with little difficulty they will soon subdue them.'

'Our men are over there,' I said with a shudder.

Gordon's eyes did not meet mine.

'Oh, Gordon, what can be happening?' I asked.

'Those people are fighting for the homeland. That gives them extra strength,' he said. 'The tide will turn one day. Sometimes I feel I should be there, but we need to keep the estate going. Some of us have to stay. You will know, of course, that there is a fear that Germany might not only subdue the Netherlands, but France as well.'

'There is the Maginot Line.'

'That has not been tested yet, but the situation looks very bad. You know there is an organization being formed to protect our own country?'

'Is it the Local Defence Volunteers?'

'Anthony Eden is the new Secretary for War and he was talking about it the other day. You know what it means?'

'To protect us against invasion?'

'If France falls . . .'

'Surely that can't be!'

'As you say, there is the Maginot Line. But Belgium and Holland, in spite of the bravery of their people, cannot be a difficult conquest, and as France, like ourselves, was not prepared beforehand . . . we must be ready for anything.'

'Surely Hitler could never succeed in invading England?'

'It would not be easy. There is the Channel.'

'Thank God for the Channel.'

'Well, we are preparing now. That is why the Local Defence Volunteers are being formed. You know how I feel about being at home, so . . . I have joined.'

'I do know. But you could not have been spared, Gordon.'

'That was pointed out to me. So I have joined this new organization. It will be run like an army. I am to be in charge of our group in this area.'

'I am glad, Gordon. I know you will do it very well.'

'I hope it never comes to invasion. But perhaps it is best to be realistic and look on the dark side, as well as the bright.'

'I agree with you. Because we are preparing for an invasion, it does not mean that it will come.'

'The more prepared we are, the less likely it is to happen.'

I fell silent, thinking, as always, of Jowan and Edward who were out there. I tried not to imagine the hardships they might be suffering, what danger they were in. But that was not possible.

Gordon knew this. It was typical of him that he did not attempt to make light conversation as many would have done. He understood too well that that would not turn my mind from my anxieties. Instead, he went on to talk of the new organization and how enthusiastic were those men who were too old for, or were otherwise not eligible for, active service.

And when we came out of Smithy's, Samson was ready and we returned to Tregarland's together.

There is no need for me to say much of what happened during the rest of that beautiful May month. It is well known that disaster followed disaster. The Germans bypassed the much-vaunted Maginot Line quickly. They made their way across France and were in Boulogne by the last Sunday of the month.

We all went to church on that day. It was a day of prayer throughout the country and the Empire; and the King and Queen, with the Queen of the Netherlands, who had sought refuge in England when her country was invaded, attended a service in Westminster Abbey.

The British Expeditionary Force and other Allied troops had been driven towards the town of Dunkirk by the advancing Germans and were cut off from the rest of the armies; and the historic rescue had begun. The Navy sent all available ships to bring the men home and hundreds of civilian boats joined in the rescue.

There followed a time of deep anxiety and a fierce determination among all who could be of help to bring our men home.

What happened in those never-to-be-forgotten days was little short of a miracle. The sea was calm and it was as though our prayers were being answered. The Germans were broadcasting that the British Army had been annihilated and victory was in their grasp and that the British Isles would soon be under their domination as well as France, Belgium, Holland and the whole of Western Europe.

The story of the determination and valour, the fight against desperate odds, is well known in our history – and the name of Dunkirk will always be remembered with reverence.

There was subdued rejoicing when the Prime Minister told us that nearly three-quarters of a million men had been brought safely back to Britain. It was no victory, he told us in sombre tones. It was a miracle of deliverance. But we had to face the facts. The French were collapsing; they would give way to German dominance to ensure peace; the Netherlands were in the hands of the enemy; now there would be the battle for Britain.

The Prime Minister spoke with all that fiery eloquence which was characteristic of him and an inspiration to us all. '*Britain will never surrender*,' he declared.

Our men were coming home. There was a hope in my heart that Jowan would be one of those who had been picked up at Dunkirk and brought back to safety.

And so I waited.

The days were passing and there was no news of Jowan.

Dorabella said: 'You can imagine the confusion. Three-quarters of a million men arriving suddenly. Of course there will be delays.'

My mother was on the telephone. She had great news. Gretchen must be told at once. Edward was home. He had been evacuated with the Expeditionary Force from Dunkirk. He was in hospital at this very moment in Sussex.

'Gretchen! Gretchen!' I cried. 'Edward is home!'

She was beside me, crying: 'What? What?'

'Gretchen must come home at once,' my mother was saying. 'Yes, yes, Gretchen, isn't it wonderful news?' No, she had not seen him yet. They would go to the hospital in Horsham. She had just had news. No, he was not badly hurt. Some little thing. Gretchen must not worry. My mother was planning practically. Perhaps we could keep Hildegarde down at Tregarland's for the time being.

Then Gretchen could come straight to Caddington and they would arrange everything from there.

Gretchen looked bewildered but blissful. Dorabella was hugging her. I was loath to let my mother go.

She was saying: 'No . . . no news of Jowan yet?'

'No,' I replied.

'It will come,' she said brightly.

'I pray so.'

'Darling,' said my mother, 'we are all with you. Let us know if there is any news . . . at once. Things are changing. I'm sure we're going to get some good news soon.'

I smiled wanly. With the enemy on our doorstep? With the country alert for invasion? With the might of Germany facing us across a strip of water? And no news of Jowan.

Still, I must remember that Edward was home. Edward was safe.

'Please God,' I prayed, 'let Jowan come back to me.'

Gretchen left that day and the waiting went on. I lifted my face to the clear blue sky and felt a vague annoyance because the world was so beautiful at this time. It was as though we were being told: This is how it could have been but for the folly of men.

Each day I waited. Where was Jowan? Had he been one of the men who had died before he could be rescued? Was he with the remains of the Army who had been left behind?

Edward was not badly wounded. He had some shrapnel lodged in his right arm which had to be taken out. Then, after a brief leave which he and Gretchen could spend together, he would join his regiment in the West Country.

If this proved to be so, my mother said, it would be better for Gretchen to rejoin us as she would be nearer to him. She was sure her stay with us had done her good.

Lucky Gretchen! Lucky Edward! And still there was no news of Jowan.

How the days dragged on! Each morning when I awoke after a generally listless night, tormented by dreams which reflected my daytime fears, I wondered what the day held. Events were moving rapidly, but I was obsessed by one thing. Where was Jowan? What if I should never know! How could fate be so cruel as to show me what happiness I might have had and then snatch it away from me!

The French were fast collapsing; the myth of the impassable Maginot Line was being exploded; Marshal Pétain had asked for an armistice; and we stood alone.

And I was beginning to fear that Jowan would never return.

The position was grim. The Germans had control of the Channel ports and the Battle of Britain had started. We were in constant danger, not knowing from one moment to the next whether this would be our last.

Dorabella and I came down to breakfast one morning, finding Gordon drinking a cup of coffee before leaving.

'I wanted to talk to you,' he said. 'There is a possibility of enemy agents coming into the country disguised as refugees. Small boats are still getting across the Channel. We have to watch. The idea is that when these boats come in, we will examine everyone in them before they are allowed to land. It is tricky because they will, in the main, be genuine refugees, but there will no doubt be people who would do a great deal to get through. We are setting up a watch along the coast. The most likely spots will be farther east, of course, as the distance is so much shorter there. But some might try Cornwall in spite of that because it would be easier to be undetected. Anyway, we have to be prepared.'

'This gets more and more fantastic,' said Dorabella.

Gordon gave her a slightly exasperated look.

'Fantastic indeed,' he said. 'And more than that. We are in acute danger, you know. We have to be prepared night and day. During the day any boats could be seen. Fortunately, there are not many places along this coast where it would be easy to land. But they must be watched and I am arranging for this to be done. The beach below this house is certainly one of them and this little stretch of coast is our responsibility. I am preparing a rota and the beach will be watched throughout the hours of darkness by two observers. You two will naturally want to do your part. With the servants and the people from the cottages around here there will be several available, so your periods of duty will not come round so frequently.'

'Certainly we shall do our share,' I said. 'Tell us more.'

'We shall watch in pairs for two hours each night. Fortunately at this time of year there are not many hours of darkness. You and Dorabella can watch together. Some of the older couples can join in. It will give them the satisfaction of helping the war effort.'

Charley and Bert Trimmell wanted to be on the rota and Gordon thought it was a good idea that they should be. He had discovered that Charley was quite interested in the estate and he was giving him tasks now and then for which he was receiving small payments. He and Gordon seemed to get on very well together.

Dorabella and I quite looked forward to those nocturnal duties. It was good to have something worthwhile to do and be able to do it together.

It was one o'clock in the morning. We had been on duty since midnight and at two o'clock the next pair would come to take over.

We sat looking across the sea, talking desultorily.

'How strange life has become,' said Dorabella. 'At least it's not exactly boring. I found it so once . . .'

'That was when you had the urge to run away with your Frenchman,' I said.

'You wouldn't understand. I saw life stretching out before me . . . year after year . . . the same old thing day after day. And the impulse came. Oh no, you wouldn't understand. Violetta would always do her duty.'

'You left Tristan,' I said. 'That was what I could not understand.'

'He was only a child. Oh, it's no use trying to explain. I thought I'd settle in Paris, and Dermot would divorce me. I would marry Jacques Dubois and you would come over to see me. I thought it would work somehow.'

'That's just like you. You make a wild plan and then imagine everything is going to work out to make it come right.'

'Don't scold.'

'Well, it was all rather stupid, as it turned out.'

'You'll never understand.'

'I think I do . . . quite well.'

Then suddenly I saw the light on the water. It was a long way out, almost on the horizon. It flickered for a moment and then went out.

'Did you see that?' I whispered.

'Where?'

'Look. No. Towards the horizon there. It's gone. No. There it is again.'

Dorabella was staring ahead of her. 'Lights,' she whispered. 'Oh, Violetta, they've come. The invasion has started!'

'Wait a minute,' I whispered. 'It's gone. No, there it is.'

For a few seconds we watched the unearthly lights on the water.

'There's another, and another,' I cried.

It was light and then dark . . . and the lights seemed to be bobbing on the water.

I said: 'We must give the alarm at once. I'll call Gordon. You wait here and watch.'

I hurried to the house and up to Gordon's room. I knocked on his door. There was no answer, so I went in.

He was fast asleep.

'Gordon!' I cried. 'They've come. It's the invasion.'

He was out of bed and thrusting on some clothes.

As we came out of his room, one of the servants appeared.

'Wake everyone up,' cried Gordon. 'Raise the alarm!'

We hurried down. Dorabella came to meet us.

The sea was dark now. I wondered whether the enemy had realized their lights had been seen.

There were voices everywhere, and several people on the cliff looking out to sea. The whole company of the Local Defence Volunteers arrived.

'Should us alert them in Plymouth, sir?' asked one.

'We'm getting the church bells ringing down in Poldown, sir,' said another.

And then we heard the bells ringing out.

Dorabella and I were aghast, because the sea was in darkness and the lights we had seen seemed to have disappeared entirely. We looked at each other in dismay. We could not have been mistaken. We had seen them clearly.

And then suddenly there was a flash of brightness.

We were vindicated. They were really there. For a moment I felt almost a relief, and then immediately I was ashamed of myself.

There were several fishermen in the crowd of watchers. I heard one of them laugh and the others joined in.

'They be fish,' cried one of them. 'They Germans be naught but a shoal of fish.'

There was a deep silence, and then everyone started to laugh with relief.

Dorabella and I could not hide the fact that we were deeply mortified.

'Don't 'ee fret, Miss,' said one of the old men. 'Couldn't be expected to know 'em . . . not coming from these parts. Us 'as seen 'em time and time again. 'Tis familiar-like to us.'

Gordon said: 'You did well.' And, raising his voice, he added: 'We have been shown tonight that we are well protected. If anything should happen we should have had our warning.'

It was something which would never be forgotten. Of course, it was the phosphorescence of fishes' scales we had seen and which had deluded us into thinking they were lights on boats. It was something of a joke and people tittered when they saw us.

We knew what they were saying. 'What could 'ee expect from a batch of foreigners? Didn't know the difference between fish and Germans.'

But everyone was delighted, of course, that it had been a false alarm and the night we called out the guard for a shoal of fish would never be forgotten.

We could scarcely believe what was happening. Across that strip of water, which mercifully divided us from the scene of disaster, were the Germans occupying more than half of France, including all the ports; the Army was demobilized, the fleet in enemy hands; and the French, who had agreed not to make a separate peace, were now being required by the Germans not only to surrender, but to help them in the war against Britain.

All through the days we waited for fresh disasters.

We heard the Prime Minister express his grief and

amazement that our one-time allies could have accepted such terms.

One evening there was a broadcast by General de Gaulle, who was in England and determined to free his country; his plan was to preserve the independence of France and help Britain in the war against Germany. Only an actual invasion could have made the situation worse.

I think we were all in a state of shock listening to the rallying call of our Prime Minister, which never failed to bring us out of our despondency and give hope – and a touch of excitement – to us all. He assured us that we would be ready. We would fight the enemy in any place on our island, wherever he dared to show his face. We would succeed – and somehow he made us believe that.

Gretchen came down. She had a great deal to tell us. There was a change in her. Edward was home and the immediate terror of imagined disaster was lifted. His wound had been slight and she admitted that she had wished it had not healed so quickly. Now he had rejoined his regiment and was ready to defend the country, but at least that would be here, on our own soil, and not in some foreign land.

She was very careful in what she said. I knew she was afraid to appear too happy at Edward's return because she feared that would call attention to the fact that Jowan had not been one of those who came back. I could read her thoughts as I knew she did mine, and I could feel closer to her at that time than I could even to Dorabella.

One day Gretchen said to me: 'What is the matter with that boy – I mean Charley, the one from London?'

'What do you mean, Gretchen? Gordon thinks he is rather bright.'

'He certainly seems very bright. I find him watching me. I suddenly look up and find his eyes on me, and he is giving me such a strange look. He turns away when he realizes I am looking at him and tries to pretend he was doing no such thing. Do you know, it's a little upsetting.'

'Perhaps you are imagining it.'

'At first I thought so, but it happens all the time. I have been in the garden and looked up at a window. And I saw him there . . . watching. What can it mean? I thought perhaps you could find out.'

'I'll try, but I can't imagine what.'

'The young boy is doing it, too.'

'Bert?'

'The brother, yes. It is like some game. I can't explain it. It's creepy in a way.'

'I'll see if I can find out what it's all about.'

'I somehow feel they don't like me.'

'Why should they not? They are just interested in everybody and everything here. It must be such a change for them. I think they have settled in rather well.'

Nothing would convince Gretchen that there was not something behind the boys' behaviour.

I decided the easiest way would be to try Bert, who might betray something more readily than his brother would.

I found him alone and said: 'Bert, do you like Mrs Denver?'

Bert opened his eyes wide, caught his breath and put on an air of wariness.

'Well, Miss . . .' he began and stopped.

'What is it? What don't you like about her? Why are you always watching her?'

'Well,' said Bert, 'you've got to watch 'em, ain't you?'

'Have you? Why?'

'Well, 'cos . . .'

'Because what?' I asked.

'Well, you know, Miss, we go to watch out for 'em every night, don't we? Charley says . . .'

'Yes, what does Charley say?'

Bert wriggled a little.

'Charley says you've got to watch 'em. You never know what they'll be up to.'

'What do you think Mrs Denver will be "up to"?'

'Well, she's one of 'em, ain't she? She's a German.'

I felt sick. I was reminded of that scene in the schloss when those violent young men had tried to break up the furniture.

I said: 'Listen, Bert. Mrs Denver is our friend. In a way she is related to me. She is good and kind and this war has nothing to do with her. She is on our side. She wants us to win this war. It is very important to her and her family that we do.'

'But we watch out for 'em, don't we? And she's one of 'em. Charley says we ought to watch her.'

'I must talk to Charley,' I said. 'Will you bring him to me?'

Bert nodded and willingly ran off. Soon after he returned with his brother.

'Charley,' I said, 'I want to talk to you about Mrs Denver.'

Charley's eyes narrowed and he looked wise.

'She's on our side, Charley,' I said.

Charley looked disbelieving and gave me a look of mild contempt.

'I have to explain something to you,' I said. 'It is true that Mrs Denver is a German.' I went on: 'But they are not all bad, you know. Moreover, she and her family have been treated very badly by them. Hitler is as much her enemy as ours – perhaps more so.' I tried to explain briefly and vividly what had happened at the schloss on that never-to-be-forgotten night; and I think I must have done so effectively. His eyes narrowed. He was a shrewd boy. He understood something about violence, I could see.

I finished: 'You see, Charley, it is of as great importance to her as to us that we win this war.'

He nodded gravely and I knew that I had brought home my point.

It must have been a month after the incident of the phosphorescent fish, and Dorabella and I were on one of our seats in the garden watching the sea. A dark night, with a thin crescent moon, a midnight blue sky, and a smooth, almost silent sea.

The first fears of invasion no longer enveloped us. It is amazing how quickly one can become accustomed to disaster. Our spirits had been considerably lifted by the Prime Minister's frequent broadcasts to the nation, and each passing week meant that we were more prepared. We were told that the nine divisions brought back from Dunkirk were now reinforced and at full strength; and here, in our country, there were forces from the Colonies, also Poles, Norwegians, Dutch and French – the latter being built up by General de Gaulle. All over the country men were rallying to the Local Defence Volunteers; and even in the last few weeks our position had improved considerably.

We were by no means lulled into security, but we were optimistic and we were certain that, when it came to conflict, we could stand firm and win.

'Do you realize,' Dorabella said to me, 'it is nearly a year since all this started? It seems it is going on for ever.'

She smiled wistfully. She knew I was thinking of Jowan, as I always must be. Where was he? Should I ever see him again?

Then suddenly I noticed it. It was a faint light – not on the horizon, as we had seen the fish – but much nearer to land.

'Do you see . . . ?' I began.

Dorabella was staring out to sea.

'Fish?' she said.

'Yes, perhaps it is . . .'

The light disappeared and then there was darkness.

'They are still laughing at us because of that night,' said Dorabella. 'Only the other day . . . Oh, look, there it is again!'

It was there and then gone. There was darkness and no sound but the gentle swishing of the waves on the beach below.

Dorabella yawned.

'Well,' she said, 'we learned our lesson. No more raising the alarm for a shoal of fish.'

'They all enjoyed it and the locals were glad to have a laugh at our expense.'

'There's something in that. Anything that can make people laugh these days can't be all bad.'

'Gretchen is happier now.'

'It must be wonderful for her. I wish . . .'

She stopped, and I said: 'I know. I've just got to go on hoping.'

'There'll be some news soon. I feel it in my bones. I've got some very reliable bones.'

She was trying to cheer me. I wondered if she really believed that Jowan would come back safely.

Then I was back again, thinking of those places where we had met, going over what had been said between us, how we had gradually become aware of our feelings for each other. How unhappy I had been when I thought Dorabella was dead, how he had comforted me and how different I had been then. Experiences change people, force them into maturity. How young I must have been before that visit to Germany!

Dorabella gave a sudden start.

'Look! Down there! I saw it on the water, a dark object bobbing about on the tide.'

'It's a boat,' I said, and I heard the drumming of an engine.

'Probably one of the fishermen coming in late,' replied Dorabella.

We waited for a few seconds. We could not see the boat coming in to the beach.

'Should we give the alarm?' I asked.

'And make ourselves a laughing-stock again?'

'It's what we're supposed to do.'

'Gordon said we did the right thing. How were we to know about those wretched fishes?'

'Let's go down and see who it is,' I said. 'I bet it's old Jim Treglow or Harry Penlore, or one of them. They might be just doing it to catch us . . . to get another laugh at the expense of "they foreigners".'

'Suppose it's some secret agent?'

'Don't make me laugh! That's one of the old fishing-boats. There are lots of them in the harbour.'

I hesitated. We must not call the alarm again unless it was really necessary. If we had waited a while on that other occasion, we might have realized that what we had seen was a shoal of fish and not an invading army.

'Come on,' said Dorabella. 'We'll watch them come in and, if it is anyone we don't know, we'll run up and give the alarm. There'll be time.'

We sped down the path to the beach and stood close together in the shelter of an overhanging rock. The engine had been shut off and there were no lights showing now. Nearer and nearer came the boat. It touched the sand and then I heard a man's voice say something in French.

Dorabella caught her breath as the man looked up at the cliff face towards the house. He had not seen us.

Then he turned and another figure had started to climb

out of the boat. It was slight, wrapped in a cloak. A woman, I thought.

We must act. We must slip away unseen. We must give the alarm. No one must be allowed to come ashore without some interrogation.

The man was looking our way. He had seen us. He spoke almost in a whisper but his voice was clear on the night air.

Dorabella said: 'Jacques . . .'

The man heard. He stepped towards us, the girl beside him.

Dorabella came out of the shelter of the rock. She walked towards the pair.

She said: 'Jacques, what are you doing here?'

He turned and faced her.

'Dorabella, *ma petite* . . .' Then he held out his hands.

They stood facing each other, then he turned to his companion and said: 'This is my sister, Simone.'

I knew who he was now. I had seen him before at the Christmas party at Jermyn's Priory when he had first met Dorabella. He was the French artist who had been painting the Cornish coast, and for the sake of whom she had faked a drowning accident and fled to France, leaving her husband and her little son Tristan.

He released her and turned to me, stretching out a hand and taking mine in his.

'I am so glad to see you,' he said in his accented English. 'I did not think we would arrive. The sea is calm but the craft is frail . . . and it is a long way to come.'

'Why . . . why?' stammered Dorabella.

'You ask that! We cannot live in France . . . not till we are free again. Neither Simone, nor I. It is impossible. We are two of many who are making this journey. They take to the sea . . . they take the small boat . . . and they risk their lives . . . but what good is life as slaves, eh? So, we escape.'

'I see,' said Dorabella. 'It was very brave of you.'

She was studying Simone, a small, dark girl who looked romantically beautiful in the darkness of the night. She was shaking, I saw, and I said: 'You must be cold.'

'We had long at sea,' she answered. 'It is not easy . . . this Manche. No . . . even on such a night as this. We are cold and hungry but we rejoice to have succeed. We are here . . . as we planned to be.'

'We can give you some food and something to drink,' I said. 'Come up to the house. You can tell us all about what is happening over there.'

'And you . . . out at this time?' asked Jacques.

'On the watch,' replied Dorabella. 'For people like you. No, really, we are looking for Germans.'

'The enemy . . . you expect . . . ?'

'Any minute,' said Dorabella. 'We are on watch every night.'

'And you find us! I did not expect to see you so soon. I planned to land and wait till morning somewhere along the coast. I thought we should land and wait until morning. Then we should throw ourselves on your mercy. We want to work for the overthrow of these tyrants who have taken our country. I shall join General de Gaulle as soon as possible . . . and there will be some work Simone can do.'

I said: 'I think you had better tie up your boat. I'll go and tell Gordon what has happened.'

'My sister is so practical,' Dorabella told them.

'Ah yes,' said Jacques. 'I remember this Gordon. The good manager, is that not so? You must tell him?'

'Yes. He is in control here and you will understand we have to report to him.'

'Of course, of course.'

I left them and went ahead into the house. My thoughts were in a whirl. What a coincidence! Dorabella's lover, escaping and coming to our beach! But then, I supposed he had made for it, thinking how much easier it would be to explain himself to those who already knew him than to strangers.

It was all very strange, but then so many strange things were happening now.

Dorabella

Encounter in Paris

I could not describe my feelings when, waiting with Violetta in the shelter of the rocks, I heard that voice from the past. Jacques in England! And at such a time! Here was the past, which I had hoped was buried for ever, come back to confront me. It seems that everything we do remains for ever; there is no escaping from it.

I can remember Violetta quoting something like this once:

> *'The moving finger writes, and having writ*
> *Moves on, nor all thy piety nor wit*
> *Can lure it back to cancel half a line,*
> *Nor all thy tears wash out a word of it.'*

Violetta always liked poetry and often quotes it to effect. I thought of this now. How true it was. Many a trouble had she covered up for me throughout our childhood; and this was the biggest of them all. And she had helped me to emerge from it with as little discredit as possible.

The war had helped too, for I returned just when it was declared and people had other things with which to occupy their minds than the affairs of an erring wife.

Yes, I was indeed impulsive. It was always act first and think afterwards; and Violetta was there to help if need be. But, of course, when I was about to become involved in a mad escapade, I never thought of the consequences until afterwards.

There had been that time in Germany when I first met

Dermot. There he was – an Englishman on holiday – as we were. It was all so natural – a holiday romance which ended in wedding bells. Quite an ordinary story, really. I enjoyed every minute of it at the time. Dermot had all the qualities of a romantic hero – handsome, presentable, heir to a large estate and very much in love with me. Up to that time, I had been a little disappointed in the holiday. All that intense nationalism, all that clicking of heels, the great Hitler and the rise of the new Germany – and then, of course, it became a little sinister. But it was all so far removed from our lives. When the holiday was over, we should go home and what was happening in Germany seemed of little importance to us. I was wrong about that – as I was about so many things.

Then we came home and my family visited Dermot's and everything went smoothly and it seemed the most natural thing in the world that we should marry and live happily ever after.

Perhaps I began to feel a few twinges before the wedding. It is strange how different people can be in certain settings.

In Germany Dermot was the romantic hero, rescuing us when we were lost in the forest, defending us during that frightful scene in the schloss when the Hitler Youth tried to break up the place because the owners – our friends – were Jewish. Yes, he was wonderful during that time.

Then back in Cornwall he seemed less heroic, seen against the background of Tregarland's, the ancestral home. He was in awe of that strange old man, his father, and he was overshadowed by Gordon Lewyth; there was, in truth, something sinister about the entire household. It was not quite as I had imagined it.

I realized then what I had done. It had been like that often during my life. It seems fun to do something until one begins to count the cost and the advantages dwindle away, overcome by the difficulties.

My sister came and I felt better then. There is this close bond between us. It has always been there and I know it always will be. When she is not around I feel a certain anxiety. She is like a part of myself – the reasoning, sensible part. It never occurred to me until I went away how very important she was to me.

Well, there I was, in the house in which I had never felt entirely comfortable, married to a man with whom I was falling rapidly out of love. I was very fond of my little son; but I am not the maternal type, and a child could never make up to me for the lack of a satisfactory lover. It was not that Dermot's affections for me had wandered. He remained devoted to me, but he was no longer exciting. I found Tregarland's overpowering; the closeness of the sea disturbed me; and I wanted to get away. There was no one to whom I could explain – not even Violetta.

And then Jacques arrived.

That silly feud between the houses of Tregarland and Jermyn has played quite a part in our lives. It goes back a hundred years or so when a Jermyn girl and Tregarland boy were lovers – our Cornish Montague and Capulet – and the girl drowned herself on the Tregarland beach while the lover who had tried to elope with her had been caught in a mantrap set by the Jermyns and maimed for life. This resulted in years of enmity between the two families.

My dear sister Violetta and the charming Jowan Jermyn decided that the whole thing was ridiculous and they shocked the whole neighbourhood by meeting, falling in love, becoming engaged to be married and making a continuation of the feud a nonsense.

I think the locals shook their heads and said no good would come of it and they might be right, because Jowan has not returned from Dunkirk. I tremble for Violetta. She is not like I am. She will not love lightly.

There were times when I felt I had been caught. I could picture the years ahead. I had been trapped here. I was married to a man who had ceased to attract me. I had a child who was more fond of Violetta and Nanny Crabtree than of me. I was not meant for the domestic life. I had always wanted excitement and admiration. Kind, gentle as Dermot was, he was not the ardent lover whom I required to give me contentment.

And then I had met Jacques.

It was Christmas. The feud was being thrust aside by Jowan, his grandmother and Violetta. The grandmother was one of those sensible, down-to-earth women; she lived for her adored grandson in whom she could see no fault. She liked Violetta, which was fortunate – though she might think she was not quite good enough for her wonderful Jowan, but who could be? And everything seemed set fair in that direction. Then came this wretched war and the possibility of Jowan's being removed from the scene for ever.

That was something I dared not contemplate. I feared it would have such an effect on my sister and I could not bear her to change.

It was Christmastime when Jacques was in Cornwall and it was at Jermyn Priory that I first met him. I was feeling particularly disillusioned with my life at that time, deeply aware of the mistake I had made, seeing the dreary years ahead – and there was Jacques.

It seemed that Jowan had met him somewhere on the Continent. He must have talked to Jacques about Cornwall and said something like, 'You must come and see us if you are ever our way.' It was one of those casual meetings at which such invitations are lightly issued and seem little likely to come to anything at the time. And then fate plays an unexpected trick, and that seemingly insignificant fact is the catalyst which changes our lives.

Certainly it would have been better for me if Jowan had not met Jacques Dubois and issued that casual invitation.

Well, Jacques came. He was staying at one of the inns in Poldown. He had a friend with him – Hans Fleisch, I remember, a German and an artist, as Jacques was.

They had arrived with their sketchpads and declared themselves excited by the beauty of the Cornish coast. I remember so vividly how I felt at that time – depressed by the dullness and monotony of life. I was really desperate and there was Jacques.

He was different from anyone I had known, very worldly, everything that Dermot was not. He seemed to sense how I felt and he understood it. He was sympathetic and very attentive. I went home from that gathering at Jermyn's in that state of excitement which I needed in my life.

The next day I met him when he was painting on the cliffs. It was one of those mild winter days which one gets hereabouts. He looked remarkably pleased to see me. I sat beside him and asked if I were interrupting his work. Indeed not, he said. The work could only interrupt his meeting with me and could be set aside with the greatest pleasure. At times like this, Jacques always knew the right thing to say.

We walked and the time flew by. I had no idea I was with him so long.

'I am here every day,' he told me. 'The weather is not always as good as this, but if it is not, I shall be at the inn. I'd like to show you my work sometime.'

For three days we met on the cliffs. Then I began to see how it was between us. To me it was more than a passing flirtation. It was arranged that I should go along to the inn to see him. Of course, if anyone observed my going to his room, there would be a good deal of talk. It seemed an added excitement to plan my visits and seek an opportunity to slip up to his room unseen.

The outcome was inevitable. In a short time we were lovers. And what an exciting lover he was! How different from Dermot!

I knew how shocked my family would have been if they had known, and that included Violetta. She had always been rather conventional. I could not imagine her straying from the path of virtue. I think I was more apprehensive of her discovering than I was of Dermot.

I have always been the sort of person who lives in the present. Violetta calls it the 'butterfly existence'.

'Fluttering hither and thither,' she said, 'round the candle like a moth until you scorch your wings.'

It could not last, of course. Though I made myself believe it would. Jacques would not stay for ever and then it would be a return to my old, dull existence.

Then one day Jacques said: 'Why not come with me? You'd like Paris.'

I said: 'How wonderful!' and let myself believe it was possible.

I suppose Jacques's nature is really like mine. We started to plan. I love planning. I think up the wildest ideas, which I make myself believe in while they last. In the past Violetta has been there with her common sense. 'How absurd you are being!' 'How could you possibly do that? You're not being logical.' And she would have shown me right from the beginning how stupid I was. But she was not there and Jacques and I used to lie in the bed in the inn where there was scarcely room for us both, and float into that world of fantasy. We made plans and deluded ourselves into thinking they were not impossible.

'I have it!' I cried. 'The feud.'

Jacques's eyes sparkled. He was enjoying these plans as

much as I was. They certainly helped me to evade the unpleasant fact that parting could not be far off.

I said: 'In the feud . . . this Jermyn girl – I can't remember her name, so I'll call her Juliet – was so heartbroken because they wouldn't let her marry the man she wanted to that she went down to the beach and walked into the sea. Dermot's first wife was also drowned in that way. She was murdered by Gordon's mother who wanted Tregarland's for him. It's a good story. I'll tell you all about it in detail one day. Suppose I arranged a "drowning accident"? I know. I'll go down to the beach every morning to have a bathe, and one day they'll find my bathrobe and shoes and I shall have disappeared.'

Jacques laughed. It was a brilliant idea. His eyes sparkled and he started to plan how we would do it.

We made the wildest suggestions. It was not impossible. They would think I was drowned. I did not want poor Dermot to know I was tired of him. That would hurt him too much. We would fix it all beautifully. I would simply have gone bathing and not come back. Just as Juliet Jermyn had done – as they had thought Dermot's first wife had done until the truth was discovered.

We must make sure that the truth about my departure was never discovered.

We planned and planned. We were caught up in the idea – and then somehow it became a reality. Jacques said: 'You can bring a few things with you. Not much, or they'll get suspicious. There's a snag. You'll want your passport.'

We were thoughtful.

'Why should they think to look for a passport?' I asked.

'They might not immediately. But sometime perhaps somebody will.'

'We can't worry about a detail like that. They'd think I'd lost it. I do lose things.'

So the plan was that I should slip a few things out of the house while Jacques would be waiting for me in the car Hans Fleisch had hired. He would lend it to Jacques without demur. And so we should be ready for the day of departure. I must make a habit of taking a bathe in the early morning just for a few days before we left. Then on the night we were to get away, I would slip out of the house and join Jacques. First I would put my bathrobe and shoes on the beach and people would believe I had gone for my early morning swim.

Hans Fleisch would drive us to the coast and return to Poldown afterwards, for he planned to stay another week or so. It was all quite simple.

My conscience worried me that night. I was glad Violetta was not then at Tregarland's. I was sure she would have guessed I was, as she would say, 'up to something'. I promised myself that later I would find some way of seeing her. I would write to her and she would come to Paris. I had a miniature of her – a beautiful thing, and she had one of me – and I took it with me.

And it all went according to plan.

I know now that my clothes were found on the beach, just as I intended, and they all believed I had been drowned – except Violetta. There was that strong bond between us and instinctively she knew I was not dead.

Well, she knows the truth now, and when I did come back, she helped me to concoct a story of my loss of memory and being picked up by a yacht. Violetta said this talk would never have been accepted but for the fact that the war had come and such affairs as mine were trivial compared with that.

Such was my nature that I could forget all the difficulties, even the enormity of what I was doing, in the excitement of the moment. I know I am shallow and pleasure-seeking, but I found Jacques so exciting and amusing, and I had convinced myself that I must escape from the eerie atmosphere of Tregarland's and that at some time in the future I should be able to justify myself in what I had done.

There is something intoxicating about the very air of Paris. During my first days there I was so exhilarated that I told myself that everything that came after would be worth it. During that period, I stilled my conscience which, in spite of myself, kept intruding. I would think of Tristan, Violetta, Dermot and my parents all mourning for me – for they would mourn deeply, in spite of my unworthiness. I wished that I could find some means of telling them that I was alive. Violetta will know, I promised myself. She must. And that comforted me a little, and for those days when I walked the streets of Paris, buying the clothes I needed, absorbing that atmosphere which is indigenous to the city, I lived on excitement. I loved the cafés with their gay awnings, and the little tables at which people sat, drinking their coffee or wine. I loved the famous streets and the narrow ones, and the shops, the smell of freshly baked bread which came from some of them, and the remains of the old city before Haussman had rebuilt it.

I spent a certain amount of time strolling through the streets, looking at the places which had been only names to me before. I loved the ancient bridges, and I gazed in wonder at the majestic Notre Dame. I wished I had paid more attention to my lessons, and I thought that if Violetta was here she would be able to tell me a great deal about these places.

Jacques did not accompany me on these journeys. He

was not the type to wander round gaping at everything like a tourist. He had work to do. He had changed a little. He was no less the ardent lover, and that part of our relationship remained. It was just that, when I expressed the excitement I felt in Paris and wished that he would show me certain places, he became remote and evasive. He had some sketches to do. He was not free that day.

'If only Violetta were here,' I said.

He smiled and nodded vaguely. He could not understand what existed between me and Violetta.

I had always imagined that artists lived in attics in abject poverty and went to cafés to celebrate when they sold a picture and there caroused with their impecunious friends.

This was not the case with Jacques.

He had a small house on the Left Bank, it was true, but he lived in a certain degree of comfort. There was an attic in which he worked because the light was from the north. But it was just his working area and below was an ordinary dwelling which one might expect anywhere.

In the basement were a husband and wife who looked after his needs. They were Jean and Marie, middle-aged, eager to please and not really surprised to see me, which was a little disconcerting.

Jacques was clearly by no means poor. He gave me money to buy clothes and, providing I could subdue my conscience, I was happy during those first weeks.

Jacques worked now and then in the attic which he called his studio. People called often. Some of them were sitters, I presumed; but others came and he would take them up to the studio to talk. He did show me one or two portraits. I was hoping he would suggest painting me, but he did not.

People sometimes called in the evenings. Marie would cook a meal for them and Jean would wait at table. I would be present on such occasions, of course, but they talked such rapid French that I could understand little of what they said. When I told Jacques this, he laughed and said I had missed nothing I needed to know. It was all gossip.

'Do they talk about what is going on in Europe?' I asked. 'People were always on about that at home.'

'It is mentioned.'

'They were all worked up about it in England. I expect they are here. Yet usually they all seem so much more excitable than we do.'

He shrugged his shoulders and I sensed he did not want to talk about the possibilities of war. I was in agreement with that. I had grown weary of the subject before I left home.

About ten days after I had been there, Hans Fleisch came to the house. We greeted each other warmly. He had been a great help to us. He bowed, and clicked his heels, which took me right back to that awful time at the schloss. He asked me in his stilted and rather Germanic English if I were enjoying France. I told him I found it most exciting.

'Jacques is very happy that you are here.'

'What happened in Poldown when they discovered I had gone?' I asked.

He was thoughtful and then said: 'They believed you were drowned. That you had gone swimming. It was not a wise thing to do, they said. The sea can be treacherous, and you were lost.'

'Did you happen to see any member of my family?'

'No, but I heard they had come to the house.'

'My sister . . . ?'

'Yes, I think your sister.'

'I see. So . . . the story was accepted.'

'It would seem so.'

I thought to myself: Oh, Violetta, dear mother, dear father, I hope you don't mourn me too much.

I think it was then that I began to regard what I had done more seriously.

I was still fascinated by Jacques. The physical relationship between us was perfect – for him, too, I was sure; but I had built up such an image of life in the Latin Quarter that I was vaguely disappointed because ours seemed so conventional. I had pictured artists coming in every day. I remembered stories I had heard of Manet, Monet, Gauguin, Cézanne, and the café life of the Bohemians. That was completely missing. Jacques seemed quite affluent. This was perverse of me. I should be grateful. Did I want to live in poverty because it seemed artistic for a moment or two?

I began to know one or two people who came fairly frequently to the studio. One of these, to whom I took a liking, was Georges Mansard. He was a tall man with a ready smile and blue, rather penetrating eyes. He was very fair and did not look very French. He spoke good English and was very interested in me. I was always drawn to people who were. It was something to do with an inferiority complex I had acquired, having grown up lacking Violetta's intelligence. I enjoyed feeling superior to her in the matter of feminine charm.

The first time Georges Mansard came to the house, I was there alone, for Jacques had gone out that morning. He had a way of going off suddenly, not saying where, and when he returned I learned not to protest. Jacques was the sort of man who did not like his actions questioned. It was a trait which was beginning to irritate me.

I heard someone talking to Jean and Marie below and I went down to see who it was.

Jean said: 'Monsieur has come to see Monsieur Dubois.'

Delighted to have a visitor, I said: 'Oh, do come up. It may be he will not be long.'

The visitor looked pleased and turned to nod at Jean, who looked faintly disturbed, but I said: 'That's all right, Jean. Perhaps,' I went on, 'you would bring some coffee.' Then to the guest: 'Or would you prefer wine?'

The French seemed to consume a great deal of wine, so I was not surprised when he chose it.

We went up into the room which was called the *salon*. It was not exactly large but was comfortably furnished. I waved to a chair with a little table beside it and went to the cabinet to get the wine.

Then he told me his name was Georges Mansard and he was a friend of Jacques.

'I heard that you had arrived from England,' he said. 'Tell me, how do you like Paris?'

'Enchanting,' I told him.

'You have visited the well-known spots, I hear. Notre Dame, the Eiffel Tower. What do you think of Montmartre?'

'I was delighted by it all,' I said.

'Your home was . . . ?'

'In Cornwall. We had a place right on the coast.'

'That must also have been enchanting.'

'It is reckoned to be so.'

He lifted his glass. 'Welcome to France.'

We talked easily and his English, being only slightly accented, was not difficult to understand. He knew England. He had even been to Cornwall. He himself came from the south, near Bordeaux.

'Where the wine comes from,' I said.

'Exactly so. All the best wine in France – in the world – comes from the Médoc.' He lifted his hands and smiled whimsically. 'Of course, there will be many who deny this . . . for instance those who do not have the good fortune to live among those delectable vines.' He smiled and looked into his glass. 'This is a good claret.'

'I am glad. I am sure that Monsieur Dubois, like most of his countrymen, would drink only the best.'

He told me a great deal about Bordeaux and how he came to Paris on business, marketing his wines.

'We have an office here, you see.'

'So I suppose you travel back and forth to Bordeaux frequently,' I said.

'That is so.'

'I thought you must be an artist when you first came.'

'Oh, do I look like one?'

'No . . . I don't think so. How does an artist look? One imagines them in flowing smocks, splashed with paint – but I have found them not like that at all.'

'This is the Latin Quarter. This is where they abound.'

'I suppose the days of La Bohème are no more.'

'I expect things have changed now. There is the art of commerce. What do you say, commercial art? This is more now to employ the artists. They are not so poor. It is not a matter of exchanging a picture for a meal, if you understand.'

'I do.'

He stayed for two hours and I felt elated by his visit.

When Jacques returned and I told him Georges Mansard had called, he received the news nonchalantly.

'He's a charming man,' I commented. 'We got on very well.'

'I am sure you did. I knew he would be enchanted by my little cabbage.'

He seized me and swung me round. We danced. Our steps, like everything else, fitted perfectly.

He stopped suddenly, kissed me intensely and said: 'It seems years since I saw you.'

That was how it was with Jacques.

Georges Mansard called the next day and went up to the attic where he remained with Jacques for a long time. He greeted me like an old friend before he went up. I guessed they were talking about wine and Georges was going to get an order.

He had talked very enthusiastically about his products during our conversation the previous day and had betrayed his pride in them.

'I hope you got a good order,' I said to him as he was leaving.

Georges Mansard smiled broadly.

'Very good,' he said. 'Very good indeed.'

He came fairly frequently. I gathered that he was a friend of Jacques besides being his wine merchant, but I met him often in the streets. In fact, so often that I began to think he sought me out.

Violetta always said that I changed when I was in the company of men. I opened out, she said, like a flower does in the sun or when it is given needed water. She is right, of course. I am frivolous and susceptible to admiration, but I do pride myself on knowing my weaknesses.

When we met he would suggest we take a glass of wine together; he knew the right place to take me. It was a kind of wine bar with secluded corners where people could talk in peace. He told me a great deal about his family's winery and was quite eulogistic describing the gathering of grapes; then he would tell me about the pests, the inclement weather and all the hazards that had to be watched.

He knew, of course, that I had left my home to go off with Jacques. He talked often of Jacques and the people who called at the studio; he was one of those people who are very interested in others and in what is going on.

I liked to stroll in and out of the second-hand bookshops which abound on the Left Bank. I constantly thought how much Violetta would like to have been there. Then I would grow morbid, wishing that she were with me and thinking how different it would have been if she were and we were on holiday together, carefree, eventually to return to our real home in Caddington. Then the enormity of what I had done would be brought home to me. I thought of them all mourning me for dead.

If I had known then that Violetta would become engaged to Jowan Jermyn and in the course of events would become my neighbour, I might never have left Tregarland's. But what was the use? It was done now. Characteristically, I had plunged into this adventure. It was the sort of thing I had been doing all my life – but never so irrevocably as I had now.

I had realized it was a mistake – perhaps the greatest of my life. What I had felt for Jacques was slowly slipping away. Not only for me, but for him. I recognized the signs. As for myself, here I was, in a foreign land, dead to all I had known in the past . . . my sister . . . my beloved family . . . my husband who, after all, had cared for me, and my child.

It was no use. I deserved whatever was coming to me. I knew I did. But that does not make it any easier to bear – harder in fact, because of the knowledge that it was my own actions which had brought it about.

One day when I was wandering rather aimlessly round the second-hand bookshops, I met the Baileys. It was one of those encounters which happen simply because one meets fellow countrymen abroad, like that other occasion when we had met Dermot. He had heard us speaking English in the café near the schloss and had stopped. Then he noticed me. I believe that he would have found some way of getting to know me, but it was the language which had first attracted his attention.

I had paused by a shelf to look at a book – a very old one. It was called *Castles of France*. As I stood there, a middle-aged man standing close to me reached out to take a book from a shelf and, as he did so, another book was dislodged. It was a heavy one and it fell, touching my arm as it dropped to the floor.

The man turned to me in dismay. '*Mademoiselle*,' he stammered, '*pardonnez-moi*.'

The accent was unmistakably English and I replied in our tongue. 'That's all right. It hardly touched me.'

'You're English,' he said with a delighted smile.

The woman who was obviously with him was beaming at me. I guessed that they were in their late forties. Their look of pleasure at finding a compatriot amused me.

'And you knew that we were,' added the man.

'As soon as you spoke,' I said.

He grimaced. 'Was it so obvious?'

'I'm afraid so,' I said.

We all laughed. We might have passed on and that would have been an end of it, but the man showed concern about the book which had hit me. He picked it up and said: 'It's rather heavy.'

He replaced it on the shelf while the woman said: 'Are you on holiday?'

'No. I'm staying with a friend.'

'Oh, that's nice.'

'I hope the book didn't hurt you,' said the man. 'Look, why don't we sit down for a bit? Have a coffee. There's a nice place a step or two away.'

'I do like those little cafés,' said the woman. 'And isn't it a relief not to have to think how to say what you want to for a little while? And if you do get it out fairly well, they rush back at you so fast that I for one am completely lost.'

I was thinking: Why shouldn't I have a coffee with them? It will be something to do.

So I found myself sitting with them in the café near the bookshop. They told me they were Geoffrey and Janet Bailey. He was working in the Paris branch of an insurance company and they had been here for six months or so. They were not sure how long they would stay. They had a house at home near Watford, convenient for the City, and they had a married daughter who lived close by who was keeping an eye on things for them.

They asked where my home was.

'Well . . . er . . .' I said. 'It's in Cornwall.'

'Cornwall! A delightful place. Geoff and I thought of having a cottage there. In fact, we might retire down there, mightn't we, Geoff?'

He nodded.

'Looe,' she went on. 'Fowey . . . somewhere like that. We have had many a holiday there. Are you near there?'

'Not very far . . .' I was getting a little embarrassed. I could not tell them then that I used to live there before I ran away with my lover.

I felt a sudden insecurity. I had really thought of my home as Tregarland's. But I had abandoned all that. Their mention of their home and retirement had had an effect on me. They could see ahead. I could not.

Then Geoffrey Bailey said: 'I don't like the way things are going, do you?'

'Things?' I said vaguely.

'The political situation. This man Hitler . . . what will he be up to next?'

'Didn't Mr Chamberlain come back with that agreement from him?'

'Oh, you mean Munich? Do you trust Hitler? Our people in London don't like the way things are going, Czechoslovakia and all that. It will be Poland next, and if he dares . . . well, I think we shall be in it . . . deep.'

'Well, let's hope for the best,' said Mrs Bailey. 'I'm so glad we spoke to you in that bookshop.'

'My clumsiness turned out well in the end,' added Geoffrey.

They talked about Paris then and I was relieved that they asked no more questions about me. They thought I was staying with a friend; but I must have seemed somewhat reticent about my background.

It was only a casual meeting and I should not have got as far as drinking coffee with them if they had not had a guilty conscience about letting a book drop on me.

I was wrong about it being a casual meeting. They insisted on seeing me home, as they said, and they took me to the house. I did not ask them in but said goodbye in the street.

I think that after that Mrs Bailey was so determined to see me again that she did. It was not really difficult.

She was a motherly type of woman, and I realized later that she had sensed that there was something rather mysterious about me. The fact that I had been evasive about my home had not escaped her. I was staying with friends apparently indefinitely, but I had said nothing of these friends. I must have given an impression of frailty. Violetta had always said that drew men to me. I looked helpless and they longed to protect me. Perhaps Mrs Bailey felt this, too.

However, I had caught her interest and the idea had come to her that I might need help.

About a week after our encounter, when I came out of the house, I saw her strolling towards me. She expressed surprise, which did not seem quite natural, and I guessed at once that she had been looking for me since our meeting. She said why didn't I go along with her and have a nice cup of tea in their apartment. Not that the tea tasted like it did at home, but it would be more comfortable than a café, and she would enjoy being able to talk to someone in English.

I was persuaded. Jacques had gone out and if he did return it would do him good to know that I could amuse myself quite happily without him. So I went to the Bailey apartment.

It was a pleasant place in a block of such apartments and she told me that it was the company's and staff used the place when they were over to work, which several of them did for spells from time to time.

We had a pleasant two hours together, which I thoroughly enjoyed, until I realized that she might expect to be invited back. I suppose I could do it. Jacques wouldn't object. It would have to be when he was out, for I was sure he would find the Baileys dull and not his type. He was worldly and sophisticated. It was that which had attracted me in the first place. But the Baileys were comforting. I knew instinctively that in an emergency they would be there. And I was not sure of Jacques. That was the truth. It was beginning to be brought home to me how very rash I had been.

Mimi

It was summer – that long, hot summer when war clouds were gathering over Europe. I was not particularly interested in the war situation. I was too deeply concerned with my own affairs – but then, as Violetta had said, I always had been.

I was feeling definitely uneasy. Things were not the same between Jacques and me. I had a feeling that something was going on all around me – something which I should know because it was important to me.

Georges Mansard, the wine merchant, came frequently and I looked forward to his visits. With my usual vanity, I thought he might be falling in love with me and, as Jacques seemed less ardent, that was gratifying.

I began to ask myself during those summer days what would become of me. It was, of course, a question I should have asked myself before I embarked on this adventure, but, as I have admitted, I always ask myself these questions too late.

What a fool I had been! I knew I had been bored at Tregarland's but my sister was not far off, and my parents would always have provided a refuge. And now they believed me to be dead. It is only when one realizes how much one may need a refuge that it becomes of paramount importance.

I looked forward to those days when Georges Mansard took me to the wine bar for a glass of wine. He asked a great many questions. I was a little evasive about myself, but I expect I betrayed a good deal.

He was very interested to know if I did any work for Jacques.

'You mean modelling?'

'That . . . or anything else.'

'What else should there be?'

He shrugged his shoulders. 'Just . . . anything.'

'Nothing at all.'

He did say on another occasion: 'Still not helping Jacques with his work?'

'No.'

'He just paints all the time, does he?'

'He is out a good deal.'

'Travelling around Paris.'

'Yes, and sometimes farther afield.'

'And never takes you with him?'

'No. He has not done so.'

'It would be very pleasant for you to see a little of France.'

'Very pleasant,' I said. I went on: 'My friends, the Baileys – those English people I met in the bookshop . . . do you remember?'

He nodded. He had been very interested in them at first and asked a lot of questions about them, and then seemed to forget them.

I went on: 'They are always talking about Hitler. They think there will be war.'

'My dear, everyone in Paris thinks there will be war.'

'And you?'

He lifted his shoulders and rocked to and fro as though to say he was not sure. It could go any way.

'If it comes to that, they will go back to England at once.'

'And you?'

'I don't know. I don't see how I could.'

'It would be better for you. You should consider it.'

'I don't see how I could, after what happened.'

'Nevertheless . . .' he murmured.

I saw the Baileys frequently at that time. I told Jacques about them and he had not seemed very pleased.

'But they are very friendly people,' I said. 'They take a parental interest in me and I have often been to their apartment.'

Rather as Georges Mansard had done, he asked questions about them and did not find them very interesting. When I said that, as I had visited them many times, I thought I should return the hospitality, he shook his head rather irritably and said, 'We don't want them here. They sound very boring.'

I supposed they would be to him, but I felt I owed Janet Bailey some explanation, and one day, over a cup of tea, I blurted out the whole story to her. I went right back to the beginning, the meeting in Germany with Dermot, our whirlwind romance and marriage, the birth of Tristan, and the realization that I could endure it no more.

She listened intently as I did so and I saw her expressions of bewilderment, horror and amazement that I could abandon my baby son.

It was a long time before she spoke.

Then she turned to me. 'You poor child,' she said. 'For that is all you are. A child . . . just like Marian. I'd say to her, "Don't touch the stove, dear." That was when she was three years old. "If you do, you'll burn your fingers." Then, as soon as my back's turned, out come her little fingers. A nasty burn, but, as I said to Geoff, "It's experience. That will teach her better than anything."'

'I'm afraid my experience is more than a burned finger.'

'I think you should go home. You don't want to stay with this Frenchman, do you?'

'I don't know.'

'That's good enough. If you don't know, you'd better

get away and the sooner the better. That sister of yours . . . she seems a sensible sort.'

'I must show you a picture of her. It's a miniature. I couldn't leave it behind when I went.'

'Why don't you write to her?'

'She thinks I'm dead.'

'Yes, it is a mess, isn't it? Oh, Dorabella, how could you!'

'I don't know. Looking back I don't understand how I could.'

'It was a heartless thing to do,' said Mrs Bailey slowly.

I stared ahead and felt the tears in my eyes.

Suddenly she put her arms around me.

'I think you have been rather a spoiled baby,' she said. 'But babies grow up. I think you should . . . now, quickly. It's not right for you to be here. What is this artist of yours like?'

'He is good-looking . . . very worldly . . . very sophisticated.'

She nodded. 'I know. It's a pity you couldn't see things a bit more clearly. I know the sort. And when it's over, what shall you do?'

'I just don't know.'

'There's a way out. You could go back and tell your people all about it. They'll be shocked . . . but I reckon they'll be so glad to have you back that they'll forgive you.'

'I don't know if I could face it.'

'I've got a daughter of my own. I know how mothers feel. I know how Geoff and I would be if it were Marian in this mess. Not that she would be. She's happily married with two of the sweetest little things you ever saw – a girl and a boy. But if it were us, we'd be saying, "Give us back our daughter and never mind the rest." Look here, my dear, do you mind if I talk this over with Geoff?'

'No,' I said. I felt as though I were drowning and they wanted to help me at all cost.

After that I saw them very often and we always discussed my position.

Geoffrey was of Janet's opinion. Some means must be found of getting me home.

In the midst of all this I met Mimi.

It was one afternoon. I had been visiting the Baileys. Jacques was aware of my friendship with them, but had expressed no wish to meet them. I had come home a little earlier than usual. I sat down in the *salon*, thinking over my conversation with Janet. She had been telling me that the company had suggested that, because of the way things were going in Europe, it might be necessary for their staff in Paris to make a hasty exit.

'It is looking more and more grim,' she said. 'Things are really working up to a climax. Geoff says that it was inevitable after Hitler had taken Czechoslovakia. That really was the last straw. And now, all this talk of *Lebensraum* and his designs on Poland . . . I know he says he has no quarrel with Britain, but, unprepared as we are, Geoff thinks that if he sets foot in Poland we shall declare war.'

I have to confess that my own affairs concerned me so much that I had little thought to spare for those of Europe, which indicated how foolish I was, for Europe's troubles were those of us all.

However, that day I was early coming back, and as I sat in the *salon* the door opened and a woman, whom I had never seen before, walked into the room with the casual air of one who is very familiar with her surroundings.

She was attired in a *peignoir* merely, and her feet were bare. For a moment I thought I must be in the wrong house.

Her long black hair hung loose; she had almond-shaped dark eyes, a pert *retroussé* nose with a short upper lip. She was tall and I could detect beneath her *peignoir* her full bosom and narrow hips. She was very attractive.

I had risen to my feet in amazement and then, immediately behind her, I saw Jacques.

He said casually: 'Hello. You are back, then. This is Mimi.'

'Mimi?' I said.

'Mimi the model,' she said. She had a very strong French accent.

'I am Dorabella,' I stammered.

Her gaze flickered over me. I returned it, summing her up as coolly as she did me.

Then I said to myself: But it is natural that an artist's model should be in an artist's studio in a state of undress since she would have been posing for him.

'Dorabella has come from England,' said Jacques.

He went to the cabinet and poured out wine.

I felt bewildered. I was asking myself what relationship there was between Jacques and Mimi. I really knew. But Jacques did not seem in the least embarrassed. But then I supposed he would not. That worldliness which I had once so admired was obvious, but now I was less enchanted by it.

I tried to appear as nonchalant as they were.

'Mimi,' I said lightly. '"They call me Mimi, but my name is Lucia."'

Mimi looked puzzled and Jacques said: '*La Bohème*.'

I went on. 'I am Dorabella from *Così Fan Tutte*, and my sister is Violetta from *Traviata*. You see, my mother was very interested in opera.'

Mimi nodded. 'It is amusing, yes.'

'Very,' said Jacques coolly, implying that it was not in the least so.

We sat there sipping our wine; they talked in French too rapid for me to follow all the time. I caught names of various people, some of whom I had met, but I could not really get the gist of their conversation. Once or twice they turned to me and said something in English.

I finished the wine, set down my glass and said I had something to do.

I guessed the relationship between them and I was not quite sure how I felt about his infidelity. Being myself, my first consideration was what effect it would have on me.

What a position I was in! Here was I, alone in a strange country, having left my own in a manner which would make it difficult for me to return. We were on the brink of war. The man whom in my absurd dreaming I had imagined I would be with for ever, had made it clear that he had never intended our liaison to be anything but a passing one.

What a fool I had been! Never in my worthless life had I been in such danger. In every other petty escapade my sister had been at hand to rescue me. Now she was mourning me for dead.

What should I do? Where should I turn?

As usual, one side of me sought to placate the other. She is only a model. Artists have their models. They are casual in their behaviour.

Casual indeed . . . in their love-affairs, slipping from one to the next, and the last one is as dead as the first one they ever had. This was the Bohemian life which I had been so eager to sample. Oh, if only I could go back! But no . . . '*The moving finger writes* . . .' Well, it had written and where now? Oh, Violetta, why are you not here with me at this moment?

I must be careful. I must work out what I should do. Was I going to leave Jacques before he told me to go? Where could I go to? How? Return to Caddington? Face Violetta, my parents? It was the only way.

They loved me. They would be happy to have me back. But how could I explain? And yet . . . what else?

Think, I told myself. Don't rush into something as you usually do – as you did into this. You have to do something. You can't go on here. This is over . . . for him and for you. Thank your stars you are not in love with him any more than he is with you.

I would speak to him. I would ask him exactly what his relationship with Mimi was. How many others were there? I would be calm, practical. I must be.

I sat in the bedroom I shared with him. I heard footsteps in the attic above. I thought, when she left I would speak to him.

I waited and after some time I heard the front door shut.

I would go to the *salon* and confront him. But when I arrived the *salon* was empty. I went up to the studio. He was not there and I realized he had left with Mimi. I felt uncertain. Waiting had always been trying for me. I wanted to strike quickly. I wanted to be on my way. Where to? That was the question.

I rehearsed what I would say to him. I was ready and waiting, but still he did not come back.

He did not return that night. Was he with Mimi? It seemed possible. Perhaps there was someone else. But surely he was staying away to show he cared nothing for my feelings.

It was early afternoon of the next day when he came into the house.

I waited for him in the *salon*. When he came I said with the utmost restraint, tinged only slightly with sarcasm, 'You have had a pleasant time?'

'Very, thank you.'

'With Mimi, the model?'

'Is that your affair?'

'I imagine it is yours.'

He lifted his shoulders and smiled at me benignly.

'Are you telling me she is your mistress?'

'I did not speak of it,' he said.

'Listen, Jacques . . .'

He continued to smile. 'I listen,' he said.

'You can't expect me to accept this.'

He raised his eyebrows questioningly.

This was maddening. He was behaving as though it were perfectly natural for me to find him in the company of a semi-clad woman and then go off and spend the night with her. I could be calm no longer.

'This is unacceptable!' I cried.

'Unacceptable?' He repeated the word as though puzzled. 'Why so?'

'How dare you treat me like this?'

'Treat? What is this treat?'

He was seeking refuge behind an imperfect knowledge of the language. I had seen him do this before. But I knew he understood.

'I left home,' I said, 'to come here . . . and now . . .'

'You left your home because you no longer wanted to stay there.'

'I gave up everything . . . for you.'

'You are being very . . . provincial.'

'And you are so worldly, so sophisticated.'

'I thought you had grown up, too.'

'How can you do this . . . right under my nose?'

'Your nose?' he said, puzzled again.

'You know exactly what I mean. You make no secret of what is going on.'

'Secret? What is this secret?'

'She is your mistress.'

'So?'

I could not go on. I would burst into recriminations if I did, and that would not help me.

'I hate you,' I said.

He lifted his shoulders and regarded me with that benevolent tolerance an adult might show towards a recalcitrant child.

I could bear no more. I ran out of the room, took a coat and left the house.

There was only one place I could go. Janet Bailey had said: 'You know where we are, dear. You can always come to us and we shall be glad to see you.'

I was so relieved to find she was at home.

'I am so glad you came,' she said at once. 'Geoff and I are getting ready to leave.'

I stared at her in dismay. This was another blow. What should I do now?

'Come in,' she went on. 'And I'll tell you all about it.'

I sat down in a daze.

'Cup of tea?' she asked.

'Tell me about your going first,' I said.

'It's on company advice . . . well, orders, more like. It's the way things are going. They're sure there'll be war. They think it's better for us to get home. All the English staff will be leaving and the office will be run by French employees. Heaven knows what will happen! Anyway, we'll be leaving.'

'When?' I stammered.

'In a few days. Just time to get ourselves together.'

'Oh,' I said blankly. Then she noticed something was wrong.

'What is it?' she said, and I blurted out what had happened.

'You can't stay with him!'

'No . . . but what can I do?'

'You'll have to go home. Why not come with us? We'll talk to Geoff about it. He should be home in a couple of hours. Things are in a whirl at the office. They're all saying

Hitler won't stop at Poland and then the balloon will go up. It will be a stampede back once it's started.'

I was seeing a way out. I could go with them. They would help me.

Janet went on as though reading my thoughts.

'Yes, you must come with us. I am sure that will be the best for you.'

'How can I go home?'

'You'll have to make a clean breast of it, dear. There's no help for it.'

'Oh . . . I couldn't do that.'

'What, then? Stay here? Have you any money?'

'I haven't bothered much about money. I have a little at the moment. Jacques always seemed to have plenty and he was quite generous. He liked me to buy clothes and things. I still have most of the last lot he gave me. I think he had a private income. I don't believe he earned much with his paintings. That was one of the reasons I found life in the Latin Quarter so different from what I expected it to be. I've spent hardly anything recently. I suppose it was due to this growing resentment against him. Perhaps I had some notion of getting home. I am not sure. My plans are so vague.'

I could not remember how much I had, but I thought it would pay my fare home.

'Never mind,' said Janet. 'We'd help, of course. You will, of course, have to leave with us, dear. It's the only way. You will have to go back to your husband. Perhaps he will forgive you.'

'I couldn't,' I said.

'But what will you do? You can't stay with that man. I don't suppose he'll want you now he's got this other one. Then you've always got that nice sister of yours – and your mother and father, too. They'll look after you. I know it's not nice having to eat humble pie, but sometimes it's the only way.'

I could see that she was right, and I was wondering how I could work something out.

'Besides,' she went on, 'what work could you do here? I can see something terrible happening to you if you stayed. No, you've got to come home with us. If you can't go back to your husband, there are your sister and your parents.'

She was right, of course. The more I thought about it, the more I could see that I would go home with her and Geoffrey and in the meantime I would make a plan.

We talked in this strain until Geoffrey came home.

'We are leaving at the end of the week,' he said.

He listened to my tale of woe and said of course I must go back with them. I embraced them warmly and said I did not deserve such good friends.

I stayed the night there and the next morning went back to Jacques's house and packed my clothes. I was hoping to leave without seeing Jacques, but he arrived just as I was about to go.

'I'm leaving,' I said.

I fancied I saw a certain relief in his face.

'As you wish,' he replied.

'I am going home.'

'That will be wise.'

I felt a certain exultation because I felt no love for him now. I just wanted to forget the whole episode. If only he had never come to Cornwall! '*The moving finger writes . . .*'

But at least I would be free of him. I would find some way out of this. Violetta would help, as she always had.

'You'll need money,' he said. 'Your fare . . .'

'I can manage, thank you.'

He looked surprised. Then, characteristically, he made that gesture of lifting his shoulders, which had begun to irritate me.

'I would most happily . . .'

'No, thank you. Goodbye.'

'*Bon voyage.*'

And so I left Jacques.

Violetta had once said that feckless people such as I was often seemed to have helpers who arrive at the right moment. So it was with the Baileys. I have often thought since of that happy incident when the book fell from its place on the shelves. What I should have done without the Baileys at that time, I do not know. I shall always be grateful to them – and how fortuitous it was that they should be leaving at that time!

So the first stage was comfortably managed.

There were certain delays on the trains and we were late in reaching Calais. The ferries were uncertain, too.

'It seems,' said Geoffrey, not for the first time, 'that we are leaving at the right moment.'

We had to wait three hours for the ferry.

'That will give us time to have a leisurely meal,' said Janet.

We went to the restaurant near the docks and on the way Geoffrey bought a newspaper.

'I wonder if there is any fresh news?' he said as we settled down and ordered the meal. He opened the paper.

'Hitler signs non-aggression pact with Soviet Union. That's not good. It means he's about to launch an attack on Poland.'

'And if he does,' said Janet, 'that means war. Britain and France won't allow that.'

'Well, we are on our way home, thank goodness. Oh . . .' He paused, and went on: 'There's been a murder . . . a body's been found in the Rue du Singe.'

'Where?' cried Janet.

'It's in the Latin Quarter. I remembering seeing it once. Odd name. Not a very salubrious spot. The sort of street you'd hesitate to go down after dark. As a matter of fact, I was interested in the name when I saw it and I asked them in the nearby café why it was called that. They said a man who had a monkey had lived there. He used to take it into the street and people dropped money into a cap he held out.'

He went on: 'The body seems to be of a man ... a Monsieur Georges Mansard, a wine merchant from Bordeaux.'

I was staring at Geoffrey.

'What?' I said. 'May I see?'

'You look quite shocked, dear,' said Janet.

'I knew him slightly. He used to come to the house now and then. Jacques used to get his wine from him.'

'It's always a shock when it's someone you know. You never think these things are going to happen to people you know.'

I felt very shaken and I wondered who could have murdered pleasant, inoffensive Georges Mansard.

It was getting late when we boarded the ferry. Wrapped in a rug, I sat on deck with the Baileys and kept thinking of Georges Mansard's body lying in that street ... dead ... shot through the heart, it had said. Who had done that to him, I wondered? Was it a love-affair ... a jealous husband? It was hard to imagine Georges involved in anything of that sort.

Then my mind was occupied with what I should do when I reached home. I should go direct to London on reaching Dover and I would telephone Caddington, for that would be the most likely place to find Violetta, and I wanted to ask her advice before I spoke to anyone else. It would be a terrible shock to them all to find me returned from the dead, and I needed Violetta's help as I never had before.

Suppose my mother answered the telephone? Could I speak to her? I could disguise my voice and ask for Violetta. I would beg her to come to see me before I spoke to anyone else. If my mother or father answered the telephone, I should put down the receiver without answering.

We were nearly home now. It was a quiet night. Then I caught a glimpse of the white cliffs of Dover. The curtain was about to rise on a new act in my drama.

The Baileys insisted on my going home with them until I had really made up my mind what I was going to do. They had a pleasant house in a place called Bushey, which had grown out of Watford and was almost an extension of London, for there was mostly a built-up area between it and the capital.

'Convenient for the City,' Geoffrey commented.

Their daughter was there with her husband and I was introduced as a friend they had met in Paris who had had to leave as they had.

I managed, with Janet's help, to avoid mentioning embarrassing details, and as the imminence of war was on everyone's mind to such an extent, this was not really difficult.

I spent a rather restless night in the Baileys' spare room and in the morning had made up my mind that I would telephone Caddington and ask Violetta to come here so that we could plan what had to be done.

I was trembling as I made the call, ready to cut off if anyone but Violetta answered . . . even my parents . . . though I should feel very guilty, remembering all the love they had showered on me throughout my life. But I simply could not face them, telling them the truth. If I had merely eloped it would have been different, but to have staged my disappearance to make it look like death was a terrible thing to have done.

Yes, I must speak first to Violetta.

A voice came over the line to me. It is amazing what emotions one can feel in the space of a second.

'Caddington Hall,' said the voice, which I recognized as Amy's, one of the maids. I felt relieved, then fearful that, if I remembered her voice, she might mine, so I assumed a French accent.

'Could I speak please to Mademoiselle Denver . . . Mademoiselle Violetta.'

'Miss Violetta isn't here now.'

'Not there?'

'No. She's gone to Cornwall.'

'Oh . . . er . . . thank you very much.'

I rang off.

She was in Cornwall, of course. I had asked her to look after Tristan if I should not be there. That was when the thought had come to me that I should make a poor sort of mother, and that Violetta would be a perfect one. My little Tristan would need her in his life. And indeed he had!

So she was with him. And now what must I do? I must go to Cornwall. I must speak to Violetta. She would help me to decide the best way to get back.

I spent another restless night trying to decide the best way to settle the matter. I was forming a plan. I would have to tell Violetta the truth, of course, and together we must concoct a scheme. It occurred to me that I might have become unconscious during that early morning swim and been picked up by a fishing-boat. I had lost my memory, which I had only just regained. I knew that they would all believe me dead and my returning to life would be a shock to them. I must see Violetta first. She would help me break it gently. Turning to Violetta had been a lifelong habit with me. She will get me out of this, I told myself, as I had so many times before.

I had explained to the Baileys that my sister was in

Cornwall and I wanted to break the news to her first, so I should go to her immediately.

I set off the next day. I should arrive in the evening when there were few people about. I must not be recognized. Of course, no one would be expecting to see me, but many of them had known me when I was at Tregarland's and I could imagine the stories which would go round if I were seen.

I realized that I could not call at Tregarland's where, of course, Violetta would be. She would be looking after Tristan.

Then a wild idea came to me. There was a Mrs Pardell, who lived on the west side of Poldown on the cliff in a rather isolated spot. She was the mother of Dermot's first wife and Violetta had struck up a friendship with her when she was trying to find out the truth about my predecessor.

Violetta had said she was a blunt and honest North Countrywoman and she firmly believed that her daughter had been murdered – by poor Dermot, of course, who would not have hurt a fly.

I arrived at Poldown, as planned, late in the afternoon. I decided I would go first to Mrs Pardell. I would tell her that I was afraid to go to Tregarland's. If she believed Dermot had murdered his first wife, she would understand the fears the second might feel. I would tell her this tale of loss of memory. I had embellished it a little since I first thought of it; and I would ask her advice. People loved to be asked for their advice. It made them feel wise.

This is what I did and, to my tremendous relief and not a little surprise, it worked.

I knocked at her door; she opened it and regarded me suspiciously. Then I saw her expression change. She had recognized me.

'Don't be afraid,' I said. 'I am not a ghost. I am myself.'

She seemed unable to speak. Then she said: 'You're Mrs Tregarland . . . the second one, I mean.'

'That's right. I lost my memory. I can explain. I'd like to tell you about it. I know I can trust you.'

That was another point. People liked to be trusted.

'It is all so difficult,' I went on. 'I know you will help me.'

They liked to be asked for help, and to give it – if it was not too inconvenient to themselves.

'You'd better come in,' she said.

I could see she was trying to suppress her uneasiness in talking to what might be a ghost, but she was determined to cling to her North Country good sense and have 'nowt to do with any of that ghost nonsense'.

She was really rather brave, I thought; and I must say her conduct was admirable.

I was taken into a sitting-room and seated near a picture of the first Mrs Tregarland – a handsome girl, with somewhat overripe attractions. A good sort, I thought. Easy-going, just right to bring people into the inn where she had worked as a barmaid before her marriage. Poor Dermot! He had been very young at the time.

I told my story. I had gone swimming one day, had lost my memory, had been taken into a hospital some way off. I could not remember where or who I was.

'Well, there was an awful fuss when you went. Your sister was very cut up. I reckon she'll be as pleased as a dog with two tails when she knows you're back. You'd better get to her right away.'

'I want to make sure of seeing her alone first. I shall have to explain. I am very undecided, Mrs Pardell. It will be a shock, and I am a little frightened about my husband.'

She was silent, staring at me.

I said: 'I'm afraid to go back . . . afraid . . .'

'I know what you mean,' she said. 'There's something funny about that place. But you needn't be afraid of him any more. He got his come-uppance, he did.'

'What do you mean, Mrs Pardell?'

'He's dead. Fell off his horse. He was crippled . . . badly. Then he took too many pills. Some said it was by accident, some said he meant to do it. They weren't sure.'

I could not speak. I was too shocked. I kept saying to myself: It was my fault. Oh, my poor Dermot. You fell off your horse and I wasn't there and you died. How much better it would have been if you had never taken that holiday in the German forest! How much better for us all!

'Well,' went on Mrs Pardell, 'he went . . . and then there was all that trouble with the housekeeper . . . or was she a housekeeper? No one knew quite . . . some sort of relation. Went off her head. Had to be put away. And there she is in Bodmin. It was one thing after another up at Tregarland's.'

I thought: How can I face them now . . . even Violetta? She will blame me. This changes everything.

I had planned to tell them the story of losing my memory. No one except Violetta must ever know about Jacques. I had planned to reform and be a good wife to Dermot for ever after. Now . . . he was dead.

I stammered: 'I find it all so difficult. It wasn't what I had expected. I don't know how I shall face them . . . even my sister.'

'Your sister is a nice, sensible girl.'

'I know . . . but even her . . . after this. My husband . . . dead.'

'Don't take it so hard. I'll never believe he didn't have a hand in my girl's death.'

'No . . . not Dermot. He would never hurt anyone.'

'Well, he was your husband. It's natural, I suppose, for you to stand up for him.'

'Mrs Pardell, may I stay here for a while? I've a little money. Suppose I could stay for about a week? I'll pay for everything. I've got to think how I am going to get back.'

She hesitated for a moment, then she said: 'You're welcome to stay.'

'Oh, thank you. I only want a few days. I couldn't even see my sister now . . . not just yet. I have to think . . .'

When I look back on that time, I can't remember the order in which things happened. I went over my plans, deciding what I could tell Violetta. I should need all my courage to face her. The news about Dermot had unnerved me.

I was in a panic now. I felt sick and ashamed. I could not stop thinking of Dermot's going out riding . . . recklessly, I imagined, for he had always been decidedly at home on a horse. Mrs Pardell had hinted darkly that he had been drinking. Oh, Dermot, I thought, what did I do to you?

I longed to see Violetta, while I wondered how I could face her.

There was one day when I was alone in the house. Mrs Pardell had gone into West Poldown to shop. I thought how fortunate it was that she was, as she said, one to 'keep herself to herself'. She would not gossip in the town. She was what they called a 'foreigner' in these parts, not even coming from the South of England, and so she was placed in a category lower than mine. In times of stress, one is thankful for these small blessings.

There was a knock on the door. I was startled. Mrs Pardell had had no visitors since I had arrived. I looked from the window of my bedroom and emotion swept over me, for Violetta was standing below.

Now was my moment. Yet I stood still. Panic rushed over me. I could not move. I had been waiting to see her and now that the opportunity had come to do so, I was filled with dismay. I was unprepared. I kept seeing heartbroken Dermot, drinking too much, taking his horse out in a reckless mood and then being injured – and later ending his life.

I had done that. I stood at the window and I said to myself: Not yet.

Again she knocked. I felt limp. I wanted to go down and throw myself into her arms. But I did not do so. I watched her walk away and immediately she had gone I wanted to rush after her.

What a fool I was! What would Mrs Pardell think if I told her? I stood leaning against the curtains, cursing myself for being an idiot. I had lost the best opportunity that could be offered.

I did not tell Mrs Pardell. She would have despised me for a coward, and rightly so.

There was another stupid thing I did. I had not gone outside the house during the daylight hours for fear of being seen and recognized. But after a while I was so distraught that I just could not bear to remain indoors any longer. I felt as though I were in a cage. I was imprisoned by my own folly and cowardice. I had to get out. Late one afternoon, in a mood of recklessness, I left the house. It was unfortunate that on the cliff path I came face to face with one of the maids from Tregarland's. I had at least taken the precaution of wearing a scarf over my head.

To my horror, I realized she had recognized me, for she turned pale and stared at me. She thought I was a ghost, that was clear. I tried to look vague and unearthly. I stared ahead of her and went past.

I knew she would go back to Tregarland's and tell them she had seen my ghost. And what would Violetta think? She could not believe the girl, of course, but she would start thinking of me and I knew she would be mourning for me afresh.

I went back to the cottage. I lay tossing all that night. This state of affairs could not go on. I suggested to Mrs

Pardell that she write to Violetta and ask her to call. That would seem reasonable.

This she agreed to do.

And that was how I was reunited with Violetta.

I remember every detail of that meeting. I opened the door and stood before her. I shall never forget her look of amazement, of disbelief, and the sudden dawning of joy when she realized that I was alive.

As always, Violetta set me on the right course. Not that it had been easy. She immediately pointed out that, of course. I had to tell her the truth and she agreed that this was something which, for all our sakes, should not be revealed. Life would be impossible if such stories were kept alive in the neighbourhood in which we were living, and they would be embellished in the process. There was Tristan to think of. He must not grow up learning of the scandal.

Violetta brought her practical mind to bear on a solution. To have been picked up off our coast and taken to Grimsby was ridiculous, she said. If I were picked up by a fishing vessel, it would have been a Cornish one. I should have been known immediately and taken to the hospital in Poldown, and, lost memory or not, Tregarland's would have been notified without delay.

The loss of memory would have to stay, but Violetta suggested I could have been picked up by a yacht, the owners of which were on their way home to the North of England. They had been in Spain. They did not realize immediately that I had lost my memory and, by the time they did, we were on the north coast. So they took me to a hospital there.

'It is not very good,' she said, 'but it will have to do.'

She arranged it as she always did. My parents came down to Tregarland's at once. They had to know the truth. No one else there did.

Violetta said we should never have got away with such a tale but for the fact that, just about this time, war was declared and people had something other to think about than the exploits of a wayward wife.

I had done my best to forget that incident with Jacques, as I did with all the unpleasant incidents in my life. It was a comforting habit I had developed.

And then . . . there he was, arriving on our shore, in the middle of the night, with a sister of whom I had never heard before.

Violetta

Suspicions

There was great excitement in the Poldowns over the arrival of the French refugees. People welcomed them. They were our allies, escaping from German tyranny and eager to come over to us and help with the war effort.

I wished they had arrived somewhere else and not on our coast, for I could see what effect the advent of the lover whom she had left not long before was having on Dorabella. She was deeply disconcerted, though he was nonchalant enough, as though meeting up with a past passion was an ordinary event for him.

Gordon Lewyth helped in his practical way. He found out where Jacques could join General de Gaulle's headquarters and very soon Jacques left us. Simone remained. She wanted to do some work and Gordon was looking round to find something for her.

By this time people were feeling they should all be doing something, for, as the weeks passed, the situation was becoming more menacing. The Germans were now dropping bombs on England and London was attacked with particular ferocity. We all knew, even if the Prime Minister had not told us, that the enemy was attempting to destroy our air defence as a prelude to an invasion of our island.

We must be prepared.

I was seeing Mrs Jermyn frequently, and we found a great deal of comfort in each other's society. We shared our mourning for Jowan, as no one else could, and we both refused to believe that he was dead.

I used to go and sit with her while we had tea served by her maid, Morwenna, just as we always had, although the cakes now were made without butter and the tea was weak; but when we spoke of Jowan, it was as though he were somewhere over there and would come home to us in time.

Mrs Jermyn was not given to self-pity. She just kept herself – and me – convinced that he would come home one day.

When she heard about the arrival of Jacques and his sister, she invited them to come and see her, for she remembered that Jacques had come over for a painting holiday before the war.

She also asked Dorabella, who declined on the pretext of a previous engagement, for naturally she did not want to be in the company of Jacques any more than was necessary.

We talked, of course, about the situation. Mrs Jermyn understood why they did not want to live in France with Pétain, who had not only surrendered but was actually helping the enemy. She saw that the only thing they could do was come and join de Gaulle.

'And you, my dear,' she said to Simone, 'they tell me that you want to do something. What sort of thing?'

Simone replied that she would do anything needed to help. Perhaps she could go and make munitions somewhere. 'Mr Lewyth . . . he is very kind. Is he not, Jacques?' she said.

Jacques replied that Mr Lewyth was a man of much knowledge and indeed he was kind.

'How do you feel about going on the land?' asked Mrs Jermyn.

'The land?' said Simone. 'What is this land?'

'It's working on the farms. As so many men are going off to fight, girls are being recruited now. I heard they are shaping up very well. What of you?'

'On the farm . . .' She lifted her eyebrows and looked at Jacques.

'Would it be here . . . in these parts?' he asked.

'I think so. I know our manager, Mr Yeo, is looking for someone to replace one of the men who has just been called up.'

Jacques said: 'To work here . . . on this estate . . . on Jermyn's . . . that would be very good, would it not, Simone?'

'Well, yes. If I can do . . . this land. I must have means to live . . . we could bring very little with us, you understand?'

'But of course. I tell you what we will do. When we have had our tea, I shall send for Mr Yeo. He was a little sceptical about landgirls, I'm afraid, but naturally he would be, wouldn't he, Violetta? We will talk to him and then decide.'

'Soon it will not be for us to decide,' I said. 'They are talking about calling up the women as well as the men. They will draft them into suitable occupations, I expect.'

'Well, Mademoiselle,' said Mrs Jermyn to Simone, 'you must see Mr Yeo.'

It was amazing how well it worked out. Mr Yeo was sure he could find a place for Simone, and shortly after the Dubois had arrived on our shores Jacques had joined the Free French Army and Simone was working on the Jermyn estate.

Dorabella had admitted to me that she was relieved that Jacques was not staying in the neighbourhood.

'Did you fear that he might revive your passion?' I asked.

I was alarmed because she did not answer immediately. She seemed as though she were going to confide something. Then I saw the look in her eyes. No use trying to explain to Violetta. She would never understand.

Then she said: 'Oh no, nothing of the sort.'

But I continued to feel a little uneasy. I feared that, though she knew him for a philanderer and an inconstant lover, she was still attracted by him.

I was very glad that he had gone away.

The war news was becoming more and more depressing. It was heartrending to hear of the terrible damage that was being inflicted on London. There were rumours of barges being constructed on the other side of the Channel in preparation for invasion.

It was amazing how people steeled themselves for the worst. I think what we dreaded most was to have the enemy on our soil. There was a general feeling of kindness towards each other. It was noticeable. The awareness of what could happen to us made us tolerant and want to help others.

We heard stories of the heroism of the people of London. Many of them had already sent their children away from home and now they faced bombardment with stoicism flavoured by grim humour.

It was indeed a strange time to live in and I knew that I should never forget it through all the days left to me.

And still there was no news of Jowan.

I was having tea with Mrs Jermyn one day when she said: 'Your family used to run that place in Essex. They made it into a hospital during the first war.'

'That's so. It was my grandmother, and my mother helped too. She has often told us about it.'

'I was thinking of this place. Not exactly as a hospital, but lots of those men will need somewhere to get over their illnesses and operations. I thought . . . with all this space, we could have some of them here. It would give them a rest . . . a sort of convalescent home. What do you think?'

'Would it be too much for you?' I remembered when I had first met her she had seemed almost an invalid.

'I should have people to help. I thought about you.'

'But, of course!' I cried. 'I have been wondering what I could do to help. They say that soon we shall all be called up.'

'My dear,' she said, 'I should find it hard if you went away. It is so helpful for me to talk to you. You know how I feel. You understand . . .'

She meant that we were the two who loved Jowan and we had to keep the belief that he would come back alive. We helped each other in that.

I said: 'It seems an excellent idea. There are several bedrooms. It would make a wonderful convalescent home.'

'So I thought. We could get your mother to give us a few hints of how they ran their place.'

'She would be delighted to help.'

'You and I together could run the place. And perhaps your sister would like to help.'

'I am sure she would. It is a wonderful idea.'

We talked excitedly. It took our minds from the fear of what might come – and chiefly what might have happened to Jowan.

How grateful I was for all that had to be done in the next few weeks! I was constantly at Jermyn's Priory. The authorities came to look at the place and we were in touch with the hospital in Poldown. It seemed that the idea of a convalescent home for the war-wounded was very acceptable.

The rooms were made ready and we were expecting the first arrivals. There were several servants at Jermyn's and these would stay and help with the running of the place instead of going into factories or on the land, as so many of them would be called upon to do. There was no doubt that running Jermyn's Priory in this way was considered to be essential war work.

In the midst of this something very tragic occurred.

I was leaving the house on my way to Jermyn's, where I now went each day, when Gordon opened the door of his study and asked me to come in for a moment.

He was very grave.

'It's bad news,' he said. 'The boys' parents, Mr and Mrs Trimmell . . . their house has been hit. It happened last night.'

'Oh no! And . . . ?'

He nodded. 'Both parents killed instantly.'

'How terrible! Those poor boys. What will become of them?'

'They'll stay here for a while . . . well, as long as they want to. Is it not tragic? Mother and father . . . gone like that. Apparently the father was home on leave from the Navy, so both were there.'

'The boys will have to be told,' I said.

He looked at me helplessly. 'It's what I dread. How can I, Violetta? I thought you would know how to do it better than I.'

I was silent, thinking of the boys. How best to break the news to them. It was going to be difficult. But I could see that Gordon would not be the best one to do it.

I pondered. I said I thought I would speak to Charley first and then we could tell Bert afterwards. Charley was a shrewd boy. I always felt he was far older than his years. There were times when it seemed as though I were talking to a young man of eighteen; at others he would seem just like a child. He would have need of his maturity now.

I went up to the nursery where I was greeted with vociferous pleasure by Tristan, while Hildegarde, who always imitated Tristan, showed her delight in my arrival.

I told Nanny Crabtree what had happened.

Her face creased with tenderness.

'The poor mites,' she cried. 'I wish I had that Hitler

here. I'd give him a dose of the medicine he's giving to little children.'

I arranged with her that when the boys came home from school Charley should be told I wanted to see him. I would break the news to him and with his help tell Bert – or perhaps it would be better for him to do it alone.

I felt sick at heart when he came and still could not decide what was the best way to tell him.

His face was bright with expectancy, and I heard myself say hesitatingly: 'Charley, there's something I have to tell you . . .'

I paused. 'Yes, Miss,' he said.

I bit my lip and turned away. Then I stammered: 'Something has happened. It's very sad. You know London has been badly bombed?'

He stared at me. 'Is it my mum . . . or Aunt Lil . . . or someone like that?'

I said: 'Charley, it is your father and mother. Your father was home on leave . . .'

He stood very still; he had turned very pale and then the colour rushed into his cheeks.

'Charley, you know how dreadful this war is . . .'

He nodded. 'Does Bert know?' he asked. ''Course he don't. You told me first.'

'Yes. I thought you would know how best to tell him.'

He nodded.

'Charley, we're all very sorry.'

'If we'd 'a bin there,' he said.

'You couldn't have done anything for them, you know.'

'Why wasn't they in one of them shelters?'

'I don't know. Perhaps we'll hear. I suppose sometimes the raids start before people can get there.'

He nodded again.

'This is your home now, you know, Charley. Mr Lewyth wanted you to know that.'

He was silent for a moment, then he said: 'I'd better tell Bert.'

'You'll know how to do that.'

He looked bewildered and, on a sudden impulse, I went to him and put my arms round him. I held him tightly for a few seconds. He did not respond, but I sensed he was glad I did it.

Then he went off to tell Bert.

Nanny Crabtree was very gentle with them that night. She called Bert 'my pet' when she addressed him.

They were strange boys. I guessed their parents had never been demonstrative in their affection. I kept thinking about them throughout the evening and I could not resist going up to their rooms that night when they had gone to bed.

I looked in at Charley's first. He was not there. Then I went into Bert's room. Charley was on Bert's bed, holding him in his arms. The night light on the table beside the bed was still on.

Charley looked at me rather aggressively as I came in.

I said: 'I thought I'd just look in to see how you were feeling.'

'All right,' said Charley, almost defiantly.

'And Bert?' I asked. It was clear that Bert was not 'all right'.

'He couldn't sleep,' said Charley, by way of explaining his presence. 'So I just come in to talk to him.'

Bert started to cry.

Charley said: 'It's all right. This is our home now. She said so. It's nice here. Better than Oban Street, now ain't it?'

I sat down on the bed.

'Charley's right,' I said. 'This is your home now. There's

nothing to worry about.' I put my arms round him and, surprisingly, he turned to me. I stroked his hair.

'There,' I went on soothingly, 'it is very sad, and we are all very, very sorry. But you are here now and Charley's here with you.'

He nodded and kept close to me.

Charley lay back on the pillows.

'It's all right, Miss,' he said. 'I'll see to him.'

I nodded, rose and went quietly out of the room.

I saw Charley the next day. Bert was not with him. Charley seemed to feel I needed some explanation of Bert's behaviour on the previous night.

'He'll be all right,' he said. 'It wasn't much good there. Better here. I tell Bert that. Our old man, he was always drunk and when he was he'd belt us . . . Bert more than me. And Mum, she was always on at us.'

'My poor Charley,' I said.

He looked at me rather scornfully and said: 'I was all right and I looked after Bert. But, well, it was his home, like. He's only little. That's what it is with him. It was his home, see.'

I said I did see.

'It will be better here,' I assured him. 'We'll make sure of that. You like it here, don't you?'

'It's all right,' said Charley grudgingly.

I thought: We must make sure that it remains so. He was a good boy, Charley. I was not surprised that his little brother thought he was wonderful.

Mrs Jermyn was forging ahead with her plan. It had not been difficult to convert the Priory into the kind of home she had visualized, and she already had half a dozen soldiers there. Some of them walked with sticks and there were others who had to be taken into the hospital in West

Poldown for dressing of their wounds, so we had plenty to do. Mrs Jermyn had taken up the project with such enthusiasm that she seemed years younger. I could not believe she was the same woman to whom Jowan had introduced me not so long ago.

Dorabella, Gretchen and I were all working for her. Dorabella was an immediate success with the soldiers. She did them a great deal of good, I was sure, by joking with them in her mildly flirtatious way. Gretchen worked hard and I must say, so did I.

We were all tremendously enthusiastic, and we had the wholehearted approval of the authorities.

Tom Yeo had immediately found work for Simone on the estate, and she was sharing a cottage with old Mrs Penwear. It had worked out very satisfactorily, for Mrs Penwear had been recently widowed and did not like living alone. Mr Penwear had been retired for a few years before his death and his wife had been allowed to keep the cottage for her lifetime.

Simone seemed very pleased with life. She was clearly relieved to have left France and was eager to do all she could to bring about Hitler's defeat. She proved to be of a friendly nature and Mrs Penwear was obviously delighted to share her home with her.

In the evening, Simone told me, they would talk together. Mrs Penwear liked to tell her about the people in the neighbourhood. These conversations were a great help to Simone and her knowledge of English improved perceptibly. Everyone was very kind and welcoming to her. They thought she was very brave to have crossed the sea with her brother. They could all understand why she did not want to stay in her own country, and felt impelled to come over to England to work with the brave de Gaulle and help drive the enemy out of France.

Most of the soldiers who came to us stayed for two or

three weeks. Many of them seemed just like boys who had been thrust into experiences of horror and were somewhat bewildered by it; but in the main they were light-hearted and prepared to enjoy life.

I remember one rather serious young man in whom I was particularly interested because he had been in the RFA and had trained at Lark Hill; and it occurred to me that he might have known Jowan.

He was not badly hurt. He had a leg wound and walked with a stick which he hoped in a few months he would be able to discard.

One day I found him in the gardens alone and I joined him.

I said: 'You will be leaving us soon.'

'I shall always remember this place,' he told me. 'It has been a happy time here. It feels so restful . . . away from it all.'

'Scarcely that,' I replied. 'There's a lot of activity in the air and then the continual watch for invasion.'

'Ah yes, that's true, but where could one get away from this ghastly war? You and the young ladies, and Mrs Jermyn, of course, have helped a great deal.'

We were silent for a while, and then I said: 'I told you my fiancé was . . . over there?'

'Yes,' he said.

'It is some months since Dunkirk now. Do you think . . . ?'

'One can never be sure. Some of them were taken prisoner. Others may be on the run. There are some good brave people over there. They hated this patched-up peace and are working underground. I believe they help people get across the borders into neutral territory . . . Switzerland, for instance. The lucky ones could manage to get home . . . in time.'

'What of the soldiers who were taken prisoner?'

'Even the Germans should respect the rules of war and

must treat prisoners according to them. But it would mean waiting until the war is over . . .'

'Do you think it is possible for people to escape?'

'Everything is possible.'

'Do you really believe it is reasonable to go on hoping? Please tell me the truth.'

He said solemnly: 'Yes, I think it is reasonable to hope. How can we know what is happening over there?'

I did feel a little comforted after that, and I had a conviction that somewhere Jowan was alive and that he would come back.

I could not sleep that night. I kept thinking of Jowan in some prisoner-of-war camp in France . . . in Belgium . . . in Germany. It could be in any of those countries. Or perhaps he had escaped capture. Perhaps he was in hiding with some French people who were looking after him and would get him to Switzerland.

And as I lay there, I saw a sudden light flash across the sky. I got out of bed and looked out to sea. It was dark; but as I stood there I saw a beam of light. It flashed and was gone in a moment.

In view of the invasion fears, I felt I could not dismiss this lightly. At the same time, I remembered the laughter we had aroused through our shoal of fish which we had thought was an invading force. I was cautious.

I slipped on some clothes and went out. Everything was still. I could see nothing as far out as the horizon. I waited a while and went back to bed, but not to sleep. I had definitely seen those flashes.

When I went down to breakfast I saw Gordon and told him that I had seen flashes of light during the night.

'Strange,' he said. 'Could have been lightning. I don't think any invading force would flash lights to warn us of their arrival.'

'No. That's why I did not raise the alarm. I did not want

to appear ridiculous again. It was all quiet, so I just returned to bed.'

'It was almost certainly lightning.'

But it seemed that others had seen the lights. We were still keeping our watch on the cliffs, though it seemed less likely now that the Germans would try to invade.

We were, according to reports, showing a strong resistance in the air, and the battle which must be won before a landing was attempted was not yet over. Unlike the French, the British had shown they were determined to fight, no matter at what cost to themselves.

All the same, we must be on the alert.

There was a great deal of talk about the lights.

Naturally there were exaggerations and the lights had become signals and there was the inevitable conclusion that there were traitors among us who were sending messages to the enemy across the sea.

Charley came home from school one day with a bruised face and a black eye.

Nanny Crabtree seized on him.

'Fighting again!' she cried. 'You'll get really hurt one of these days, young fellow. I tell you, I won't have it. What was this all about?'

Charley looked stubborn. 'Knocked me 'ead on a post,' he said sullenly.

'Don't give me that,' said Nanny Crabtree. 'You've been having a scrap, that's what.'

She showed extreme displeasure, but Charley refused to talk and he was in disgrace. I was surprised to detect how much he cared; but he put on that defiant, almost insolent, look which always maddened Nanny Crabtree.

'I can't do with a child that gives me that look,' she explained. 'He says nothing . . . just looks at you as though he knows it all and you know nothing. And what can you do? All he's done is look. And another thing, I can't stand a child who lies. Walked into a post, my foot!'

Poor Charley, I was sorry for him. However indifferent his parents had been, they were still his family and there did not seem to be anyone else but Aunt Lil, for whom he obviously had little respect or affection. All he had was his little brother, and I was deeply touched by the protective care he bestowed on him. I liked Charley and I hated to see him on bad terms with Nanny Crabtree.

I was visiting Mrs Pardell now and then. She had been a good friend to us at the time of Dorabella's return and I knew she was pleased when I called on her, though her nature prevented her from showing this pleasure.

She was fiercely patriotic and was constantly knitting sweaters and balaclavas for the troops; she also worked a few hours a week with the Red Cross.

She gave me a glass of her homebrewed wine and, as we sat talking, she mentioned the lights which had been flashing out to sea.

I said: 'Mr Lewyth thinks they were probably lightning.'

'It could be,' she agreed. 'And yet again it might not.'

'If it were not, what was it?'

She pressed her lips tightly together and said: 'Well, I suppose there could have been something out there . . . a submarine, or something like that . . . something out of sight that could get in close . . . and someone on land could be sending out messages.'

'I suppose that is possible.'

'They're up to all sorts of things nowadays. There's some funny people about. The lights were out your way. You ought to remember that, so you could keep a special guard.'

'But . . .' I began.

'Well,' she went on, 'you've got that German girl up there. Can't be too careful these days.'

'You can't mean . . .'

'Well, she's a German. You can't trust any of them. Little Hitlers, the lot of them.'

'Gretchen!' I cried. 'Oh, but that's absurd. She hates Hitler and his regime. He has ruined the lives of her family.'

'Well, that's as may be, but once a German always a German.'

I knew from the past that once Mrs Pardell had made up her mind, there was no changing it. I was deeply disturbed, for I guessed she was not the only one who would be suspicious of Gretchen. Her accent betrayed her and since the flashing lights episode, which, as had been observed, had come from Tregarland's way, they would say: That German woman is there.

After that I was aware of the attitude towards Gretchen when we went into the Poldowns together. Sly looks were cast her way.

This was ridiculous. I could only hope that Gretchen was not aware of it. But I could see there was an inevitability about it. The people wanted to suspect someone, and naturally they looked to Gretchen.

This was confirmed when I made the discovery through Bert Trimmell.

I came across him one day, sitting on a stile near the home farm. He had been doing some little job Gordon had given him. Both boys liked to work on the farm, particularly among the animals.

He looked mournful, even near to tears. I paused and said: 'Hello, Bert. What's wrong?'

He hesitated for a moment and then said: 'Nanny Crabtree don't like us any more. Will she send us away?'

'Good gracious, no. She would never do that. She really does like you very much.'

'She don't like Charley. Charley says she could send us away.'

'She would never do that. We wouldn't let her, and she wouldn't want to either. It's just that she doesn't like fighting and Charley wouldn't tell her why he had done it when she had said he was not to.'

'Charley didn't think he ought to tell her, did he?'

I was used to the phraseology of the boys. They would ask confirmation of facts of which one could know nothing. They were not really asking, I realized. It was just a form of speech.

'To tell her what?' I asked.

'What he was fighting about.'

'Why?'

''Cos he didn't think it was right, did he?'

'What didn't he think was right?'

'To tell 'er. He said there was some things you had to keep quiet about.'

'Bert, please tell me. I promise that, if it is something which I shouldn't be told, I won't tell it.'

He paused for a moment, then he looked at me squarely.

'All right,' he said. 'It was that boy, wasn't it? He said there was a traitor in our 'ouse. She was a German spy and she was sending messages to them Germans out there.'

'Yes,' I said faintly.

'Well, Charley said it was a lie, didn't he? There wasn't no traitors in our 'ouse, and then he gave him that black eye, didn't 'e?'

'I see. So that was what it was all about.'

'Charley didn't 'arf give him a going-over,' Bert giggled. 'Charley would give him the same over again if he said anything about anybody in our 'ouse.'

'I see. Bert, I think I ought to tell Nanny Crabtree.'

'Charley won't like it. He'll go on at me for telling.'

'I think Charley will like it. It was a good thing he did. I am going to tell Nanny. Then I think she will like him . . . like him very much. Charley need not be unhappy any more.'

Bert was silent for a moment, then he said: 'All right. You'll know, Miss.'

I went to Nanny Crabtree at once.

'Nanny,' I said. 'I've discovered why Charley was fighting.'

'The young imp,' said Nanny. 'After I'd told him I'd have none of that here.'

'I think you'll change your mind when you hear. Some boy was saying that Gretchen was a spy and was sending messages out to sea. Charley wouldn't have that. He wouldn't have anyone saying anything against anyone in this house.'

Nanny Crabtree's face softened into a beatific smile.

'And he had a fight with this boy because of that? Silly lad. Why didn't he tell me?'

'He seemed to have some idea that you wouldn't like it to be mentioned.'

'Well, well, what would you do with them, then?'

'So it was rather a noble act,' I said.

'What goes on in their minds, bless 'em. I'm going to give him my sweet ration, that's what.'

I put my arms round her and hugged her. Nanny loved sweet things and her sweet ration was rather important to her.

After that, Charley knew he was forgiven.

I said to Nanny: 'I am so pleased. It shows, doesn't it, that he thinks of Tregarland's as his home?'

'More of a home than he had back with those parents of his. And that Aunt Lil. I don't much like the sound of her.'

'Yes,' I said. 'He feels he has to defend us all. It means, Nanny, that he looks on this now as his home.'

We had a caller at the Priory. He drove over one afternoon when I happened to be in the gardens getting some flowers for one of the rooms, so I heard the car arrive and went to see who it was.

A tall, pleasant-looking man in the uniform of a captain alighted from the car.

'I wonder if I could see Mrs Jermyn,' he asked me. 'My name is Brent.'

'I am sure you can. Do come in.'

I took him to a sitting-room on the ground floor and asked one of the maids to tell Mrs Jermyn that we had a visitor.

'A lovely place you have here,' he said. 'Highly suitable for your convalescent home. It is that I have come to see you about, really.'

'We have had visits from the authorities and from the hospital. That was when we started.'

'Yes, I know, and everyone is delighted with what you are doing. I'm actually an army doctor. My captain's rank is complimentary. I thought you might allow me to call occasionally to see the men who are here. Many of them, although they are physically well enough to leave hospital, have suffered gruelling experiences and need special care.'

Mrs Jermyn arrived. They shook hands and he said: 'I'm James Brent – attached to the medical staff. I have been explaining to Miss . . .'

'Denver,' I supplied.

He smiled. '. . . to Miss Denver that we want to keep an eye on some of the men. They have been through some shattering ordeals and we want to make sure they're all right. I was hoping you wouldn't mind if I called from time to time . . . just to see that all's well. There are one or two who have given us cause for anxiety.'

'But of course, you are welcome at any time,' said Mrs Jermyn.

'We think you are doing a wonderful job here. These few weeks of recuperation are just what the men need.'

Mrs Jermyn smiled with pleasure.

'It seems such a small thing to do at such a time.'

'It is all the small things which add up. I was saying to Miss Denver what a lovely place you have. Ideal for the rest these men deserve and need. I suppose you have always lived here, Mrs Jermyn?'

'Oh yes. It's the ancestral home. It came with my marriage. The family have been here for three hundred years. It belongs to my grandson. He . . .'

'He was with the forces,' I heard myself say. 'We were hoping he would come back from Dunkirk . . .'

'Miss Denver is his fiancée,' said Mrs Jermyn quietly. 'We feel . . .'

'There are a lot of our men over there,' he said quickly. 'Quite a few of them were taken prisoner.'

'It is the not knowing . . .' began Mrs Jermyn.

'I am very sorry. But it does not do to give up hope.'

'That is what we tell each other,' I said.

'And you are helping in this enterprise, Miss Denver. If you could hear what some of the men are saying about you all, you would feel it was very rewarding. And you have several helpers, I believe?'

'Oh, the servants have thrown themselves wholeheartedly into the project, haven't they, Violetta?' said Mrs Jermyn.

'Indeed yes.'

'And you have other young ladies here to help you?'

'I have three helpers,' said Mrs Jermyn.

'I should like to meet them and express my appreciation.'

Mrs Jermyn looked at me. 'They would be around somewhere, wouldn't they?'

'Yes,' I said. 'I'll ask Morwenna to bring them. I am sure they would be delighted to meet you, Captain Brent. They will enjoy hearing that the men have been happy here.'

'Just tell me a little about them first, would you?'

'There is my sister, Mrs Tregarland. She is a widow. She was married to young Mr Tregarland. It's the big house just along the cliff. She has a young child and we are twins actually. We have been together most of our lives.'

He nodded, smiling. 'And there is another young lady, I believe.'

'That is Mrs Denver.'

'Oh? She is related to you?'

'Well, it is a little difficult to explain. She married . . . a sort of adopted brother. My mother took him when he was a baby and he was brought up mainly by my grandparents.'

'Would they be the people who made such an excellent job of turning their home into a hospital during the last war?'

'Yes. Marchlands, my grandparents' home. Briefly, my mother was at school in Belgium in 1914 and she found a baby who had lost its foster parents. She brought him to England. He took our name of Denver. Mrs Denver is his wife.'

'Is it true that she is German?'

'Yes. She is Jewish. Her parents and brothers may be dead. We don't know where they are. They were persecuted by the Nazis.'

'That's very sad. And she is helping here now?'

'She is of great help,' said Mrs Jermyn. 'Tell Morwenna to bring them here if she can find them, Violetta. Then they can meet Captain Brent.'

I did so. Dorabella was the first to arrive.

'Dorabella,' I said, 'this is Captain Brent. He has come to see some of the men here. Captain Brent, my sister Mrs Tregarland.'

They shook hands and I saw Dorabella's eyes brighten. Captain Brent was, I supposed, attractive, and she was as susceptible as ever.

He told her how much the men enjoyed their time with us and what good it had done them.

'So our efforts are not in vain,' she said lightly.

'Far, far from it.'

Gretchen had come in. She looked slightly flustered and a shade fearful. She had been uneasy since she had been aware of people's suspicions, and her accent became more pronounced when she was nervous.

'Captain Brent has been paying us some nice compliments,' said Mrs Jermyn. 'He wants to compliment all those who have been taking part in our venture.'

'That is goot,' she said.

'It must be hard work looking after all these men.'

'We enjoy it,' I said.

'Are you staying near here, Captain Brent?' asked Dorabella.

'For a while. I move around, you see.'

'I see. And I understand you will be visiting us now and then to make sure everything is going well.'

'That's the idea. It will be a great pleasure for me.'

'And for us,' said Dorabella.

The days passed quickly. Summer had gone and November was approaching. Captain Brent had paid several visits to the Priory, and I knew Dorabella enjoyed these.

One morning Gordon came to breakfast when I was there. He was working very hard and we saw little of each other. He was short-handed and was very much concerned with what was now known as the Home Guard. The Prime Minister had thought this a more appropriate title than the Local Defence Volunteers.

He said that he had a spare few hours during the day and he proposed to go into Bodmin. He wondered if I could take the time off to accompany him. He wanted to look at a couple of bicycles which he proposed to get for Charley and Bert.

'They have done so many little jobs on the estate and they are so keen,' he said. 'They really have been a help and they need some way of getting round the country. I think this would suit them very well.'

'It is an excellent idea!' I cried. 'They will be delighted.'

He looked at me rather pleadingly. 'I see so little of you nowadays,' he said.

'We are all very busy. When do you propose to go to Bodmin?'

'Tomorrow . . . or the next day.'

'I'll tell Mrs Jermyn and I'll see if I can shift some of my duties.'

The next day we set out.

Gordon made this journey frequently to visit his mother, and I was wondering whether he was thinking of her as we drove along. I supposed he could not fail to.

I felt I had never really known Gordon. From the first moment when I had come to Tregarland's, he had aroused certain misgivings in me, but he had behaved admirably always. The prosperity of Tregarland's was due to him and his mother could not have had a more devoted son.

On arriving in the town, the first thing we did was find the bicycles. I was so pleased that he had thought of this, for I could imagine the joy on the boys' faces when they saw them. It was a very kind and thoughtful gesture on Gordon's part.

We decided to stow the bicycles in the car and have

lunch. There was an old inn Gordon knew on the edge of the moor; it was not far and after that we should have to go back.

I had gone to an inn on the moor once with Jowan, and I was not sure whether I hoped it would be the same one or not. Memories could be painful, and yet I felt a constant urge to go back into the past.

It was called the *Inn on the Moor* and it was quite new to me. There were not many people in the dining-room and we found a secluded table.

It was difficult for the host to find dishes with which to feed his guests, and instead of the traditional roast beef, such a feature of the past, there was meat roll. The meat was conspicuously invisible, but it was tasty enough with beans and vegetables to supplement the beef; and there were roast potatoes. We drank cider with the meal.

Gordon talked about the Home Guard and the difficulties of running the estate in wartime; but I guessed his mind was on other matters.

He said: 'I am glad you are here, Violetta. I've always had a feeling that you might go back to your parents' home.'

'I want to be here. If there is news of Jowan, it would come to his grandmother first, I suppose, so I should know at once. Then Dorabella is here . . . and Tristan, of course. And now there is work for me to do here.'

'We've been through some bad times, Violetta.'

'We have indeed. Gordon, how is your mother? Is there any change?'

'No . . . not really. Some days she is better than others. I think she will not change. And if she did recover her sanity, she would remember what she had done . . . and what she had tried to do to that child. It doesn't really bear thinking of.'

His hand was lying on the table and I reached over and touched it. His grasped mine firmly.

'You understand, Violetta. You more than any.'

'I should not have mentioned it.'

'It makes no difference. It is there all the time, whether one mentions it or not.'

'And you come here regularly. We should have gone to another town . . . not Bodmin.'

'Well, this is the nearest and we must not let these things affect us. They are part of one's life.'

He changed the subject. 'What do you think of Captain Brent?'

'Oh . . . a charming man.'

'I mean this business of visiting men at the Priory?'

'Well, I suppose they feel it is necessary. They have been through terrible experiences and the doctors are not sure whether or not they need some psychiatric treatment.'

'I think there is something else.'

'Such as what?'

'I think we may be under suspicion.'

'Suspicion?'

'Those lights were said to be flashing out to sea. It is very possible that they were lightning, but they were noticed and rumours have grown up. Everything, however remote, would have to be investigated. Think of the position we are in! Hitler has been shown that our air forces are not to be lightly set aside and invasion does not seem imminent, as it did some little time ago; and this would not be the time of year to attempt such an undertaking. But we must still be watchful.'

'You are saying that they suspect someone in our neighbourhood of sending signals to the enemy?'

'I suppose it's a possibility.'

'What message could they send?'

'All sorts of information could be useful to the enemy. Positions of factories . . . news about shipping . . .'

'How could someone here know about shipping?'

'It might be someone who is in touch with others. There must be spies all over the country . . . planted before the war, some of them. That sort of thing goes on, you know.'

'It sounds fantastic.'

'We live in fantastic times. The idea has come to me that Captain Brent is here to watch. I saw him on the cliffs the other day. He was looking at the countryside through his binoculars. I can't help feeling that his mission is not merely looking after those wounded soldiers, but something else as well.'

'But why look for trouble at the Priory?'

'I wondered . . . because of Gretchen, perhaps.'

'Oh no, that's absurd. Gretchen helping people who have behaved so badly to her own family!'

'The fact that she is German is bound to make her a suspicious character in the eyes of some people.'

'You know about Charley and his fight?'

He did not, so I told him.

He said: 'There. You see what I mean.'

'Poor Gretchen. It's hard on her. I hope she does not realize all this.'

'I thought I would talk to you about it. It's as well to be aware of what is going on.'

'Gordon, suppose there is someone sending signals . . . someone close to us. I know it is not Gretchen. But who . . . ?'

'Well, if someone is sending messages, and there will always be wild rumours in wartime, we must do our best to find out who. It is not easy to send out messages across the water, as has been seen. We must watch for anything unusual. I think we should not talk about it openly. Perhaps it is better not to say anything of this to Gretchen. Let her stay well out of it. You might have a word with Dorabella. Depend upon it, I shall be on the watch.'

We were silent for a while before he said: 'Violetta, you are still hoping?'

'I can only hope. What else is there?'

'It is a long time now . . .'

'Gordon, do you think we shall ever know?'

'If we don't, you will have to accept the fact . . .'

'That he is dead? I could not do that. I must hope until I know . . .'

'It could go on and on.'

'The war, you mean?'

'This not knowing.'

'I don't want to look too far ahead.'

'Of course not. I want you to know that I think of you a good deal. If there is anything I can do to help . . .'

He was looking at me wistfully. It was unlike Gordon to display his feelings. I thought he might be telling me that, if Jowan did not return, he, Gordon, would be there to help me through my grief.

Dorabella and I had acquired a car which we used jointly. It was so useful for driving into the Poldowns when we wanted to shop. It saved carrying heavy bags over the cliffs or waiting to have goods sent.

It was particularly good for driving some of the men to and from the hospital, as many of them were unable to do the steep walk.

We often went together, and on this occasion had taken in Jack Brayston, a young man of no more than eighteen who had to have a dressing on his leg.

We deposited him at the hospital, parked the car, and were strolling on into the town when we came face to face with Jacques Dubois.

I heard Dorabella give a start of surprise as she cried out:

'Look who's there!' She had drawn back slightly, but he had already seen us.

He advanced smiling.

'This is a delightful surprise,' he began.

Dorabella replied: 'Well, this is a shopping centre, you know, and we live just along the cliff. We are the ones who are surprised to see you, aren't we, Violetta? What are you doing here?'

'Making a quick visit,' he said.

'Have you just arrived?'

'I came last night. I stay a night at the hotel . . . what is it? The Black Rock. I come to see my sister. This day we shall meet. I return this night.'

'Where are you living now?'

He lifted his hands and shook his head from side to side.

'I am in London . . . I am here . . . I am there . . . But we must talk . . . in the comfort, eh? Why do we not go into the hotel? We could have a glass of wine, yes?'

I looked at Dorabella. I fancied she was not entirely pleased to have this ghost from the past in her company. I left it to her to decide.

She hesitated and looked at her watch.

'We have certain things to do. I could not stay long.'

'Oh, come. It would be such a disappointment. Just for a little, eh? One glass of wine?'

'Well, I suppose we have to wait for Jack,' she said. 'He's one of the soldiers staying at the Priory. We have taken him in for a dressing and will have to take him back.'

'Then you will come? That is good. You know this hotel?'

'Yes,' I said. 'Is it good?'

'The views are superb,' he said.

I laughed. 'Well, it is wartime,' I said. 'You can't expect *haute cuisine*.'

We went into the hotel; he found a corner in the lounge and ordered a bottle of claret.

'Now,' he said, 'you must tell me how life goes with you.'

'I dare say yours is more interesting,' said Dorabella.

'What is happening with the General?' I asked.

'He is very busy. He broadcasts to the French nation. His plan is to get his men together.'

'Are many coming to join him?'

'All the time.'

'You mean they escape from France and get across the Channel?'

'Some do. It is not impossible. Ah, here is our wine.' He watched while it was poured and then lifted his glass. 'To you both, my friends. A speedy end to the war, eh? Then we can all be 'appy again.'

We drank and he savoured the wine, implying that he did not think a great deal of it.

'It was so strange,' said Dorabella, 'that you should land up on our beach. Was it really by accident or was it by design?'

'Well, I had been to that coast, had I not? To cross the Channel where it is most narrow is best . . . but it is very quiet . . . very deserted . . . along this coast. It would have not been easy to ship out from Calais . . . from Boulogne . . . Dunkirk. But the quiet coast . . . it seemed best to try.'

'It must have been very dangerous,' I said.

'Mademoiselle Violetta, the danger was there, yes, but there was danger all around . . . and neither Simone nor I wished to live in France in chains.'

'I never knew until you arrived that you had a sister,' said Dorabella.

'So? For the last few years we have not met often. She did not live in Paris, you see. She was with our aunt near Lyon.

I see her now and then, but not much. But when she saw what was happening she came to me. She could not live in a humbled France. Nor could I. So we came together.'

'You were very brave to come in that little boat.'

'The sea was very kind to us and when I landed I rejoiced. I knew I was with friends.'

'Friends?' said Dorabella, a little tersely.

'We should always be friends,' he said, smiling smoothly.

'And you came straight to Tregarland's. That was a coincidence.'

He smiled at me impishly. 'I confess . . . I knew roughly where we were. Remember, I had come here to paint. An artist has a special eye, shall we say. There is this – this form of the rocks. Exciting. Fascinating.'

'It was dark when you came in.'

'I knew – just a little – and had an idea where we were. I could hardly believe we had come in just beneath Tregarland's. I thought we should be farther west . . . Falmouth or the Lizard perhaps. But by great good luck we were with friends.'

'It was certainly very clever of you,' I said.

'Oh no, Mademoiselle. Just luck. It comes to us in life sometimes, you know.'

'Have you seen Simone?' I asked.

'Not yet. I have heard that she is very happy here. The people, she say, are very kind and she is living with this Mrs . . .'

'Penwear,' I said.

'Yes, Mrs Penwear, who thinks she is a very brave young lady to leave her country and come to fight for freedom.'

'She seems to be liking working on the land.'

'Simone will adapt herself to whatever must be done.'

'Has she ever done any work like this before?'

'They had a small estate in France – my uncle and aunt,

I mean. It may be that she learned something of the kind there. More wine?'

'No, thanks,' said Dorabella, and added: 'By the way, did you ever hear what happened about that wine merchant?'

'Wine merchant?' he asked, raising his eyebrows.

'We read in the newspaper, just as we were leaving, that Georges Mansard was found murdered. It would be the same man, wouldn't it?'

'Who was that?' I asked.

'He was a friend of Jacques. He used to come to the studio to sell his wine. That was what reminded me, when you asked us to have more wine.'

'I remember now,' said Jacques. 'Yes, it was robbery. I had warned him not to walk about with so much cash in his pockets. He was not, as you would say . . . discreet. I said to him, "*Mon ami*, one day you will be set upon by thieves." And it was so.'

'Did they ever find the ones who did it?'

Jacques lifted his shoulders. 'It was in that street . . .'

'Something about a monkey, wasn't it?' said Dorabella.

'The Rue du Singe. Not a very good place to be late at night.'

'I am sorry,' said Dorabella. 'I liked him.'

'Oh yes, he was charming. But, alas, he courted danger.'

'And nothing was heard of the murderer?'

'It passed away. The war was nearly upon us.'

'What a terrible way to die!' said Dorabella.

'Have you been to see Simone before?' I asked.

'This will be our first meeting since we came. It will be so good to see her and to hear from her own lips that she is well and happy.'

'You are in the General's army now, then?' I asked.

'Yes . . . yes. But there is much to do yet. We have to get ourselves how is it you say? – in order? Much work to be done, yes, but when the time comes we shall be ready.'

'Do you think Germany will invade?'

He lifted his shoulders. 'It is what they thought to do. It has changed, has it not? A little, yes? It is not so easy as they thought. They believed they would cripple Britain in the air, which they must do if they invade. But they have not done this, and it is said that their losses are great. We shall see.' He lifted his glass. 'But when they come – if they come – we shall be ready.'

I said: 'We should be going. Jack will be ready to leave the hospital now.'

We left Jacques, who said with fervour that he hoped we should meet again soon.

As we drove to the hospital, I said to Dorabella: 'He has a habit of turning up unexpectedly, that man. First he arrives on the beach and then we find him strolling in Poldown.'

Dorabella agreed.

A new year had come and there had been no attempt at invasion, though there had been scares in plenty.

It had been a dreary Christmas. London had been battered with incendiary as well as high-explosive bombs. The Guildhall and eight Wren churches had been destroyed, and, although London bore the brunt of these attacks, other towns had suffered as well.

Yet the mood had lightened since the evacuation of Dunkirk. We stood alone and we had begun to feel that we were capable of doing so.

Life went on for us much as usual. We had grown accustomed to being careful with food and never wasting anything that was edible. We seemed to have realized that, whatever happened, we had to go on living our lives as well as we could.

Charley and Bert Trimmell had been delighted with their bicycles. They would speed along the lanes and up and down the cliff path with the carefree abandonment of happy children. They, at least, were contented.

Spring came and went. It was June again. Soon we should be saying: It is two years since the war started and then they said it would not last until Christmas. How wrong they had proved to be!

And we were growing stronger every day.

Then came the news that, without even a declaration of war, Germany had invaded Russia.

This could mean only one thing. Hitler believed he could not make a successful invasion of Britain. What our Prime Minister had said of our airmen was true, that 'never in the whole history of human conflict has so much been owed by so many to so few.' They had saved the world and now the full fury of Hitler's attack was not turned against us only. We shared it with the Russians.

The time was passing – and still Jowan had not come home.

Dorabella

Break-in at Riverside

I was deeply shocked when I found that the man and woman in the boat were Jacques and his sister. Who would not have been, faced with such a situation so suddenly, and in the middle of the night at that!

I had never wanted to see Jacques again. He had disappointed me, humiliated me by bringing his objectionable Mimi right into the house with what I could only call insolent nonchalance, as though it were the most ordinary conduct for one mistress to be presented to another in such a casual manner.

The arrogance of the man was unacceptable and I had wanted to cast off all memory of it for ever.

And then, there he was!

I was thankful when he went away, but I quite liked Simone. She was very different from Jacques – quite modest, in fact. Of course, Jacques had been the artist living in the Latin Quarter, thinking he was a Degas, Manet or Monet, or that little one with the short legs, Toulouse-Lautrec, I think. Simone was more of a country girl – very eager to please, and Tom Yeo said she was a good worker and he was glad to have her.

I struck up quite a friendship with her; she seemed a little lonely and I did not see why my relationship with her brother should affect ours.

In spite of the war and having to see my poor sister grieving for a lover who, I believed, would never come back, I was not displeased with life. I enjoyed being with the recuperating soldiers. They had a special feeling for me,

I knew. They liked to chatter in a jolly way, pretending to fall in love with me. It was all very light-hearted and pleasant.

But I could not stop worrying about Violetta. She tried to be cheerful but she did not deceive me. It was there all the time . . . a cloud to spoil the complete enjoyment of the fun. And fun there was in the silly little things of everyday life. I wished above everything that Jowan Jermyn would come home – or if that was asking too much, that we might at least know what had happened to him. If he had been killed, it would be better for her to know it. Then perhaps she could begin to forget. I thought Gordon Lewyth was in love with her in his way. I never understood the man. Violetta would say that because he had not been attracted by me, I thought there was something wrong with him. Well, she did say things like that to me, and often there was some truth in them.

But Gordon is a strange man. There is some hidden depth there. After all, his mother is a murderess and now in an asylum. I know he visits her frequently and must be constantly reminded of the terrible things that had happened at Tregarland's. I do think he cares for Violetta, and I am sure he would be a very faithful husband. But she loves Jowan, and I suppose will go on doing so throughout her life – even though he is lost for ever somewhere over there.

I have changed a little. Experience does change one; the bigger the experience, the greater the change. I am not the same woman who blithely gave up her home, her husband and child to go off with a French artist. I sometimes think of Dermot as he was when I first met him in Germany. He never seemed quite the same afterwards, and it was certainly eerie when I first came to Tregarland's. No wonder, with all that was going on in the house! Violetta tried to tell me that Dermot's death was not due to me.

He fell from his horse. They said he had been drinking too much. Yes, but why? Poor Dermot! He had been so crippled that it is possible that he took his own life, though it is not certain whether it was an accident. I tell myself it was. It makes me feel better. And then there is my baby.

Tristan is such a darling. He is beginning to like me at last. At first he turned to Violetta and Nanny Crabtree when I wanted to pick him up. It is different now. When he calls me Mummy, I want to hug him and cry: 'I'm going to make up for leaving you, my darling. I will, I will!'

So, in spite of the war and my twinges of conscience, which I have to admit grow less as time passes, I could enjoy life if Violetta could be her old self – and she won't until we have news of Jowan.

Recently I have discovered a new interest in life.

I liked him from the moment I saw him. He is rather tall, not conventionally good-looking, but I like him better for that, and he has an authoritative manner which appeals to me.

The day after he came to inspect us, I met him on the cliffs.

'It's Mrs Tregarland, isn't it?' he said.

'And you are Captain Brent.'

'I recognized you at once,' he went on.

'So you should,' I retorted. 'It was only yesterday.'

We laughed.

'What a wonderful old place the Priory is!' he went on.

'Tregarland's is as good.'

'Your home, of course.'

'Yes. They are the two big houses around here.'

'And your husband . . .'

'I am a widow. It is Mr Gordon Lewyth who looks after the place. He always did when my husband was alive. He's very good at it and is quite a personage around here. He runs the Home Guard. I think in a way he would like to join the Army but the place would fall to pieces if he did.'

'Well, he is doing the best job possible at home.'

'We're thinking of using some of the rooms at Tregarland's to extend the convalescent home. Then we could take in more at a time.'

'That's an excellent idea, and you and the other young ladies will be in charge, I suppose.'

'Well, Mrs Jermyn had the idea in the first place, and Tregarland's would be a sort of extension. It would be rather like that, I suppose.'

'And your sister is the fiancée of the heir of the Priory?'

'That's so.'

'It's a wonderful job you are doing. All of you work very hard, I'm sure. It is interesting that you are all related.'

'In a way . . . though Gretchen isn't really. She's married to Edward.'

It was so easy to talk to him that I found myself telling him the story of Edward's being brought out of Belgium when he was a baby by my mother. He listened intently. Then I went on to the incident in the Bavarian forest when we had all been brought face to face with the Nazi menace.

'That was like an introductory chapter,' he said. 'It set the scene for the drama to come.'

'Yes, it was exactly like that. Though we didn't see how important it was at the time.'

'Few saw the significance of it and those who did were not able to do anything about it.'

He turned to me, dispelling the gloom.

'Well, this is a great pleasure meeting you, Mrs Tregarland.'

'I do not find it at all unpleasant meeting you, Captain Brent,' I replied.

We laughed a great deal during that morning and when we were about to part he said: 'Do you often go out for these walks?'

'Not often. There is usually too much to do. I have a little boy and I like to spend some time with him. He has the best nanny in the world. She was mine and Violetta's at one time and my mother thought so highly of her that she acquired her for Tristan.'

'Tristan?' he repeated.

'You will like this! My mother was a devotee of the opera. So my sister was Violetta and I am Dorabella, and I thought we should keep the tradition, hence Tristan. If he had been a girl, he would have been Isolde.'

He laughed at that. It was a very happy interlude.

I said to him: 'By the way, what do you think of Jowan Jermyn's chances of getting home? My sister is engaged to him, you know.'

He was silent for a moment. Then he said: 'Well, it is not impossible.'

'But . . . remote?'

'I suppose I should say that.'

'It's better to face the truth.'

'Always.'

'I must go,' I said.

'It has been such a pleasure to meet you, Mrs Tregarland.'

'That is what you said when we met.'

'It bears repetition and I repeat it with emphasis.'

We said goodbye – and that was the first time. After that our meetings were frequent. They were not exactly arranged, but we somehow contrived to meet in the same place at the same time.

Violetta would have said I should see the way things were going. But that was how I was. I had married Dermot in haste and it had not taken me long to discover what a mistake that was. Then there was the affair with Jacques, from which I had but recently emerged. Violetta had been there to help me out of that, so I should have been wary; but when people like me embark on an adventure, they are carried along by their belief in what the outcome will be – and that is, of course, the way they want it to go – and they sometimes find themselves in awkward predicaments.

However, my meetings with Captain Brent were the highlights of those dark days.

At first, there were those seemingly accidental meetings. Later, of course, it was different.

There was so much to talk about. He was interested in everyone and everything. Nothing seemed too trivial. All the people who lived thereabouts, even the maids. Nothing was too insignificant to interest him.

We laughed a great deal. That was one of the reasons we enjoyed each other's company so much. It was a light-hearted relationship and even things which would not ordinarily be amusing seemed so with him.

He even asked about Nanny Crabtree and Tristan and Hildegarde. Then Charley and Bert. I had never known anyone so interested in people. It was all a lot of fun and irresistible to me.

He was living in a small furnished cottage on the edge of East Poldown. He told me the Army had taken it for a year and it was for the use of personnel who had to be in the neighbourhood for any length of time. He was not sure how long he would be there; and indeed there were times when he was called away.

I suppose uncertainty does give a touch of urgency to a relationship, and it develops more quickly than it might otherwise.

He was looked after by his batman, Joe Gummer, who did housework and cooking and looked after the Captain with a rare efficiency. He was a Cockney with a perpetual grin and a habit of winking exaggeratedly to let one know when he was making a joke, which was frequently. There was no doubt in my mind that he was devoted to James Brent. I found it all very amusing.

The cottage was small; two bedrooms and a bathroom on the top floor, and two rooms and a kitchen below. It was rather sparsely furnished and had obviously been prepared for letting to holidaymakers in peacetime. It had an impersonal look.

The garden was pleasant. It ran down to the river. One could look southwards and see the ancient bridge which separated the two Poldowns and yet feel isolated. Rhododendrons, azaleas and buddleia grew prolifically. I became fond of the place.

Those days were full of excitement for me. I took every opportunity of going into Poldown. I would take the car round by the road which meant I had to pass Riverside Cottage. I would look in and Joe would give me the information, 'Sir's off out, Miss. I'll tell him you called. That'll please him. How are you, Miss? I've been run off me plates of meat this morning.' I had to get used to his Cockney rhyming slang and discovered that his 'plates of meat' were his feet. He told me his trouble and strife (his wife) had been bombed in her place in Bow.

'Kitchen ceiling come down. What a mess! It was a job to clear it up. She said: Did that Hitler think she was his housemaid? Pity he couldn't clear up his own mess.'

His conversation was always accompanied by those winks, to which I had now become accustomed, and bursts of laughter. I always felt the better for having seen him.

Yes, I did enjoy those days. I had made a habit of spending an hour or so with Tristan in the mornings before I left for the Priory and again after I returned home. I would sit with the children and read them a story while Nanny Crabtree watched, nodding with pleasure. I was sure she was thinking that this was how a mother should behave . . . not going off gallivanting, with foreigners.

For, of course, Nanny Crabtree had never accepted that amnesia story.

'Loss of memory, my foot,' she had said. 'That Dorabella's not the sort to go losing her memory. No, she'll be up to something.' And Violetta had said: 'We must tell Nanny the truth. She'll be terribly shocked, but she'll forgive you, and in any case, she won't rest until she knows what really did happen.'

Then there was Simone. I met her frequently about the estate. She had turned out to be different from the quiet, earnest girl who had arrived in England with her one desire to fight for her country.

She never seemed to want to talk about Jacques. Well, nor did I, so that was no hardship. She had seen very little of him during their childhood, and then she had gone to live with the aunt in the country. She was light-hearted and frivolous in a way – not unlike myself.

She told me about one of the men on the farm who was pursuing her. He was a typical Cornishman, Daniel Killick by name, and she made me laugh by her efforts to reproduce his accent, and was really funny about their efforts to communicate – her English being a little limited and her accent not helping, the Cornish expressions were incomprehensible to her.

We giggled a good deal together, and, I must say, it was a relief at that time, for the gloom of war could be very depressing.

Of course, she wanted to know about me. I told her about Dermot and she was naturally aware of my affair with Jacques. She said he had always had love-affairs and he had stayed with me longer than with most and, after all, it was I who had walked out on him.

Very soon I was telling her about Captain Brent.

'He is charming, that one,' she said. 'Like my poor Daniel? Oh no! *Quelle différence!* Tell me. I am all nose.'

'Ears,' I corrected her and we giggled. I told her of my meeting with the Captain on the cliffs and how our friendship had progressed from there.

Life was full of interest at that time. Even those boring Germans had turned to the Russians, which everyone thought was a 'good thing' for us, if not for the Russians.

It was a warm day – oppressively so. I decided to go down to the town to order a few things. There were always certain goods we needed. I had plenty of time, so I walked over the cliffs, did the ordering and then made my way to the cottage. A storm had been threatening all the afternoon, and there were thunder clouds over the sea. As I emerged from the town I heard the first clap of thunder. Then the rain came teeming down and by the time I reached the cottage my thin dress was soaked; there was water in my sandals and my hair was streaking round my face.

James was in.

He cried, stating the obvious: 'You're drenched!'

'That's putting it mildly,' I said.

'Hurry and get those things off.'

'Where's Joe?'

'Gone into Bodmin to get some stores. Get to the bathroom and I'll find something for you to put on. Then we'll dry those wet things.'

I went up the stairs to the small bathroom. James left me there and in a few moments returned and handed me a towelling dressing-gown. I took off my clothes, dried myself vigorously and wrapped the dressing-gown about me. It was huge – being his own.

I came out. He was in the bedroom, sitting on the bed.

He said: 'That's quite becoming. I thought it was an insignificant thing . . . until now.'

'It's rather large.'

'Well, I am a little bigger than you.'

He stood up and put his hands on my shoulders.

There is no need for me to go into details: it was inevitable. It was so romantic, if a somewhat stereotyped situation. It was like something in a play. The hero and heroine are thrown together . . . the car breaks down . . . or the girl is caught in the storm . . . never mind what manipulations are undergone to get them into this situation. But there it is . . . thrust upon them.

He slipped the dressing-gown from my shoulders. Now was the time for me to express outraged protests. But did I? Of course not. That was not my way. I wanted this to happen as much as he did, so it was no use pretending I did not. So, of course, it did.

Afterwards we lay in the bed together. I thought of Joe's coming back. I could imagine his pronounced wink; I knew he would not be altogether surprised. After all, he was only the old 'bucket and spade' (housemaid), as he sometimes called himself.

I just lay there in a state of delicious euphoria.

James said how wonderful it was for him to have found me. I said it was wonderful that we had found each other. And we knew that this was the beginning.

After that there were many meetings. Joe knew about it and reacted with the nonchalance I had expected. Sometimes we heard him bustling about below. I was now choosing every moment I possibly could to go to the cottage where James would be waiting for me.

Afterwards we would sit downstairs, or perhaps in the garden; and James would bring out a bottle of his favourite French wine and we would talk.

He told me that he had been married. It hadn't worked. That was before the war. They had lived in London for a time, but they were always moving around. She hadn't liked the lifestyle marriage with him offered; she had wanted to settle in the country. So they had parted. They were lucky to have arranged an amicable divorce without bitterness on either side. That had happened three months before the outbreak of war.

They were wonderful days for me. There was an element of excitement in the affair. I enjoyed that. The only one who knew was Joe. But, before long, I was to learn that that was not entirely true.

Of course, I am a somewhat irresponsible person. It came out one day when I was with Simone.

She said unexpectedly: 'You look . . . how is it? Different? Has something happened?'

'Oh,' I said evasively, 'life is tolerable. How is Daniel?'

'Much the same as ever.'

'Adoring?'

She lifted her shoulders. 'And the good Capitaine?'

I imitated her gesture.

'I had expected to see you yesterday. You were busy?'

'Very.'

'With the good . . . James?'

'I did see him.'

'That is a pleasant little *maison*. I passed it the other day. I thought – nice.'

'Oh yes, it is.'

'You know it well, I think.'

'I've been there once or twice.'

She nodded, smiling. Then she went on to tell me of some encounter with Daniel. I was not really listening.

My love-affair with James Brent continued. I knew it was important to us both. It is difficult to explain one's feelings sometimes to people who have not experienced them. Those who have would understand immediately.

I never knew when I arrived at the cottage whether he

would be there, and he had told me that he could be called away at any moment. He did not think that would be for any length of time, but he could never be sure.

How could any of us, in those days, be sure of anything? How did we know when any of us would come face to face with death? It gave a transience to life, an urgency. It was: 'Eat, drink and be merry, for tomorrow we die.' It was true that we lived precariously. I suppose I wanted to squeeze as much pleasure from each day as I possibly could, for how did I know how long I would be able to enjoy it? If one found something good, one wanted to cling to it before it was snatched away.

This gave an added flavour to my relationship with James.

There were times when I almost confided in Violetta. I could not imagine what her reaction would be. She thought my recent experiences with Jacques had sobered me. Sometimes I thought I should never be sobered.

I needed James at that time. He did a great deal for me. Nanny Crabtree had once said to Violetta – so my sister told me – that when I came into a room it was like the sun breaking through the clouds. 'Things don't bother her much, do they? And she has a way of making you feel the same. Well, there's something to be said for it after all is said and done.'

I thought: Yes, it is wonderful to be able to find something to be happy about in all this mess. That was my excuse. I was good at finding excuses for myself.

So I lived through those days, dancing close to the flame like the proverbial moth – never thinking of scorching my wings.

The recuperating soldiers could now make use of those rooms at Tregarland's which had been made ready. The two houses being fairly close together made this a convenient arrangement. We were always going back and forth between the two places.

'What an excellent outcome!' said Violetta. 'Particularly when you remember the old feud between the two houses.'

'Sorted out, my dear sister, by you and . . .'

How thoughtless I was! I was going to say: 'By you and Jowan.' Although he was always in her thoughts and she did not need a careless comment of mine to remind her of him.

I said quickly: 'I think we are doing quite a good job.'

'I think so, too,' agreed Violetta.

Between the two houses our days were busy, though I still found time to slip down to Riverside Cottage. There was always an excuse for going into town and, if my trips were noticeably extended, nobody called attention to the fact.

James had given me a key to the cottage.

'It will be convenient,' he said, 'if I am not there and Joe neither. We can leave notes for each other.'

We were now into October and the days were fast shortening. It was the season of gales which were a feature of our coast.

One morning when I went down, Violetta was already at the table with Gretchen, and while we sat talking one of the maids came in with the post. There were letters for the three of us. We knew they were from my mother before we looked at them, for when she wrote to one she wrote to the others. We had laughed about it – Violetta and I – when we were at school, for the letters were almost identical. Not that we would have wanted it to change. It made us more aware of the closeness between us all.

Gretchen read her letter and looked up with excited eyes.

'It's wonderful news,' she said. 'Edward is being posted to Hampshire. There will be occasions when he can get away for short spells. I should be closer. Your mother says I should return to Caddington. It will not be difficult for him to slip over. She says: "I think you should come soon, Gretchen. We shall have you and Hildegarde with us. It will be wonderful for us to have a child in the house."'

'That is good news,' I said.

'It is so long since Edward has seen Hildegarde,' added Gretchen. Then she hesitated for a moment. 'But my job here . . .'

'You'll find something to do,' Violetta assured her. 'I don't think there will be any difficulty, do you, Dorabella?'

I shook my head, and went on: 'Our first duty is to keep the troops happy, is it not? Well, one of them wouldn't be if his darling wife and child were kept away from him.'

Gretchen laughed. She could not hide her excitement.

We would leave her to pack, we said, and go over to see Mrs Jermyn about Gretchen's replacement.

As we drove over the short distance, Violetta said: 'I suppose your letter was the same as mine?'

'I imagine so. We did tell her that there had been some unpleasantness about Gretchen here, didn't we?'

'We did.'

'She thinks in that case it will be good for her to get away.'

'She's right, of course. Gretchen was very upset about it. It is something that people don't forget. If anything went wrong, she would be under suspicion.'

'It could be the same there.'

'Yes, but Edward will be there. He's a soldier – something of a hero, having come back from Dunkirk, and the parents are such paragons of patriotic zeal. And then she will be seeing Edward fairly often, perhaps.'

Nanny Crabtree was sad. She hated to see her nursery depleted, and Hildegarde was such a good girl, she said. I reckoned she was more virtuous in retrospect than in actuality, and that Tristan would hear frequently of her excellence, that Hildegarde had never done things like that, Hildegarde had been such a good little girl.

In a few weeks Nanny Crabtree became philosophical. 'Well, I've got my hands full with his lordship – and as for that Charley and Bert!' She clicked her tongue and raised her eyes heavenwards, calling in divine corroboration of what she had to suffer.

'Racing about on them bikes! My goodness me! They scare the wits out of me, them two do. Give me little girls.'

'If I remember rightly, Nanny,' I said, 'you have had two who on occasion were not such little angels.'

'You get along with you,' she said, her eyes twinkling. 'You were always the saucy one, you were!'

Tristan missed Hildegarde. He said to me one day: 'Want Hilgar.'

'Well,' I told him, 'you've got Mummy.'

He smiled suddenly and held out his arms. I picked him up and he planted a wet kiss on my cheek.

'Got Mummy,' he said with evident satisfaction.

I hugged him. My little angel. He loved me now. He had forgotten that I had once deserted him.

My darling child, I thought, as I had a thousand times. I'll make up for that.

When I look back over those months, they seem like an oasis in the midst of the fearful conflict which was going on in the world.

And Tristan loved me. There is nothing to compare with a child's innocent belief in his mother's ability to make everything come right. Even I, who am certainly not the maternal type, could rejoice in it. I swore that never again would I disappoint him. I should always be there. I had Tristan then. I had my constant comfort, Violetta, my dear parents . . . and James Brent.

Yes, it was a good time.

I had driven down to Poldown and hastily shopped and then gone to Riverside Cottage. There was just a possibility that James would be there.

When I stayed for any length of time, I made sure that the car was well out of sight from the road. It was possible to do this by parking at the back of the cottage. On this occasion, I was just looking in and, if I were to stay, I should, of course, move the car.

I let myself in, saw no one was at home, scribbled a note to James and went back to the car. As I was getting in, a car drove up. It was Simone in the estate car which belonged to Jermyn's and which she drove round collecting things for Tom Yeo.

She drew up and grinned at me.

'He is not . . . *chez lui*?'

'No,' I said.

'*Quel dommage!*' she murmured. 'Then . . . you will have a moment to spare? Perhaps we have a *café* together? Just for thirty minutes . . . twenty . . . or fifteen?'

'Yes,' I said. 'Let's do that.'

So we drove down to East Poldown. There was a small place on the front looking over the sea and Mrs Yelton, who ran the place, came to take our order.

'How be 'ee today, me dears?' she said. 'Nice cup of coffee, is it?'

'Yes, please, Mrs Yelton.'

'What they do call a well-earned rest, I'll be bound. You young ladies are doing a good job up there, the both of you. You should hear what some of the boys say about the home. Angels of Mercy, that's what they called the young ladies.'

I laughed. 'So, I look like an angel?' I asked.

'To tell you the truth, I always thought you had a bit of the devil in you, Mrs Tregarland. And, as for you,

Mam'selle . . . coming over here in that boat . . . well, that was something.'

We laughed and she went away to get the coffee.

'It's nice here,' said Simone, as she stirred the beverage.

'Yes, if they accept you,' I replied, thinking of Gretchen.

She knew at once what I meant. That was like Simone. She was always quick to catch my meaning.

'It's wonderful for her to have her husband coming home now and then,' I said. 'It would have been impossible for her to have seen him so often if she had stayed here.'

'And being German did not help her. All is well with you and the good Capitaine?'

'As well as it can be in such times.'

'I see you 'ave the key to the door.'

'Oh yes. He gave it to me. It's quite convenient. I can slip in when I like and, if he is not there, leave a note.'

'He is a thoughtful man. It is so romantic. It is good that we have this romance in wartime.'

'As long as the world goes round, love goes on.' Had I made that up, or was I just stating the obvious? It was a real old cliché anyway; but when you consider them, they are very often true.

We sat there gossiping for a while, then said goodbye to Mrs Yelton and got into our respective cars.

Returning to Tregarland's one early evening, Violetta and I found Nanny Crabtree in what she herself called 'a state'.

'I've told them time after time, if I've told them once, I won't have them dashing round the country after dark. It's them imps, Charley and Bert. What they don't seem to understand is that six o'clock in May is not the same as at this time of year. It's the dark I won't have them out in. It's them bikes, that's what it is. Fancy themselves as goodness knows what, I shouldn't wonder. Spy catchers one day, despatch riders the next. Flying round . . . I don't know . . . but I won't have it.'

'Were they going anywhere special?' asked Violetta.

'No, they wasn't. I've said to them time and time again: After school, it's home. Then they can get back and wash their dirty selves and sit down to a nice meal. You'd think they'd be satisfied with that, wouldn't you? But no. They must go dashing about the countryside.'

'I expect they'll be back soon, Nanny,' I said.

'They'd better be.'

I thought: She loves those boys. That is just how she used to be with us. Dear old Nanny, I think she is really worried about them.

As a matter of fact, Violetta and I were beginning to get anxious. Violetta said she had seen Gordon and he thought they should be back by now.

'I hope there's not been an accident,' said Violetta.

When we heard the sound of the boys' bicycles in the courtyard, we were very relieved.

They were safe, and now she was no longer afraid for them, Nanny was growing more and more bellicose. She went into action without delay. She wanted to know what excuses they had, and I could see from her expression that they would have to be very good to satisfy her.

The boys put their bicycles away and came running upstairs, their faces alight with excitement.

Nanny faced them squarely, Violetta and I on either side of her.

Charley burst out: 'There's been a burglary. Or would 'a bin, if we 'adn't stopped 'em.'

'A burglary?' I cried. 'Where?'

'At that cottage by the river.'

'Riverside Cottage?' I asked quickly.

'That's it, Mrs Tregarland. That's the one. Me and Bert

was cycling along, wasn't we? You can cut round the back if you know the way . . . by the river.'

'That's trespassing,' I said.

'It's only a little way. Well, Bert and me was there, wasn't we? You could see the back of the place, and I knew Captain Brent wasn't there, didn't I?'

'Did you?' I said. 'How?'

'Well, he wasn't there, was he? Hadn't been for some time. I heard one of the soldiers say he reckoned he'd be away for a bit. I knew it wasn't him, 'cos I saw this torch, didn't I? It was moving about . . . just like in a film, and I said to Bert, I said: "P'raps the 'lectricity's off." But then I see the light on the road was on. Well, we left our bikes and went up to the house and then I see the back door was broke open. Then I knew.'

'What did you do then, Charley?' I asked.

'I said to Bert, "I reckon they're burglars. We got to catch 'em." I didn't think me and Bert could do it on our own, so I said to him: "You wait 'ere and watch. If you see 'em get into a car, take the number . . . just like they do in the pictures. I'm going to Constable Darkin. He's not far off."'

'That was very ingenious of you, Charley,' said Violetta.

'What, Miss?'

'Very clever. Very resourceful to go to Constable Darkin.'

'He was just going to have his tea. I said, "I've come to report a burglary." He wasn't that shook up, was he? He said, "Oh yes, son." Just as if I was a little boy playing a game. Then I said, "At Captain Brent's place . . . that Riverside Cottage." It was different then. He left his tea and said, "You'd better get back home, son." Then he got on to the telephone and I couldn't hear what he said, 'cos Mrs Darkin was talking and taking us to the door. She said, "You've done well, and now it's time you was home." So I went to find Bert. He was still there watching. He hadn't seen no more lights in the house. Then we heard the cars and two men came running out. We couldn't see them very well. They got away, though, before the police got there. It wasn't half something, wasn't it, Bert?'

Bert agreed that it was.

I was thinking of James and wondering how the thieves had known he and Joe would be away at that time and what they could have hoped to steal in a cottage furnished for summer visitors.

Later on Constable Darkin came to Tregarland's to tell the boys they had done very well. It was just an ordinary break-in, and the thieves had escaped before they could be caught.

'You did the right thing, son,' said Constable Darkin to Charley. 'Always let us know if you see anything fishy round here.'

Then he roared with laughter.

'That be a good 'un,' he said, in case any of us failed to catch the aptness of the allusion.

And so it all ended happily and Nanny Crabtree withdrew her disapproval of the boys and their bicycles. In fact, she was rather proud of her protégés.

Kidnapped

It was only two weeks later when there was another alarm. This was a very serious one.

Again it started when Violetta and I returned from the Priory. If Nanny Crabtree had been in 'a state' because the boys had not come home, now she was in a panic.

And so were we all.

Tristan was missing. He had been having his nap after he had had his meal; and Nanny herself liked to doze off at that time. It gave her a chance, as she said, to put her feet up. She would lie on her bed, which was the only way to rest properly, and she would leave open her bedroom door, which led into Tristan's room.

He had been a little lively during the morning and did not drop off as quickly as he usually did, so that made it a little late and it must have been after three when Nanny settled down. She did not awaken until just on five, and was amazed when she did. It was not like her to sleep so long. She was usually a light sleeper. She would have expected Tristan to waken her before that. But when she went into his room she saw that he was not in his bed. She had been surprised, but not then unduly alarmed. He must have wandered downstairs, she thought. But Tristan was nowhere to be found. We were all very worried by this time. We had hunted everywhere. Tregarland's was a very large house and there were all sorts of places where he could hide.

We searched and searched. Nanny kept moaning: 'I can't believe this. I'm a light sleeper, I am. I've always been ready to wake at the slightest sound from any of my children. And there he is . . . getting out of bed . . . going off like that. Where is he? Where is my baby?'

In the first few moments it did not occur to me that there could be anything seriously wrong. It was only as the time began to pass and there was no sign of Tristan that we grew seriously alarmed and decided to call the police.

Constable Darkin paid another visit to Tregarland's and this was a very sombre one. The house and grounds were searched. The great fear was the sea. Suppose Tristan had gone into the garden, wandered down to the beach and thought he would paddle? Suppose he had been carried out to sea on the waves? Unbearable possibilities came crowding into my mind.

Violetta and I went on searching, the servants joined in. Gordon was very practical. He arranged search parties, discussed with the police what was best to be done; but as the night came on we were desperate.

I felt sick with horror. My darling child, who was learning to love me, to forgive me for my indifference, and who now loved me as much as he did Violetta and Nanny Crabtree, no, even more, because I was his mother. Where was he now? Crying for me. I could hear the satisfaction in his voice when he had said: 'Got Mummy.'

This was too cruel. I did not deserve this. And what was happening to Tristan? Once before he might have died at the hands of a murderess, but for the vigilance of my sister and Nanny Crabtree. Not again, I thought, oh not again.

I do not know how I lived through that night. We had searched the house and grounds thoroughly, so there was little hope that he was there.

Then where was he? I could hear the murmur of the sea. It was a quiet sea, but . . . was it possible that he had wandered down to the beach? He had been warned never to go down there alone. He was an obedient child on the whole, but one could never be sure what a child would do.

Violetta was beside me, close, and I knew she suffered as I did. As for Nanny Crabtree, she was quite distraught. She was muttering to herself. I think she was praying.

Gordon said: 'There must be some explanation. He has wandered off somewhere.'

'A child out alone . . . at this time of night!' I cried.

Gordon said very slowly, with an effort, as though he were wondering whether it was wise to raise such a possibility: 'We must not lose sight of the fact that someone might have taken him.'

'Taken him!' I cried.

Gordon nodded, and Violetta said: 'You mean . . . kidnapped?'

'It could be so. If it is . . . we'll get him back.'

'Who . . . ?' murmured Violetta.

'The family is not without means to pay a ransom.'

I clutched at the idea. It was better than thinking of him caught by the sea.

'Oh yes, yes,' I cried. 'He's been kidnapped. We'll pay whatever they ask and get him back.'

'It is a possibility we should not lose sight of,' said Gordon.

I felt sure of it now. Otherwise where was he? Some wicked person was putting us all to this anguish for the sake of money. Anything, anything we had was worth giving to get Tristan back. I had been so immersed in my own affairs that I did not realize how much I loved him. He was more important to me than anything else.

There was no sleep for any of us that night. I felt a fierce hatred for those people who had taken him, and a contempt for myself because I had not loved him enough. I had a great desire to blame someone. How had Nanny Crabtree allowed herself to be so fast asleep when all that was happening to him? It was so unlike her. I remembered how she and Violetta had watched over him throughout those nights when they suspected someone was trying to harm him. Then . . . Gordon. A terrible thought struck me. If Tristan died, Gordon would inherit Tregarland's. He was really holding it in trust for him now. Gordon was devoted to Tregarland's. He had worked all his life on the estate. He was the son of old James Tregarland – if illegitimate – and he would inherit the place if there was no legitimate heir to come before him. And there was Tristan. Motive indeed.

Oh no! That could not be! Gordon would not be involved in such a thing. But what did I know of what went on in people's minds?

And so it went on.

I did not know what to do. Search the grounds again? Just suppose he was somewhere there? The house . . . ?

We were frustrated and helpless. The police were searching for him.

Violetta said: 'I cannot believe there is anything else we can do. Gordon is right. We shall hear news soon. I shall keep in easy call of the telephone. It may come that way.'

I could not bear it. I felt a desire to be by myself. I kept going over the past. I had staged an elopement, I had deluded myself into believing that it would all come right in the end. I had always pictured the future the way I wanted it to go. Then I thought of the last time Tristan and I had been together. I had read him his favourite story about the elephant who never forgot. He had leaned against me and laughed at the animal's exploits and I had changed them a little, just for the pleasure of hearing him say: 'No, Mummy, he didn't *do* that.'

Take everything I have . . . everything I want . . . but give him back to me, I bargained with the unknown powers.

I went to my room. I sat staring out of the window. I saw Simone below. She was talking to Violetta. I did not want to join them. I could not bear to talk to anyone.

One of the maids was knocking at my door. She had an envelope in her hand.

'This came for you, Mrs Tregarland,' she said.

She gave it to me. My name and address were typed on it. I said: 'This hasn't come by post.'

'No, Mrs Tregarland. It was just lying there on the hall table.'

When she had gone, I opened it and stared at the paper before me. I could not take in those words for a few seconds. I felt myself grow cold and my hands trembled as I read:

> We have your son. He is safe so far. If you obey orders he will soon be back with you. You are to come alone to Hollow Cottage on the road to Pen Moroc on the Bodmin Road at five o'clock for your instructions. Hollow Cottage is about half a mile from the signpost pointing to Pen Moroc. If you show this note to anyone, your son will die. We are watching you. Bring this note with you. Remember, it will be dangerous if you try to trick us. Fail to come, and alone, and your son will die.

I could not believe it. It was the sort of thing I had read of or seen in films – and now it had come to me!

My first impulse was to find Violetta. 'If you show this note to anyone, your son will die.' No, I dared not take the risk. Then what? Go to this place, this Hollow Cottage on the road to Pen Moroc? I did know the road. I had been along it once or twice – a lonely stretch of moorland. I had not seen any cottages there, but I could find this one. At five o'clock it would be dark. I was afraid and yet excited. Any action was better than none.

At least I now knew that Tristan had been kidnapped. He was not drowned or lying dead somewhere. Never have I wanted to talk to my sister more than I did at that moment. Yet I dared not. I read the note again. This was the beginning. I was going to this place for 'instructions'. What could they want? Only one thing, I supposed. Money. They would tell me what to do and I should have him back when the ransom was paid.

I was going to this Hollow Cottage and I was going alone, for I dared not tell anyone of my plans.

Violetta would say I should tell someone . . . the police . . . Gordon . . . someone who would know what had to be done. But I could not take that risk.

My sister always said I acted rashly without due consideration. But what was there to consider when they had threatened to kill my son if I did not act as they commanded?

I left Tregarland's at four o'clock. I must be there in good time. I managed to get away without being noticed. I had only one thought in my mind. To find out what these people wanted, to give it to them and get back my son.

It was dark early that evening, for it had been a dull day, even for November. By half past four I was on the Pen Moroc Road. It was deserted.

I drove along slowly, looking out for Hollow Cottage. There was hardly any habitation in sight. I saw the signpost. Half a mile on, then.

I was peering about me in the gloom. I could see a building of some sort. It was in a small hollow, just off the road. Hollow Cottage. I felt sure this was the place.

It looked eerie. My heart was pounding so much I could not escape from the sound of it. It was like a drum in my ears. I drew up and got out of the car. I looked around me. All was silent. Was I too early?

I walked towards the cottage. It was uninhabited – a shell of a place. There was no lock on the door, so I pushed it open. It creaked as I did so. I stepped in cautiously. It was a derelict ruin of what had been a small dwelling.

I was sure I should never have had the courage to go into that place alone if I had not been overwhelmed by the need to have Tristan safe. I was thinking as I did so: perhaps I should have shown the note to Violetta. But if those people had harmed Tristan, I should never have forgiven myself. I had to do it this way.

I stepped into what had been a room. It was dark and I could see little. There was no one there. I was too early. I looked at my watch and saw that it was ten minutes to five. I should have to wait. My eyes were becoming accustomed to the gloom and I was able to make out a door at one side of the room. As I looked, it creaked and swung forward. My heart leaped in fear. A man was standing there. There was a mask of some sort over his face.

It was unreal . . . like something I had read, seen in a film or dreamed of.

A voice said: 'It was wise of you to come, and alone, Mrs Tregarland.' It was a cultured voice.

'Where is my son?' I cried.

'He shall be returned to you. It is a very small thing we want of you. All you have to do is bring it to us and your little boy will be returned to you. First, give me the note I sent to you.'

I took it from my pocket and put it into his outstretched, gloved hand.

'What is it you want from me?' I asked.

'You are a good friend of Captain Brent.'

I shivered. 'What . . . ?' I began.

'You have access to his cottage. All you have to do is

bring us a small metal box which you will find there. Today is Wednesday. On Friday at this time, you will bring the box here. Your little boy will be given to you in exchange for it.'

'I have no idea what little box . . . where is it? How can I be sure that you will give me my son?'

'There are some things you have to take on trust.'

'I could not trust anyone who hurt little children.'

'Your child will not be hurt if you do this one thing.'

'Where . . . where is this box?'

'It is in Riverside Cottage. It will be in an inconspicuous place. You have two days in which to find it.'

'Captain Brent will not allow me to take this thing.'

'He will not know that you have.'

'His batman . . .'

'Neither will be there. It should not be difficult. You have the key and they will both be absent for a week or so. Come, Mrs Tregarland, surely the fate of your little boy is worth such a small effort?'

I did not know what to say. I had discovered that this was not an ordinary kidnapping for a ransom of money. I had been thrust into a bizarre web of spies and intrigue – the sort of thing which, until now, had been entirely divorced from real life. But we were living in strange times.

I was in this position because of my relationship with James Brent, who was someone in addition to an army doctor. I saw now that his work must entail more than looking after sick soldiers.

I must get away. I had to think clearly. I wanted to shout at this man: 'I will not do this. Let me give you money.' I was being stupid. He did not want money. He wanted this box. And if I were to save Tristan, I had to find it.

I said as coolly as I could: 'How shall I know this box when I see it?'

'I am giving you a diagram of it. It is about six inches

by four. You will not fail to recognize it. Do not let anyone see it. Do your search by daylight when you do not have to show a light.'

That seemed significant. The burglars detected by Charley must have been working with this man.

I felt trapped, out of my depth, bewildered, one moment determined to go in search of the box, the next telling myself that I was caught up in something bigger even than the kidnapping of a child.

I must get away from this place . . . and think.

'Give me the diagram,' I said.

A black-gloved hand was held out. I took the folded paper and put it into my pocket.

'It is clear,' said the man. 'Your child's life depends on this. This time on Friday. Again, I must warn you not to attempt to trick us. You do not want to be responsible for your child's death, do you, Mrs Tregarland?'

I turned away and stumbled out of the house. I don't know how I managed to drive the car back to Tregarland's, but I did; and no one was aware that I had been out.

For the rest of that evening I went about in a daze. No one commented. They would think my mood was due to what I was suffering.

Gordon, Violetta and I sat at supper, pretending to eat. Old Mr Tregarland was in his own room. We had decided we would not tell him the news yet. Gordon thought it would be too great a shock for him.

We went to our rooms early. There was nothing we could do. There was an extension of the telephone in Gordon's room, so that, if a message came through, he could take it.

There would be no message, I knew; but I could not tell them that.

I undressed and sat in a chair in my dressing-gown, staring out of the window, seeing nothing but the secluded cottage with the creaking door and the eerie gloom – going over every sinister second I had spent there.

I had to find the box. Tomorrow I would go down and begin the search. Clearly it was something of great importance, possibly to the enemy of our country and, if I found it, if I gave it to them, I should be working for these spies. How could I do that? And yet, if I did not, they would kill Tristan.

I should never have gone to that cottage. I should never have become involved with Captain Brent.

I thought of the pleasure of the last month when I had been really happy. I was in love with him in a light-hearted, wartime way, as he was with me. It had been irresistible. One takes one's pleasures with open hands in wartime without question. We were two free people; neither of us had commitments with other people. Why should we not bring a little joy into those dreary, war-stricken months?

But he was clearly engaged in dangerous work. Naturally, he did not talk of it to me. And I, because of our relationship, had become involved in this without knowing what. Consequently, my child was in danger. There was something about the man in the cottage that was deadly serious. I knew he was in earnest.

If I did not produce the box on Friday, they would kill Tristan. And if I told anyone what had happened, they would doubtless kill me, too.

Not that I cared about myself. It would be an easy way out of my troubles, I thought.

That was foolish. I did not want to die. But I could never be happy again if they hurt my child. I must get that box. I must give it to them . . . and never let my child out of my sight again. But how could I do it? How could I steal this important thing from James?

It was important, not only to him, but to the country.

I had never been in such a terrible dilemma in my life.

I started. The door was opening. I knew who it was before she came into the room. She was in her dressing-gown, as I was. She said, in that straightforward way which was typical of her:

'What has happened?'

Of course, she was my twin, and there was this special bond between us. She had often known when I was in difficulties without my telling her.

'Violetta,' I said. 'It's you.'

'Who else? Something's happened, hasn't it?'

'It has,' I cried hysterically. 'Someone's taken Tristan. I'm out of my mind with worry.'

'We are all the same. But I know something's happened . . . today . . . this evening. What is it, Dorabella? You know you always tell me.'

I thought: She will stop me doing this. I know it is wrong to do it . . . but I must save Tristan.

I was silent. She took a chair and, pulling it close to mine, sat down.

'Now tell me everything,' she said.

I stammered: 'Perhaps there'll be a message soon. They . . . they'll want money. The old man will have to be told. He's rich. He'll pay anything to get Tristan back.'

'Dorabella, you know something, don't you? Something you're holding back.'

'I know my baby is taken . . .'

'We all know that. But there is something else. Come on. You know you could never keep anything from me.'

I began to cry silently and she put her arm round me.

'It's always better when we share,' she said. She was right. It always had been. Some of those difficulties had seemed gigantic when they loomed before me, and then my sister had come in with her calm common sense and straightened them out.

'If I tell you . . .'

I heard her deep breath and I knew that I had gone too far to turn back now.

'Yes,' she prompted. 'When you tell me . . .'

'You won't do anything unless I agree. Promise that.'

'I promise.'

'I have become rather friendly with Captain Brent.'

'I know.'

'You know!'

'My dear Dorabella, it was obvious. Those prolonged jaunts into town. The way you looked at each other. I am not blind, you know, particularly where you are concerned.'

'I had a note from them.'

'From whom?'

'The kidnappers.'

'When? Where is it? Why didn't you say?'

I told her how it had been brought to my room by Morwenna and that it had been lying on the hall table.

'How did it get there? Go on . . . what did it say?'

I told her.

'Where is it?'

'They took it from me when I went there.' I told her exactly what had happened, and I saw the shocked disbelief dawn on her face.

'This is terrible, Dorabella.'

'I must get Tristan safe.'

'I wouldn't have thought of anything like this. What on earth have you got caught up in?'

'You see, don't you, that I have to find that little box. I have to take it to them. I have to go alone and get Tristan.'

'It is obviously of tremendous importance for them to go to such lengths. You can't do it.'

'I must, I must.'

She said slowly. 'The burglary Charley saw . . . they must have been looking for this box.'

'I think that must have been so.'

'These are dangerous people. They are the enemy. It's the only explanation I can think of. They can't go back to the house to try again because the police have been alerted. I've always guessed that Captain Brent's job was not merely to keep an eye on the soldiers. He must be involved in secret work of some kind, and this box doubtless has something to do with it. And as they can't make another attempt at burglary, you, as the Captain's friend, can go into the Captain's house unquestioned. You can depend on it that your close relationship will be no secret. Therefore you can bring out the box and in exchange get your child.'

'How could they know . . . ?'

'These people make it their business to know everything that might be of importance. You must have been watched.'

'Oh, Violetta!' I cried. 'I'm glad I told you. What am I going to do?'

'There is only one thing you can do.'

'I must save Tristan.'

'You can't trust these people.'

'I have to. I have to get my baby.'

'You cannot do it that way, Dorabella. You will betray our country. That box is obviously important. How do you know that, by stealing it, you might not help to kill thousands of our people?'

'But what of Tristan?'

'There are clever people who could be working on this.'

'It is straightforward. I give them the box and they hand over Tristan.'

'There is no guarantee that they will give him to you. You cannot do it, Dorabella. Gordon . . . Captain Brent . . . they will know the best way to handle this. Tristan will be safer if we work through them. Captain Brent must know. He will understand the importance of this box.'

My head was throbbing. I was telling myself now that I had been a fool to tell her. I should have known she would have taken it this way. There was only one thought which was going round and round in my mind: I must save Tristan. I would do anything – anything for that.

We were silent for a while. Violetta took my hand and held it firmly. She was fully aware of my thoughts.

Then she said: 'We've always come through these difficulties working together. After all, two heads are better than one.'

I nodded.

'I know what we must do,' she went on.

'What?'

'This is too important for us to handle alone. They might not give you Tristan, whatever you did.'

'I have to trust them. What else can I do?'

'Would you trust such people?'

'I have to do anything to get Tristan back. We have to make sure that we do get him.'

'Dorabella, this is more important than you realize.'

'More important than I realize! It is the most important thing on earth to me. Those people don't want to hurt Tristan. They are just using him to get what they want. When they do, they'll give him up.'

'That may be, but you can't be sure. We know so little about this. This is what I suggest. We tell Gordon what has happened.'

'Gordon!'

'He will know what to do. He has connections with the Army through the Home Guard. Captain Brent must know what is happening. He will be aware of the importance of this box. He will know why they are so eager to get it. It must be of great importance for them to go to such lengths and expose themselves to danger. Be reasonable, Dorabella. You are more likely to get Tristan back safely if this is dealt with by experts . . . sensibly.'

'No. I must go there myself. I must go alone.'

'It would be quite wrong.'

'How can you know?'

'Instinctively. One should never deal with these people. These are not even ordinary kidnappers. They are spies.'

'Oh, what have I got into, Violetta? Why do these things happen to me?'

She paused and said musingly: 'I think people who do not live according to the conventions would be more likely to find themselves in awkward situations. Perhaps that is why we have these rules of conduct. But never mind. What we have to do is find the best way out of this.'

I was comforted by the word 'we'. We were sharing this, as we had always done.

'The first thing we should do,' she went on, 'is tell Gordon.'

'Oh no . . .'

'He will know best how we should act. Don't forget, he will know something of what is going on around us here. It's a fairly isolated coast and the enemy are just across the Channel. Remember the flashing lights? They were never fully explained. There is more going on than we know about and Gordon could have special knowledge. If we tell him exactly what has happened, he will certainly get in touch with Captain Brent.'

'Violetta, I have to have that box by Friday.'

'I know. That is why we should tell Gordon right away.'

'In the morning, then.'

'No, no. At once.'

'He's in his room. He's probably asleep.'

'Do you think any one of us in this house is asleep tonight?'

'You will tell him, then. What then? They'll know I've told.'

'They won't. He'll go to see Captain Brent. They'll have some plan. They will know what they are up against and how to deal with it. It's their work. You can't give secrets to the enemy in any circumstances. Believe me, this is the only way.'

'So you are going to tell Gordon.'

'That's the first step and we won't lose a moment.'

'And Tristan?'

'He'll be safer this way.'

'Oh, Violetta, I can't!'

'Trust me, Dorabella. I know I'm right. There is only one way to handle this and this is it.'

As she had thought, Gordon was up, sitting fully dressed in a chair near the telephone.

When we knocked, he said: 'Come in,' in a startled voice. 'Violetta! Dorabella!' he cried as we entered.

'Something has happened,' said Violetta. 'There has been a note from these people.'

'A note? Where?'

Violetta explained.

'My God!' he murmured under his breath.

He wanted to know everything. Where was the note? I had had to give it up, we told him. How was it delivered? It was on the hall table where the letters were put.

'So, someone must have been here . . . in the house.'

'Gordon,' said Violetta, 'we thought you would know how we should act.'

'And you actually saw this man. He gave you a sketch. It is so wild, so incredible . . .'

'It's something serious, isn't it?' said Violetta. 'It's more than an ordinary kidnapping for money.'

'I must have Tristan back,' I cried. 'I don't care . . .'

Violetta took my hand and pressed it while Gordon stood up and said: 'Captain Brent must see this sketch immediately. He will know what it is all about and how we should act.'

'He's away,' I said.

'I shall reach him. Listen. I am going . . . immediately.'

I looked at the clock on the mantelshelf. It was half past ten.

He went on: 'There may be little time to lose.'

'How will you find him?' asked Violetta.

'I shall find a way and I must do it right away.'

He went to the wardrobe and put on an overcoat and shoes. He opened a drawer and took out a briefcase; he put the sketch into his wallet and said: 'Go back to your rooms. Tell no one of this. When I return, behave as though I have just been out on some early morning estate matter. I shall probably know then what should be done. Now, go to your rooms.'

Violetta came back with me to mine and shortly afterwards we heard the sound of his car starting up and driving off.

We lay in the bed together. She held my hand as she used to when we were children. I was vaguely comforted because she knew.

It was about ten o'clock next morning when Gordon returned.

He came to us at once.

I cried: 'Have you seen Captain Brent?'

He nodded. 'It is better at this stage,' he said, 'if you do not know too much. You must do exactly what you are told. This morning you will drive to Riverside Cottage, park the car at the back where it cannot be seen from the road, and you will let yourself in through the back door. You will stay there for about an hour. Then you will come out, go to your car and drive back to Tregarland's. This afternoon, you will do the same again and perhaps stay a little longer. I shall leave this evening and hope to be back in a few hours.'

'If I cannot find the box . . .'

'Don't worry. You are going to take a box to them on Friday. It will be a box I shall give you. But you must do exactly as you are told. That is the best chance of getting Tristan back unharmed.'

'Oh, Gordon,' said Violetta, 'how glad I am we told you. Thank you . . . thank you!'

'My dear Violetta, we are not there yet and, of course, I want to do everything possible.'

'I know,' she said.

How did I live through that day? The minutes seemed like hours. I was so thankful that Violetta knew and I could talk to her frankly. I followed the instructions. I went to the house twice. I even looked for the box. I don't know what I should have done if I had found it. Probably ignored the instructions and taken it to the cottage on Friday. I was half mad with fear for Tristan. What was he doing now, I wondered? What did he think of being away from home, away from me, from Violetta and Nanny Crabtree?

After I returned from Riverside Cottage, I stayed with Violetta.

I said: 'I am not sure of Gordon. If Tristan died, he'd have Tregarland's.'

'Oh, Dorabella, he would never harm a child.'

'There would be much to gain and he loves Tregarland's. Perhaps we shouldn't have told him.'

'We did right to tell him. This is a highly dangerous matter. The box is of great importance. Oh no, this is the only way.'

'And if this means they kill Tristan?'

'This is the best way to bring him back safely. I am sure of that.'

I was not. I wished I could stop pictures coming into my mind. It was no use. We had to wait for the time to pass. It would have been unendurable without Violetta.

I felt an immense relief when Gordon returned.

He said: 'I have a box, and I will tell you what has to be done. Tomorrow morning you will go to Riverside Cottage. You will take a shopping-bag with you. In it will be the box. You will let yourself into the cottage by the back way as before and stay there for an hour or so. You will come out carrying the shopping-bag as though it is rather heavy. In case you are being watched, you will give the impression that you are carrying something precious. Then, at the appropriate time, you will drive to the cottage on the moor as you did on that other occasion. You will go in and tell them that you have the box. You will show it to them. I feel sure that Tristan will be there. He will be handed over to you in exchange for the box.'

'How do you know that they will give him to me?'

'There is no reason why they should not. They do not want him. They only wanted to use him as a means of getting you to work for them. Providing there is no hitch, they will hand over the child.'

'No hitch? What hitch?'

'None . . . if you obey orders.'

I was trembling with the desire to get on with it. I could not wait for the hours to pass.

Gordon had taken a box out of its wrappings. It looked exactly like the one in the sketch. I seized it. At least I should have something to offer them.

'Where did you get it?' I asked.

'You will hear more about it when this affair is over.'

'It won't be long now, Dorabella,' said my sister. She put

an arm round me. 'All you have to do is to obey instructions and all will come right.'

'Have you seen Captain Brent?' I asked Gordon.

'As I said, don't think about anything but what you have to do. I assure you this is the best way to save Tristan. You could never have found the box in the cottage because it was no longer there. Now please, Dorabella, listen to your sister.'

He gave Violetta a grateful and admiring look. I thought: He is right. She is so sensible. She would never have got involved in the first place.

I did exactly as they said. I went to the cottage with my shopping-bag on my arm. I stayed there for a while and, when I came out, I carried it very carefully. I put it beside me in the car and drove off.

The important moment was creeping nearer. How time lagged! Three o'clock. Would it never be half past? Had the clock stopped?

I was ready to leave at four. I knew that Violetta was watching me from a window. I placed the bag containing the box on the seat beside me and drove into the road.

To my dismay, Simone was there.

'Just going out, then?' she asked.

'Yes,' I stammered.

'I wondered if you would give me a lift into Poldown?'

What could I say? I was going in that direction anyway. I wanted to tell her that I was going on an important engagement, but restrained myself in time.

I reached over and opened the door. She got in and almost sat on the shopping-bag. Flustered, I grasped it.

'Let's put it at the back,' said Simone.

'No, no, I'll take it.' I settled it at my feet.

I was trembling. It was nothing to be alarmed at. She would leave as soon as we reached the town and I could turn into the road heading for Bodmin.

I was thankful that she did not ask where I was going. She said I must be feeling dreadful and she wished there was something she could do.

'I think we must hear something soon,' I said.

'The police are clever,' she added.

We did not speak much. There was nothing we could talk about with so much on our minds, and she knew if we spoke of that it would be painful.

I was glad when she left.

I drove on. That had delayed me only a minute or so, and I was in good time.

It was as it had been that other day, except that I did not now have to look for the cottage.

Grasping the bag, I went inside. Then I heard a voice which made my heart leap with joy and fear.

'I want my Mummy.'

'Tristan!'

I called out his name and the door opened. The masked man whom I had seen before was standing there.

'Well, Mrs Tregarland,' he said. 'What have you brought for me?'

'What you asked for.'

'Show me.'

I took the box from the bag and handed it to him. I thought I should faint with fear. It could not be the real one. They would never have let him have that. Would he know?

'Where is my child?' I said.

'You shall have him. We keep our promises. There is one other thing.'

'No! No!' I cried. 'Give him to me.'

'It is easy. You must say you found him wandering on the road.'

'I will say anything if you give him to me.'

He turned. I think the figure who was beside him was a woman. Then Tristan rushed into my arms.

He was half crying, half laughing. I said: 'Tristan, my darling, come with me. We're going home.'

I took his hand and ran out of the cottage. I pushed him into the car, started the engine and we were off.

I wanted to sing pæans of praise, I wanted to thank God, all His angels, Violetta and Gordon.

My baby was safe with me.

He nestled close to me, holding my skirt in a tight grip. I took a quick look at him. He was smiling and, in a tone of deep satisfaction, he announced: 'Got Mummy.'

At that moment there was pandemonium and noise broke out from every side. I heard the sound of shots. I stepped on the accelerator.

Gordon had said: 'When Tristan is handed to you, do not lose a moment. Get into the car, and drive as quickly as you can back to Tregarland's.'

So that is what I did.

I wonder if I have ever been so happy in my life as I was when I ran into the house gripping Tristan's hand.

'He's home!' I shouted. 'Listen, everybody! Tristan's here!'

They were all rushing into the hall. I shall never forget Nanny Crabtree's face. Tears were running down her cheeks. She was the first to reach him.

'My angel!' she cried. 'Come home to Nanny!'

Then I saw Violetta smile at Gordon . . . a smile of deep gratitude and admiration. Then she was hugging me and everyone was talking at once.

They would soon be asking how he was found, and I was not sure what I was expected to say.

Then the questions came.

'It's wonderful, wonderful. Where did you find him, Mrs Tregarland?'

Violetta said: 'We are all so exhausted. We'll hear about it later. I am going to take Mrs Tregarland to the nursery with Nanny.' She whispered to them: 'Better not to talk of it before the child.'

Trust Violetta to know what to do!

Nanny was holding Tristan's hand and would not let it go.

'Come on,' Violetta continued. 'We'll all go up now. Tristan is worn out.'

They dispersed, disappointed, but there was not one of them who was not overcome with delight because Tristan was home.

Tristan was examined by Nanny. He did not seem to have suffered from his ordeal.

It was difficult to get from him what had actually happened.

Did he leave his bed and go off?

He looked a little vague and nodded.

Why did he do that?

'To see the dinosaurs,' he said.

'In the picturebook?'

'No . . . real ones.'

'Where?'

'In the garden.'

'Who told you?'

'The lady.'

'What lady?'

'Her,' he said.

'Who?' I asked.

He looked vague.

'Was it a lady you hadn't seen before?' I went on. He still looked puzzled.

'And did you see the dinosaurs?' I asked.

He shook his head.

'Who was there?'

'Her.'

'Was she nice?'

He nodded.

I could see there was nothing to be learned from him. This woman had slipped into the house while Nanny was in a deep sleep; she had taken him down to see the dinosaurs and then, presumably, carried him off.

At least they had not harmed him and I could only think of one overwhelming fact: he was back.

Violetta and I had a long talk with Gordon that evening. I don't suppose he told us everything, but he realized we could not be left entirely in the dark.

Violetta had guessed that Captain Brent had apparently rented Riverside Cottage because he was going to look in on the recuperating soldiers while he was engaged in some important secret work. After the flashing lights episode, attention had been drawn to our part of the coast, where, it seemed, something subversive might be going on.

It was suspected that someone was transmitting messages to the enemy. They had made the initial mistake of using equipment which had allowed the signals to be so bright that they were visible. The furore in the neighbourhood which had ensued had been a warning to them. They must have rejoiced to have an obvious scapegoat in Gretchen.

'This sort of thing is inevitable in wartime,' said Gordon. 'Spies are planted before the war starts. Some might have been living the lives of normal people for some time and then are called into service. There are numbers of such people. And then there are the experts . . . the full-time spies who will have found some means of getting into the country.'

'What was the box?' I asked.

Gordon hesitated, and then went on: 'It has something to do with an invention which will detect the approach of aircraft miles away. It could be of great importance. Captain Brent was testing it in this part of the world and he had had it for a while in Riverside Cottage. They wished to get hold of it, which was why they burgled the place. Charley saw them and stopped that. Charley has been something of a help. I'll tell you more of that later.'

'I suppose at that time the important box was in Riverside Cottage,' said Violetta.

'Yes. But for Charley, they might have found it.'

'What happened after I drove away with Tristan?'

'Our people had the place surrounded. I think we fooled them. The box you were given was a replica of the actual one, though of course it lacked the vital parts. They were naturally deceived . . . but that would have been only temporarily. They believed you had carried out their orders, and they gave up Tristan. No doubt they thought it would not be wise to deceive you. They may have planned to use you again. We came in as soon as you left.'

'I heard shooting.'

'Inevitable in the circumstances. We got one of them in the leg.'

'How many were there?' asked Violetta.

'Six. We got them all. This is where Charley comes in again. The boys were riding round on their bicycles when they discovered a motorboat ready for departure. It was right down by the sea at Penwarlock. They reported it to me. Charley likes a bit of adventure and, since that scare about the lights, he has been keeping his eyes open. There have been a number of things he has reported to me. Well, this was something very important. We had people waiting down by this motorboat. Those people were about to get into the boat with their prize – the bogus box – when we took them all.'

'Who would believe such things could happen?' asked Violetta.

'This is wartime,' Gordon reminded her.

In a neighbourhood like ours, people were very much involved in what was going on around them; there had to be plausible explanations; and when it was assumed that Tregarland's had paid a ransom to the kidnappers, this was not contradicted.

We watched Tristan closely, to discover what effect the adventure had had on him. He was physically unharmed, so they could not have treated him badly. True, he would not stay in a room unless Violetta, Nanny Crabtree or I were there and we noticed his eyes followed us when we moved away, and often he would stretch out a hand to grip our skirts. It was rather touching.

At night, the door between his room and that of Nanny Crabtree was kept open, and I suggested that a bed should be put in his room so that I could sleep there.

His delight at this was very revealing. No one, not even a child who did not know what it was all about, could go through an experience such as he had had without being affected by it.

I was so glad that I was sleeping there. Sometimes during the night, he would creep into my bed and I would hold him tightly in my arms.

This brought us closer together and I could tell myself that I was grateful because I was able to make up for what I had lost in the past through my desertion.

Never again would I leave him, I would tell myself in the darkness. For as long as he needed me, I should be there.

We thought we should not question him too closely, but gradually, little bits of information emerged. He had been in a house. There was someone he called 'Her'. We learned by degrees that 'Her' had told him that, if he were good and did not cry, he would go back to his mummy, his Auntie Violetta and Nanny Crabtree. He had to eat his food too.

'Was the food nice?'

He wrinkled his nose.

'Not like Nanny's?' I suggested.

'Not like Nanny's,' he agreed.

'Her' was the one who had come in and told him about the dinosaurs in the garden.

'She came into your bedroom?'

He nodded.

'All by herself?'

He looked puzzled.

'Was there someone with her?'

'Outside the door,' he said.

'One of the servants?'

He did not know.

It was all very mysterious.

'It must never happen again,' I said to Violetta.

'It won't. It failed once, didn't it?'

'There might be other attempts.'

'It was all due to the box and your connection with Captain Brent.'

'Please . . . don't remind me.'

'I'm sorry. But Tristan will be all right now.'

Nanny had been very shaken by the incident – more so than we had realized at first. She could not stop blaming herself for being asleep when Tristan had been taken.

'Right from under my nose,' she would murmur to herself, shaking her head, looking bewildered and shocked. 'It was no more than one of my cosy naps after lunch. I've had them as long as I can remember.'

There were no more of those cosy little naps. I remembered that, when we were young, and she had, as she said, 'put us down to sleep for an hour', she would doze as she rocked herself in the next room. When we were older, we had been sent to the nursery to 'play nice and quiet' while she took her well-earned rest.

There were more cups of tea instead of the rest, for they were something she could not do without in her present state.

Violetta said that the worst time of Nanny Crabtree's day was that hour after lunch when she sat . . . awake . . . sipping her tea and going over that dreadful day when she had failed to be alert while her charge was in danger.

One of us liked to be with her at that time of day.

About a week after Tristan's rescue, I was sitting with Nanny. I didn't listen very intently to her conversation. She was rambling on about our childhood . . . usually of my rebellious ways, and how different my sister had been. I had heard it all before, and it usually amused me, for when Violetta was the recipient of these reminiscences, she did not come out of them quite so perfectly.

She said musingly: 'I haven't seen much of that Simone lately. What's happened to her?'

'Oh, she's around,' I said. 'I saw her only yesterday.'

'She was one for a cup of tea. She'd come in when I was having one and say, in that funny way of hers, "Dutay", or something. She said the tea I made tasted better than any she had ever tasted. Bit of flattery, if you ask me. But I must say, she liked her cup of tea.'

'I expect she's busy on the estate. I know she comes sometimes to Tregarland's on business. I suppose that's when she looked in on you.'

'Well, Jermyn's and Tregarland's . . . they're one and the same now. This home has brought them together more than ever. I suppose your sister started it with that Jowan. Oh dear, I wish he'd come home.'

'So do we all, Nanny.'

'I look forward to that Simone popping in. Nice girl. Nice

way with her. Of course she's a foreigner, but she can't help that. And I reckon she's really nice. Coming here like that with her brother. That took a bit of doing, I'd say. You wouldn't get me out in one of them boats, I can tell you.'

'I hope that will never be necessary, Nanny,' I said.

There was a sound from the next room. We were both on our feet. Tristan was just waking up and smiled with satisfaction when he saw us. He knew he was safe. It would never happen to him again while we were hovering round him like guardian angels – myself, Violetta, Nanny. We would always make sure that we knew where he was every minute of the day and night.

Even Charley had made himself a guard, and Bert, of course, was his assistant. When Tristan was in the garden, if they were not at school, Charley and Bert would be watching him. Charley had assumed an almost conspiratorial air. He was delighted because Gordon had told him he had acted in a wise way in reporting the motorboat he had seen in the cove. It had been a great help and Gordon hinted that 'very important personages' wanted to applaud him for his sagacity. Charley was overcome with pride and, since the kidnapping, which must have seemed to him like sensational fiction, he wanted to be part of the scene.

I think, too, that he felt he was part of the family; we were the only ones left to him; our tragedies were his and he wanted to stand beside us, fighting to overcome them.

Moreover, he was beginning to regard Gordon as a hero. He was never happier than when he was given some job about the estate.

Violetta noticed this.

'Poor Charley!' she said. 'Poor Bert! This dreadful war has robbed them of their home . . . their parents . . . everything that was familiar to them.'

'And has given them Tregarland's – and Gordon,' I answered. 'Charley regards him as a sort of god. Gordon must be gratified. Who wouldn't be, to be elevated to the heights of Olympus? But he pretends not to notice.'

'Which,' said Violetta, 'is typical of Gordon.'

Simone had disappeared. I was not aware of this immediately. I did not see her very frequently. Sometimes I ran into her in one of the Poldowns, sometimes on the estate when I went over to work at the Priory; but it often happened that for days we did not meet.

If I were taking the car into the Poldowns and she happened to be there and wanted a lift, I would pick her up. So I did not immediately become aware of her absence.

Mrs Penwear had reported that she had not seen her for several days. She had enjoyed Simone's company.

'She be a very nice lady,' she said. 'Always polite with that French way, which is rather nice in a young lady like Simone. She was fond of a chat and we'd often have a talk together. She'd tell me about the estate and I'd tell her about the folk round here. She never seemed to tire of listening. I didn't know she hadn't come home at first. Like as not, I'd be fast asleep when she come in. She was sometimes late. And then she'd be off again early in the morning. She always made her bed and tidied up before she went.'

But eventually Mrs Penwear had begun to be alarmed.

'I talked to Daniel Killick. She was friendly with him. A nice young man. He hadn't seen her either. Mr Yeo sent someone to look for her, but there was no sign of her.'

The news spread. Simone was missing.

What could have happened to her? What was wrong with this place? Only a little while ago a child had been kidnapped – and now a young girl was missing.

There were the usual rumours. Someone had kidnapped

her. Why? Who would pay a ransom for her? It was different with little Tristan Tregarland and his rich family. People didn't kidnap people who couldn't bring in a handsome reward for their trouble. She had been murdered, it was said, and for a while suspicion fell on poor Daniel Killick – that most inoffensive of men – simply because he had been friendly with her.

There were no arrests – and no evidence of what had become of her.

It was Gordon who found the solution. One of the soldiers had been seen talking to her. This soldier had been slightly shell-shocked, which had resulted in a temporary loss of memory. He remembered suddenly that Simone had spoken to him.

She told him she had news that her brother was dangerously ill and she had to go to him at once. She had written notes to Mr Yeo and Mrs Penwear explaining that she was leaving without delay, and had asked the soldier to deliver them, but he had forgotten to do so. When he eventually found them in his pocket, his memory of the incident began to return and he took the note to Mr Yeo.

The mystery was solved.

She had left her things behind, but they would be collected later, for she had gone to her brother who was with the Free French contingent. She would come back when her brother was better.

Nanny Crabtree said: 'At times like these, people will dream up all sorts of horrors. I am glad that poor girl is all right. And poor Dan Killick! Well, the things people were saying about him! They'll know better next time to wait a bit before they start taking away people's characters, won't they?'

* * *

But that was not the true story.

Gordon had been out all day and came back after dinner one evening. He did not want any food, but he came up to my room and asked me to bring Violetta along as he had something to say to us both which he thought we should know.

He looked grave.

'Let's sit down,' he said.

Violetta sat on the bed. I was in the armchair and Gordon on the window-seat.

'I have spoken to Captain Brent,' he said.

I felt my heart beat faster. I was missing James, now that the anxiety concerning Tristan no longer filled my mind.

'He thinks you should know, as you are to some extent involved. The Dubois have been arrested.'

'Arrested!' I cried.

'I think they will not bother us any more. They came here with the purpose of spying for the enemy.'

We stared at him in horror, and Gordon went on: 'I know everything that is happening seems to have taken a wild turn at the moment, but this is war. We are fighting for our lives, and so is the other side. Anything, however seemingly implausible, however incongruous, has to be investigated. These people made a mistake when they came here. Simone is, of course, not Jacques's sister. They came here because of his connection with you, which he thought would make him acceptable. It meant he had to keep the name of Dubois. Our people knew that name. He had used it in Paris, and he had come under suspicion when one of our men was found murdered in a Paris street, not far from the house where Dubois was living.'

'Georges Mansard!' I whispered.

Gordon nodded. 'They discovered who he was and killed him.'

'It happened just before I left,' I cried.

'I know, and Germany was about to invade Western Europe. It was an opportune time. Jacques had been over here before the war . . . with a German artist.'

'I remember them,' said Violetta.

'They were sketching the coast. All very useful to an enemy who has plans for the invasion of the country, of course. And Dorabella, you became caught up in this intrigue.'

I felt limp with shame and horror.

'Briefly,' went on Gordon, 'they came over, landing on the coast where you found them, which was what they intended. The woman who calls herself Simone Dubois is very clever and adaptable. This part of the country is very interesting to the enemy because of certain activities which you now know something about. They were hoping to get their hands on what was in that box about which you have heard so much. We not only foiled them on that, but caught them. Simone, of course, was concerned in it. We have suspected her for some time, but wanted to get our hands on Jacques and others as well.'

'So Simone was actually concerned in the kidnapping,' I said.

'Decidedly so. She made a habit of coming in to take tea with Nanny Crabtree. It was comparatively easy to slip a light sleeping draught into her cup. Nanny obviously did not think it unusual that she had come in that day since she had made a habit of calling; and then, when Nanny was drowsy, Simone let in the woman who took Tristan down to the garden to see those fictitious dinosaurs. At least that seems a logical assumption.'

'It was diabolical!' cried Violetta.

'These people will stop at nothing. They are clever . . . ingenious. They make it all work out as simply as possible.'

'Nanny did not say that Simone was there on that day.'

'She didn't think anything of it. Simone had often come in the last weeks. Well, it seems that was how it must have been done. The kidnappers thought they had got away with the box. Thanks to the perspicacity of Charley, we were waiting for them when they would have got away. We had the people immediately concerned in the plot. But not Simone. She was not with them on that occasion and, of course, there was no intention of her giving up the valuable work she was doing for our enemies. We had been watching Simone for some time, and we knew she could lead us to others.'

'Her "brother"?' I asked, and Gordon nodded.

'She has now been arrested, with her "brother". We have what we wanted and I think we can congratulate ourselves.'

'To think that for so long we have been living in the midst of all this intrigue!' I said.

'There is more going on than any of us realize. Living in wartime is living with melodrama all about one. This is a triumph for our service here.'

'And is Captain Brent involved in all this?' I asked.

'Deeply. But he thought you should be told something, as you two have been involved in it too – particularly you, Dorabella, having been in Paris and lived with this spy, and even having met Georges Mansard. In due course I shall let it be known that Simone wants to be near her "brother" and that she has taken a job on a farm near him. We shall pretend to forward on her clothes and effects. Mrs Penwear will pack them and I shall take them, letting everyone think that they are going to be sent on to her, just in case anyone should start rumours which must be suppressed. Gossip is rife. So, when Mrs Penwear has packed Simone's things, I shall tell everyone they have gone to her. No one must be aware of the purpose for which she was here. They must continue to think of her as the amusing French girl who so bravely left her country. And, if you hear anything to the contrary, you must come and tell me at once.'

'We understand,' said Violetta, looking at him with undoubted admiration. I must say, I felt the same.

Captain Brent came to visit the men as he had before. I met him in a passage in the Priory.

He looked at me quizzically. Then he put his hands on my shoulders and said: 'This business . . . it hasn't altered things, has it?'

I laughed with relief. 'Oh James,' I replied. 'It has been so awful.'

'Somewhat melodramatic, eh?'

I said: 'I can't forget what happened . . . because of us . . . Tristan . . .'

'I know,' he replied. Then: 'Come to Riverside this afternoon, can you? We could talk there.'

'Yes,' I answered, my spirits soaring.

I did care for James, and it would be good to be with him once more.

He was waiting for me when I arrived. He put his arms round me and kissed me.

'Wonderful to be with you again . . . like this,' he said.

'I didn't realize that you were not exactly what you were said to be.'

'Who is?' he asked.

'I suppose you are a very important person?'

'One of the cogs in the wheel. I have my little part to play. I am sorry you had to be drawn into all this.'

'It will be different knowing that you are not really here to look after those men. But that is something which we must not mention.'

He smiled. 'Then it makes no difference. What we are to each other is the same as it ever was. Do you agree?'

'Yes, I agree.'

It was wonderful to have him back. It was exciting. There was a secret we shared. He was not what he had seemed to be, but a man of mystery, which made everything more enthralling.

When I left Riverside Cottage, I drove into Poldown, where I sensed an excitement in the air. A little knot of men was standing by the bridge reading a newspaper. Something had clearly happened.

I got out of the car and went into the newsagent's.

'Oh, there you be then, Mrs Tregarland,' said Mrs Benn from behind the counter. 'Have 'ee heard the news, then?'

'News? What news?'

'They Japs have gone and bombed the American Fleet in a place called Pearl Harbor and they do say this 'ull bring them into the war at last.'

I bought a paper and read the headlines. Then I drove back as fast as I could to Tregarland's.

There was immediate relief. We no longer stood alone. This must be the beginning of the end.

Violetta

A Friend from the Past

Another year was with us and there was still no news of Jowan. I think I was beginning to believe, with others, that he would never return.

We had made a great effort to have a merry Christmas with the men and had succeeded fairly well. Everyone joined in, including my parents, who had come to Tregarland's to spend Christmas with us.

It was wonderful to see them. There was so much to talk about. My mother had known nothing about the kidnapping until it was over. She and my father would have been absolutely distracted and I was glad we had not told them until Tristan was safely back.

My mother was busy with all sorts of war work. She told me that my grandmother had opened Marchlands again. She would have liked to go there but she would not leave my father, who could not leave the estate. She and my father had considered turning Caddington into a hospital, but it was very useful for holding meetings for all sorts of projects and this was what it was being used for at this time.

She and my father, I knew, were deeply worried about me. Though they did not talk of Jowan, I was aware that he was continually in their thoughts, and I guessed they discussed my future when they were alone in their bedroom. Dorabella did not, I supposed, give them the same cause for concern, which was something of a turnabout, for usually she was the one to disturb them.

Dorabella had become a devoted mother, which pleased Nanny Crabtree.

'It does you good to see them together,' she said. 'Poor mite, he may have lost his father, but he has his mother to make up for that, and he thinks the world of her.'

Then there was Captain Brent. I wondered how significant that was. He certainly had great charm, and Dorabella had acquired that special radiance which I had seen before. At the same time, she was obviously aware that her affair with the Captain had brought about the kidnapping of her son and she blamed herself for that. But she was susceptible, and now it seemed that they were together again. I felt certain that it was one of those wartime romances. Well, perhaps Dorabella needed it; and she was certainly happy now. I was the one who was giving concern to our parents.

My mother gave me news of Gretchen, who was now in London because Edward's regiment was stationed in the South-East near the capital.

'Of course,' said my mother, 'the bombing has eased off a little and they seemed to get used to it.'

'It must be dangerous there.'

'Well, yes. But it is dangerous everywhere. Gretchen told me of a family she knew who thought they must get out of town, so they went to Wales. They had come through the London Blitz unscathed; they went to this remote place on the borders and an aircraft returning with its bomb load from Birmingham unloaded its bombs right over their house. They were all killed . . . the entire family. That's how life goes.'

'And Gretchen is happy there?'

'I think so. She was upset over the suspicion about her.'

'I know, it was terrible for her.'

'In London it's different. There's not so much petty gossip. People are more concerned with their own affairs. Hildegarde is a great joy. Of course, nannies are almost unobtainable and looking after the child herself in a fairly small house without much help is a full-time job.'

'She has friends, I suppose.'

'Oh yes, and Edward has a certain amount of leave. He can get home, if only for a day or so. And she is near the Dorringtons. You remember them.'

'Yes, of course. How are they?'

'Very much the same. Richard is in the Army. Like Edward, he is stationed not far from London. His mother is doing good works.'

'And Mary Grace?'

'She works in one of the Ministries. Everyone without home duties is being called up to work, as you know. Not that Mary Grace would want to be idle. Oh, wouldn't it be wonderful if we could all get back to normal?'

She was looking at me wistfully. I knew what she was thinking.

There had been a time when she had hoped I would marry Richard Dorrington, the barrister friend of Edward. He had, in fact, asked me. I admit I had been uncertain then. I had been seeing Jowan in Cornwall, but there had never been any reference to love between us and I had not really understood my feelings at that time. I had liked Richard very much, but I had realized even then that my feelings did not go deep enough for a lifetime partnership. Perhaps subconsciously I had known that it must be Jowan.

Now my mother was thinking that Jowan would never come back and there was Richard, still a bachelor and an eligible one. Perhaps old fires could be stirred.

I knew she was concerned, too, about my brother Robert, who had just joined the Army. He was younger than Dorabella and I were, full of high spirits; and she must be missing him. She wanted to tell me that I could not go on grieving for Jowan, but she must be aware that I would continue to hope for his return as long as there was the flimsiest chance.

However, we certainly tried to be bright that Christmas and to make this one as normal and lively as they used to be.

Mrs Jermyn had asked Dorabella and me to put our heads together and devise a programme which would entertain the men. We thought at first of a treasure hunt, but many of the men were disabled and would not be fit to take part, so we decided that we would put on a play in which some of them could take part.

We had chosen *The Importance of Being Earnest* and the result was a great deal of fun. Captain Brent played Ernest and Dorabella made a fascinating Gwendoline; I was Cicely; and one of the old sergeant-majors was the real star of the show as Lady Bracknell.

We all seemed to forget our troubles briefly during that day – which was, of course, the whole object of the enterprise.

In due course my parents left us with many regrets at the parting and insisted that Dorabella and I must come to Caddington soon.

We assured them we would as soon as possible, but it would be difficult to get away as we had our work with the invalid soldiers. Moreover, it would mean taking Tristan and Nanny Crabtree, for I was sure that Dorabella, in her present maternal role, would not agree to leave him; furthermore, I believed that, if there was news of Jowan, it would go to Jermyn's first, and I should be wondering if it had come all the time I was absent.

One March day there was a message for Gordon from Bodmin. Would he come as soon as possible? His mother's condition had changed.

When he returned, I was waiting for him. I went to his study where I found him looking upset and perplexed.

'What happened?' I asked.

He stared ahead and replied: 'She . . . she's changed. She is remembering.'

'You mean . . . what happened?'

'Not everything . . . some of it. She is different now. She talks of Tregarland's. It crops up again and again in her rambling conversation. She keeps saying "Where would it have been without you, Gordon? You saved that place. It should be yours." '

'Did she remember . . . what she had done?'

'She mentioned Tristan. She looked . . . haunted.'

I thought of her creeping into the nursery, preparing to kill him because he stood in the way of Gordon's inheriting Tregarland's; and she would have done so if Nanny Crabtree and I had not been ready to prevent it. Tristan, so young, yet at the centre of such dramatic events, fortunately knew little of them.

Gordon was saying: 'I am afraid for her. With the return of sanity, there will come remembrance, when she realizes what she planned to do and would have done, too. Murder! Oh, Violetta, I do not know what will become of her.'

I felt a great urge to comfort him. 'This may be a phase through which she is passing,' I said. 'And she might not remember . . .'

I thought what a terrible thing it was that we should hope for her return to that clouded world which she inhabited with people who were similarly afflicted.

'You have done everything you can for her,' I went on. 'She could not have had a better son.'

'And I had a mother who was ready to commit murder for me. I often think how different it could have been. She might have married someone – someone in circumstances like her own; she might have had a happy life. But she met my father and he took her to Tregarland's, to grandeur such as she had never known before. And she wanted a place for me in all that. It was an obsession and it led her to this.'

'It might have been different, yes,' I said. 'But that is the way life works out. It is the same with all of us. Dorabella and I might never have gone to Germany, never have met Dermot. Life hangs on chance. We might never have known Tregarland's existed.'

'There is one good thing at least which came out of it all,' said Gordon. 'You came to Tregarland's.'

He took my hand in his and held it. I let it rest there because he was so distraught and seemed to draw comfort from the gesture.

Gordon went to Bodmin the next day. I impatiently waited for his return. I could not help hoping that Matilda had lapsed into her previous state.

The news was surprising. She had been out in the grounds of the Bodmin establishment; she had left her coat indoors and the wind was cold. A little later, she had been feverish; and the doctor had diagnosed pleurisy. She was now quite ill.

'She said little,' Gordon told me. 'She just smiled at me. She was quiet and the wild look had gone from her eyes. She looked sad. I shall go again tomorrow.'

It was two days later when we heard that Matilda was dead. She had developed pneumonia and there had been little hope after that.

Gordon went to Bodmin and remained there all day. When he came home, he looked more tired and strained than I had ever seen him before.

He said: 'She looked peaceful in death . . . more so than I remembered seeing her. It is over, Violetta. I think I should not mourn too much for her. It is happier so.'

I sat very still, my mind going back once more to that

time when she had meant to kill Tristan. And I saw that this was the best thing that could happen to her, for if she had realized what she had done, she could never have been happy. She would have had to live out her life tormented by remorse.

We must realize that this was a release, not only for Matilda, but for all of us.

Old Mr Tregarland was very upset when he heard of Matilda's death. I think he had loved her in his way. He had treated her badly and he knew it. He must blame himself for his part in the tragedy which grew out of that.

Since Matilda had been taken away, he had changed; he had softened; life was no longer an amusing game to him in which he played with other people's lives for his amusement.

He ordered that Matilda's body should be brought to Tregarland's and buried at West Poldown in the family vault. She would have been pleased by that – acknowledged in death as she had not been in life. He insisted on going to the funeral, although he was hardly in a fit state to do so and the doctor had advised against it. I was deeply aware of his melancholy as he stood among the mourners.

Since then he had not left his bed for several days and Gordon called the doctor, for he was sure that the old man was more ill than he would admit.

The doctor came and said Mr Tregarland was tired. He should not have attended the funeral and stood in the cold wind.

One afternoon, Amy, one of the maids, came to me with a message from Mr Tregarland. He would like to see me.

When I went to his room, he was lying propped up on his pillows; he looked smaller and very frail, but I caught the old look of mischief in his eyes.

'Ah,' he said, 'the good Violetta – the sensible one. I noticed that from the start. It is kind of you to come to see me.'

'But of course I came.'

He nodded. 'Things have been happening here, haven't they? Odd, isn't it, how we go on for years in the same old rut and then suddenly everything erupts into drama. Well, that's happening all over the world now, and events in Tregarland's are mild enough when compared with most of today's tragedies. "Every prospect pleases, and only man is vile." Not true. There is much good in man. Don't you agree, wise Violetta?'

'I don't know why you call me wise. I am as foolish as most people, I suppose.'

'Not you. That is why I want to talk to you before I shuffle off this mortal coil singing "Nunc Dimittis". How I indulge in quotations this morning! That's a sign of something. When one looks back and considers one's past, one remembers those lines which suddenly assume a significance. Is that so, do you think?'

'I imagine it could be so.'

'When a man is drowning, they say his past life flashes before his eyes. Well, so it is with a man who has come to his end in any other way. There is the past mocking him, saying: "You should have done this." But mostly: "You should not have done that." Ah, there's the rub. I'm back again, Violetta. The time has come for repentance. I look back on my life and I say, "What good have you done, James Tregarland?" A little, perhaps, but the balance weighs more heavily on the other side. And now I am a sick man preparing for the last journey. I am bowed down by my sins and the havoc I have created . . . mostly for others. Not a pleasant conclusion, Violetta.'

'I don't suppose you have been much worse than most people,' I said.

He looked solemn for a moment.

'"The fault, dear Brutus, is not in our stars but in ourselves that we are underlings." That man Shakespeare had a tab to stick on everything, didn't he? This is a sort of confessional.'

'To be made to me?'

'Why not? You are the most suitable person in this house. You will be here after I am gone. You know a little about me. I have noticed you observing me in the past. You know my wickedness; how, when I was infirm, my life changed so that I was confined to this place for my last years. I liked to watch others – particularly Matilda. She was a source of interest to me because I was never sure how she would act. You see, she was brought up in a puritanical home, but there was nothing puritanical about Matilda underneath that veneer. Her parents had fitted her into a mould. She was bound to break out sooner or later. When we met there was a spark which ignited the future.'

'She willingly did what she did, I suppose.'

'It was not as simple in that age. Matilda had been brought up in fear of offending against the laws of the Church, which meant the laws laid down by Père and Mère Lewyth. When she was about to produce an illegitimate child, they turned their daughter out. Imagine that! I set her up in a place and when my wife died I brought her here as housekeeper. That's an old story which you have heard already. There was Dermot and there was Gordon; and how much more fitted Gordon was to be the heir of Tregarland's. I watched her. I teased her. I might make her son my heir . . . and I might not. It was like that all the way through. My poor Matty, she was in despair and she set about making possible what she believed would never be if she did nothing about it.'

'Why did you not tell her your intentions right away?'

'I wanted to watch what she would do. To have told her would have spoiled the fun.'

'The fun of tormenting her?'

'You could say that – and yet I was fond of her. And now that I have come to the end, like many before me I wish I had acted differently. The awful thing is that if I had, Matty would have ended differently. I wanted to see what she would do. And I did. I drove her mad and made a murderess of her. Do you think I am responsible for what she did?'

'You have been wrong. You have been heartless, but I am sure you never thought for one moment that there would be murder.'

'I can say with honesty that I did not. But it was only when I discovered what she was ready to do to the child that I understood what I had done.'

'It is over now,' I said, 'and there is nothing you can do about it.'

'Only regret. I have made reparations as far as I can. The estate will go to the boy. It must. It is his by right. As for Gordon, he should have been the one. It is sad that he was born on the wrong side of the blanket. Dermot was no good. He was weak and pleasure-seeking ... oh, a charming young man. Rather like his father and grandfather. But Tregarland's needed a strong steady hand to keep it on course. Gordon had that. It was one of those tricks of fate. The bastard is the one the place needed and the rightful heir is useless. Why couldn't it have been the other way round? Perversity of life, I suppose. Poor Gordon has suffered; but I will tell you this, wise Violetta. I have made what reparations I can. I have acknowledged Gordon as my son in this will of mine, and I am leaving him capital so that he can start up his own place, but I shall express the hope that Gordon will stay until Tristan is of an age to manage.'

'Then it will be too late for him to start on his own.'

'When Tristan is twenty, he will be close on fifty. Not too old for a man of his energies . . . if he keeps his health. However, it is what I shall do.'

'Do the others know of this? Does Gordon?'

'He will know when the will is read.'

'Why do you tell me?'

He was thoughtful for a moment, then he said, 'I think you have an interest in people . . . very like my own, but yours is benign where mine was mischievous. You would never have done what I did. You are too good-hearted – and, shall I say, too wise to meddle? You see, I am now brought to this stage of repentance because of what I did, and that was foolish of me, for I am now mourning as I approach death and asking the Almighty not to punish me as I deserve. How much cleverer I should have been if, at this stage to which we all must come, I could have had a balance sheet with the good deeds outweighing the evil? And you are here . . . part of the scene. Perhaps you will continue with the saga after I have gone.'

'How?'

'You have become part of Tregarland's. Your sister is the mother of the heir. Violetta, that young man of yours . . . you are still waiting?'

'I am still waiting.'

'And hoping? It is a long time.'

'It is nearly two years since Dunkirk.'

'This war will be over one day, and when it is and he has not come back you will spend your life in mourning for someone who is lost to you for ever.'

'I cannot see that far ahead.'

'Forgive me. I am making you sad. It is the last thing I want to do. You are a serious young lady. I knew that from the first. It would have been different if Dermot had married you.'

'It would have been different whomever he married.'

'The wayward delectable Dorabella was not the one for him, but she is the mother of my grandson. I should like to say a word for Gordon. He is a good man; he would make a faithful husband. If the Jermyn boy does not come back – and in time you must cease to hope – Gordon will be waiting, I am sure.'

I could find no words. I could only think of a bleak future without Jowan.

'I should like to think of you here at Tregarland's,' went on the old man. 'Gordon is calm, level-headed, a little like you, my dear. It would be pleasant for me, looking down from Heaven, or more likely from the fires of Hell, to see you at Tregarland's with Gordon, and my grandson growing up under Gordon's guidance to love the place. Here I am again, arranging people's lives for them. But, of course, they must arrange them themselves.'

We were silent for a while before he continued: 'I often think of how your mother wanted to take Tristan back with her and how she procured the good Nanny Crabtree to look after him. And thank God she did. There is another sensible woman. Do you remember how I refused to let the boy go?'

'Yes, I remember.'

'If I had not done that, he would have escaped danger. It is yet another sin to be laid at my door. When I am gone, you must take him to your mother. My dear girl, you will be happier away from this place. Memories of Jowan come back all the time. You will never escape from your grief here. You need to get away . . . you, your sister and the child. I should have let you go before.'

He was tired, I could see, and I told him he must rest a while and I would come and see him again. Our talk had been very interesting, I added.

'Not very productive,' he said. 'But what is there to

produce? Confession is a sort of self-indulgence. It is good for the soul, they say. One talks and the listener, because he or she has been specially selected by the one who confesses, makes the necessary comforting excuses, which you have done admirably, my dear. Thank you. Do you believe in premonitions?'

This abrupt change of subject disconcerted me a little.

'I am not sure,' I said.

'Nor am I, but I have just had one. The end is nigh, it says. You have unburdened your soul – and now, my dear, it is farewell. I hope your future will be a happy one. I fancy it will be. This evil war must end, and when you have made your decision, I am sure it will be the right one.'

I stopped over him and kissed his forehead.

'Thank you, my dear,' he said, and closed his eyes.

Three days later he had a massive stroke from which he did not recover. The premonition of which he had spoken had proved to be a warning of what was to come.

So there was another journey to the cemetery.

When we were back in Tregarland's, the lawyer from Plymouth read the will. Tristan had become the owner of the estate; Gordon was acknowledged as James's natural son; he was to remain administrator of the estate and was to inherit forty thousand pounds. Glasses of sherry were served and there was a hushed atmosphere throughout the house.

It was amazing how we missed the old man. We had not seen a great deal of him, but we had always been aware of his presence. What changes there had been since I had first seen Tregarland's, although it was not so very long ago. For so many years it had gone on in the same way and then, suddenly, the changes had come . . . drastic changes, death and disaster. And what now, I wondered?

The days were passing. Summer . . . autumn. My mother wrote often. She thought I should get away, come back home for a while. I knew she was thinking I would be better somewhere else so that I might escape from memories of Jowan.

They had all made up their minds that he was lost for ever. I guessed what my mother was saying to my father.

'The sooner she gets away from that place the better. She ought to be meeting people . . . young people. Dorabella is very interested in that nice Captain Brent, and it seems he is in her. Perhaps she will marry again. But Violetta, she is different. She doesn't shrug off these things like her sister does. She should get away.'

I had my work which I took very seriously. We had made over rooms at Tregarland's to the convalescing soldiers and were kept busy. I was glad of that. I tried to stop brooding. I used to have long talks with Gordon. He told me he had shelved the idea of getting a place of his own and would not leave Tregarland's until he could pass it over to Tristan.

I wondered what he would have said if he knew his father had talked of our getting together. I believed that he did have tender feelings towards me, and sometimes I let myself imagine that Jowan did not come back and that I married Gordon. No, I thought. That could not be. And Jowan *would* come back. There were two of us – his grandmother and myself – who believed he would. Though perhaps we forced ourselves to do so because we could not bear it to be otherwise.

In September Dorabella made one of her frequent visits to the Poldowns during which she was away for a longish time. I knew that she was with Captain Brent. She came back in a state of depression.

'What's wrong?' I asked.

'James says he is leaving the area in a few weeks' time.'

'Where is he going?'

'He's not sure.'

She looked wretched. I could never be sure how serious was this attachment to Captain Brent. I had thought it was a light-hearted wartime affair which had come about because they both happened to be in the same place at the same time and liked each other.

But she was certainly downcast.

'What shall you do?' I asked.

'I don't know. Everything is so uncertain. James is in an important job, you know.'

'I guessed that. I suppose you will be hearing which part of the country he's in. That won't be a secret, will it?'

'He will let me know.'

'I suppose you will keep in touch?'

'Oh yes.'

'Do you really care about him, Dorabella?'

'Quite a bit.'

'Have you talked about the future?'

'My dear prosaic old Violetta, you don't change. How do any of us know what our future will be?'

She was right in that.

Later she heard that he would be somewhere in the South-East, not far from London, and she was slightly less depressed.

Letters were arriving from our mother. Why did we not come home for a while? Surely they could do without us for a bit?

'Wouldn't it be wonderful if you could come to Caddington and bring little Tristan and Nanny Crabtree with you?'

'Why shouldn't we?' said Dorabella.

'We have our work here.'

'We're not indispensable. Mrs Jermyn could find plenty of others to take our place. There are many women round here who would like to find some work to do, something that would help the war effort. Mrs Pardell, for one, would give a hand.'

'I don't think the men would find her a good replacement for you, Dorabella.'

'She would be very efficient, and they would be amused by her North Country frankness.'

'A little different from your flirtatious chat.'

'A change is always welcome.'

'Only if it is a change for the better.'

'Well, there is that Mrs Canter staying at Seaview Cottage. She could get someone to look after her little girl. She goes to school most of the time anyway. Now she is flighty enough and Mrs Pardell would make a nice contrast.'

'I see you are determined to go.'

'You'd love it too, Violetta, so don't pretend the desire to see them all is one-sided.'

'Of course I'd love to go. But . . .'

'But me no buts. Will you explain to Mrs Jermyn? It would be better coming from you.'

So I sat with her in the solarium as I had so many times, and over a cup of tea I said: 'My family seem to think that Dorabella and I should go home for a little while. They think it would be good for us . . . for me mainly.'

'Yes,' she said. 'I see.'

'Of course, we could not go unless we were sure there was someone to take our places.'

Mrs Jermyn was silent for some moments, and I thought she was going to protest and say we could not possibly go.

But she said: 'They are right. You should get away, Violetta, and I know how it is with you and your sister. Dorabella seems self-sufficient, but she depends on you . . . far more than you do on her. And Captain Brent has left. Well, I understand. And you, my dear, you are not happy.

How could you be? The memory is here all the time. I am selfish and should like you to stay, but your parents are right. You should be with them. You must go. I tell you this: that if I have news of Jowan, I shall be in touch with you . . . instantly.'

'I know you will.'

'We are going to get that news one day. I feel sure of it. I have to feel sure of it, Violetta. It is that belief which keeps me going. We shall all be happy again . . . some day. Believe that, Violetta, and go to your family. Take an interest in what is going on there. It can't be much longer, and we shall be happy again. Then these years will seem like a bad dream. Now let us consider the practical side of this. Who can take your places?'

'Dorabella suggested Mrs Pardell and Mrs Canter.'

'Mrs Canter . . . well, yes, she's bright and she should get on well with the men. Mrs Pardell . . . a little grim, don't you think?'

'But very efficient. I think she might be an asset. There are, however, one or two other wives on the estate with time on their hands. I think they would all be eager to do something useful.'

'There won't be a great deal of difficulty, I'm sure. Of course, it won't be the same. It has been a joy having you around, Violetta, and Dorabella has always been such a favourite with the men. But these things happen, and I know a respite from this place will be a help to you. What of Gordon Lewyth?'

'What of him?'

'What does he say about your going?'

'Nothing has been said yet.'

'He must know you are thinking of it. I am sure he will be rather sad if you leave Tregarland's.'

She would have heard of the friendship between Gordon and myself. There was certain to be speculation.

I said as lightly as I could: 'We shall be back. It is only a stay with our parents.'

She took my hand and pressed it.

'God bless you, Violetta,' she said. 'I have a feeling that everything will come right for us one day.'

As we thought, there was no difficulty in filling our places. Mrs Canter readily accepted and Mrs Pardell hesitated only for a day or so. It was good work and she approved of it. There were, in fact, one or two who were piqued because they had not been asked. So the way was clear for us.

Nanny Crabtree was delighted.

'It'll be like going home,' she said. 'I'll have my old nursery and I never really took to this place. You're almost falling into the sea half the time – and after all that's gone on here, it's no wonder my nerves get on edge. You wonder what's coming next.'

I must admit that my spirits were lifted at the prospect of going home.

My parents were at the station to meet us. There were hugs, kisses and cries of delight. It was all wonderful. My mother could not stop talking; my father stood there smiling in that way I loved so much; then his arms were round me.

'You're home at last,' he said. 'We've been waiting for this for a long time.'

What a homecoming that was! I said it was worthwhile being away for so long to get such a welcome.

'It is your home,' said my mother emotionally. 'It always will be. And here is Tristan . . . hello, my little love. And Nanny. Welcome, welcome!'

Tristan hunched his shoulders to show his pleasure.

'It's nice,' he said.

Into the ancient hall – not unlike Tregarland's. The two

houses had been built round about the same period. There was a fire burning in the great fireplace and flowers at both ends of the hall. A feeling of peace came over me. If I must go on mourning for Jowan, I could feel great comfort in those who had been left for me to love.

We went to our rooms.

'Just the same as ever,' said Dorabella gleefully.

She put her arms round our mother and danced with her round the room.

'Steady,' said our father. 'She's not so young as she used to be!'

'Ungallant wretch!' cried my mother happily.

'It's so wonderful to be home,' said Dorabella, and I could not help wondering if she was already planning some rendezvous with Captain Brent.

In the nursery Nanny Crabtree was, as she said, 'settling in'. She was crowing with delight.

'That old cupboard!' She turned to Dorabella. 'That's where you hid one day, just to tease us and give us a fright. You were a pickle, you were. And those beds side by side. You remember, when you were little. Look, Tristan, this is where your mummy used to sleep . . . Auntie Violetta too, when they were your size.'

Tristan gravely examined the bed and it was clear that he found it difficult to imagine us his size.

Of course, it was wonderful to be home. My parents had been right to insist that we come. It would help me, not to forget, of course, for I could never do that, but to get through those days of waiting and to find some happiness in the love of my family, and to bring back memories of long-ago days.

I hoped so.

Dorabella had written to Captain Brent, who was delighted

that she was near to London; and we had not been at Caddington more than a week when he wrote to say that he could get away for a few days and could she come to London?

She could stay with Gretchen, who would be delighted to have her, said my mother.

And so it was arranged.

She came back radiant, with presents for us all. Gretchen was well, she said, and so glad we were at Caddington. It was wonderful to know that we were nearer and in fairly easy reach of London. She was hoping to come down to see us sometime when Edward could get enough leave to make that possible.

'London has changed,' said Dorabella. 'That ghastly blackout! One is more conscious of the war and there is that awful air raid warning going off at odd moments when it is wise to take cover. But it is still dear old London – always that little bit more exciting than anywhere else.'

A few days later my mother said: 'I've got a surprise for you. Who do you think is coming for the weekend?'

'I can't guess,' I said. 'Don't keep me in suspense.'

'Remember Mary Grace?'

'Mary Grace!' I cried. 'How is she? What is she doing these days?'

'She'll tell you all about it when she comes.'

'That will be wonderful.'

'I thought you'd be pleased.' She was smiling a little secretively, and I guessed something was pleasing her in addition to the reunion with Mary Grace.

At last it came.

'It is possible that her brother may be coming with her. He's Major Dorrington now, you know. He may – just may – be able to get a little spell of leave, and if he does, he knows we shall be pleased to see him.'

I must say I felt rather disturbed. Richard Dorrington

had at one time been interested in me – in fact, enough to suggest marriage; and I must have liked him sufficiently not to give him a direct no. It had not worked out very satisfactorily. I had discovered my true feelings for Jowan, and Richard and I had seen nothing of each other since before the war. It would be strange to meet again. My parents had selected him as a very desirable husband for me and, like most parents, they had an urgent desire to see their daughter make a good marriage; Richard Dorrington was, in their eyes, a very sensible and reliable man. After Dorabella's disastrous adventures in matrimony, naturally they hoped to see me safely settled.

I could always read my mother's thoughts. She was very much hoping that Richard would be able to come and that we would reconsider our feelings for each other. In her heart she believed that Jowan would never come back.

To see Richard's sister Mary Grace would be a great pleasure. I had always liked her, since her shy, retiring days when I had first discovered that she could paint exquisite miniatures. She had done one of me, which I gave to Dorabella, and one of my sister which Dorabella gave to me. The miniatures were important to us not only because they were delightful but because of what they had done for Mary Grace, who, through them, had received commissions to do others.

The weekend was almost upon us and we were still not sure whether Richard would be with us. We had been told that he had leave but it could be cancelled at the last moment. So it was in a mood of uncertainty that we went to the station to meet the London train.

It arrived on time and when Mary Grace stepped out, with her was the tall figure of her brother.

We hurried to meet them. Richard looked splendid in his uniform. He grasped both my hands and said with fervour: 'Violetta, it is marvellous to see you again.'

We drove back to the house where my father was waiting to receive our guests, and he immediately expressed his delight that Richard was able to come.

'Everything is so uncertain nowadays,' said Richard. 'But my luck was in. It is good to be here.'

We sat long over dinner that night. Everyone had so much to say. My father and Richard talked earnestly about the progress of the war.

'Everything has changed since Pearl Harbor,' said Richard. 'Even the most pessimistic can't doubt that we shall win.'

'Hitler must be growing very uneasy,' remarked my father.

'I think he made a mistake in starting up the second front. It is clear that he is not going to have an easy victory in Russia. I imagine he thought he would plough through as he did in Belgium, Holland and France. He ought to have given the matter more thought. Lucky for us that he didn't.'

'And now the Americans are in.'

'And it is only a matter of time,' Richard assured us.

'Meanwhile it goes on and on,' put in my mother. 'It was supposed to be over by the first Christmas.'

'We were unprepared,' commented Richard. 'Now the whole country is working all out.'

'Even I,' said Mary Grace.

She told us about her Ministry. Everyone had to work, of course, who had not domestic commitments. She was looking after her mother to some extent, although they had a housekeeper who had been with them for years and was too old to be needed for war work. However, Mary Grace worked part-time. It was interesting, she said, and she enjoyed it.

'And your painting?' I asked.

'I am still doing that, too.'

Richard could, naturally, tell us little of his activities,

but he did say that he would have to be ready to land on the Continent when the time came. We still had to see the outcome between Germany and Russia, and there was a great deal of activity in the Middle East. But the outlook was certainly more cheerful than it had been for some time.

They had arrived on Friday and would have to leave in the late afternoon of Sunday. It was a very brief visit but we did manage to get a good deal into it. On Saturday Dorabella and I went riding with Richard and Mary Grace; we stopped at one of the inns we knew well and had lunch; we were warmly welcomed by the host.

We talked and laughed a great deal, and I was sorry they had to leave. We all went to the station to see them off and wish them a quick journey back. Trains were rather uncertain and they could not be sure whether they might not be diverted. Such things happened in wartime and Richard must be back by midnight.

'Let us do this again . . . as soon as we can,' said my father, and my mother added: 'Remember, the first opportunity you get, you must come down.'

'Perhaps you would like to pay a visit to London?' said Richard, looking at me.

'My mother would be delighted to see you,' added Mary Grace. 'She often talks of you.'

The train came in and we stood on the platform, waving it out of the station.

My mother looked pleased.

'A very happy weekend,' she commented, and I knew that when she was alone with my father she would say that it had done me a world of good.

Mrs Jermyn wrote. All was well at the Priory. Mrs Canter was quite a success and the men seemed rather amused by

Mrs Pardell. They wouldn't allow her to bully them and they teased her rather shamefully. Mrs Jermyn was afraid she might have objected; but oddly enough, she seemed to like it.

> Your sister tells me that being in your old home seems to agree with you [she wrote]. I guessed it would be a help. Dear Violetta, you must stay there as long as you feel it is necessary. I know how happy it makes your parents to have you, and I am sure Dorabella is enjoying being there, too.
>
> You will always be welcome when you get back, but much as I should like to see you, I believe it is best for you to stay where you are.
>
> Don't forget. The first hint of news and you shall know it.

They were right, of course. I did feel better away from those places where Jowan and I had been together.

A letter came from Mary Grace.

> My mother was so interested to hear about our weekend. She wanted to know every detail. She is always saying how much she would love to see you both. It would be fun if you came up. There is still a great deal to see and do in London now we are only getting the occasional air raid. I talked to Gretchen about it. She said how pleased she would be if you came and stayed with her. I think she is rather lonely at times. She has only one maid living in who is a great help with Hildegarde, but it does mean that Gretchen can't get about very much and she hasn't all that many friends. She would simply love to have you.

When I showed that letter to my mother, she said: 'Yes,

I do worry about Gretchen. It's not easy for her. That business back in Cornwall upset her a lot. Poor girl. She was not wanted in her own country and here . . . well, there'll always be that tinge of suspicion. I wish she would come and stay here, but she wouldn't be near enough for Edward's brief leaves.'

'I think we should go up and see her,' I said.

The idea certainly appealed to Dorabella. She would be on the spot to see Captain Brent at short notice. As for me, I should like to be with Gretchen for a while.

'Well,' said my mother, 'Tristan will be all right. He'll have his grandparents and Nanny.'

So it was arranged that we should spend a week with Gretchen in London.

Gretchen was delighted to see us. She hoped Edward would get leave so that he could be with us, if only briefly. She was comfortable in the house they had acquired before the outbreak of war. The maid was very useful, both in looking after the house and Hildegarde, but even so Gretchen was fully occupied. I knew she brooded constantly on the plight of her family; she might never know what had become of them. It was touching to see her pleasure in our being there.

Dorabella was full of high spirits. She was delighted that her love-affair with Captain Brent was continuing; and I think the nature and secrecy of his work added to the excitement of the romance.

We were very soon invited to the Dorringtons' house where Mrs Dorrington greeted us warmly and, during the evening, Richard arrived unexpectedly.

'When I heard who your guests were,' he told his mother, 'I did a lot of contriving . . . and it worked. How are you enjoying wartime London?' he asked us.

'Enormously,' cried Dorabella.

'And Violetta?'

'The same,' I replied. 'Particularly this evening.'

There was a great deal to talk about and everyone was in a merry mood.

Richard said to me: 'If I can get the time off, would you come to a theatre with me one evening?'

I said we should love to, and when the evening was over, as Edward and Gretchen lived only a short distance away, we walked back through the blacked-out streets.

The next day there was a telephone call from him. He could get away on Thursday. Were we free?

Dorabella answered it. She always dashed up when it rang, expecting Captain Brent.

She said: 'Richard is asking us to the theatre on Thursday.' She looked a little sly. 'I can't make it,' she said into the mouthpiece. 'Another engagement, but I know Violetta is free.'

I said to her afterwards: 'Have you a date on Thursday?'

'What does it matter? He was hoping I had. I couldn't disappoint the poor man.'

'How do you know?'

'Of course I know. The trouble with you, sister, is that you have no finesse. He wants to be with you . . . not the whole family. I can see what is before my eyes, if you can't. The role of chaperone or unwanted guest is not for me.'

'You are an idiot.'

'I may well be in some respects, but in matters like this I am a sage.'

That was how I came to be at the theatre with Richard that Thursday night.

I don't recall the name of the play. It was a light comedy, but I do remember that the theatre was full of uniformed men who laughed heartily at the jokes, however feeble, as though they were determined to enjoy the evening at all cost.

During the second act a man came to the front of the stage and announced that the sirens had started and any of those who wished to leave the theatre should do so quietly so as not to disturb those who wished to remain.

No one left and the play went on as before and in about forty-five minutes the man came back to say that the all-clear had sounded.

After that we went to supper. We sat in the darkened restaurant and there I found the same air of determined merriment which I had noticed in the theatre. We had been shown the table almost deferentially, which was due to Richard's uniform. Everyone was much aware of what we owed to the airmen, soldiers and sailors of Britain.

We talked about the war, the hopes of a not-too-distant victory, of my parents, his mother and Mary Grace.

He said he would never forget what I had done for his sister. She had changed when she did that miniature of me. Did I still have it, he wanted to know?

'I gave it to Dorabella,' I said. 'And I have one Mary Grace did of her. They are very good indeed.'

'Yes, I fancy she is quite an artist and none of us realized it until you pointed it out. She changed from then on. She gained that confidence which she had always lacked before. You did a great deal for her and now she seems quite to enjoy being at this Ministry. It was a good day for us when Edward introduced you.'

'I worry about Gretchen.'

'Poor girl. It's sad. I fear she constantly broods about her family. It's natural, of course.'

'What could have become of them?'

'I do not like to think. The fate of the Jewish people in Germany sickens me to contemplate. If there ever was a reason why we should fight this war, that is it.'

'We must succeed in the end.'

'We will, but at what a cost!'

I liked Richard. He, too, had changed from the man I had known before the war. Then he had been sure of himself in a rather self-righteous way. Now he seemed different. I hesitated to apply the word 'vulnerable' to him but it came into my mind. There were times when I thought he was about to tell me something . . . something important which was bothering him. It was almost like a cry for help. That could not be. Richard would always be self-sufficient.

When we parted, he said: 'I can't get any more leave this week . . . and then you will be going back to Caddington.'

'Well, it is not so very far away.'

'You'll come up again? There is room at our house and Mary Grace would be delighted to have you. Shall you go back to Cornwall?'

'I am undecided. My mother does not want me to. She thinks I am better with them and the occasional visit to London. I had my work in Cornwall, as you know.'

'You could do something up here.'

'I suppose so. There has been no difficulty in finding replacements for me.'

'You must consider it. Cornwall is a little tucked away and travel is not easy in wartime. It has been such a pleasant evening for me.'

'For me, too.'

'We must do something like it again.'

'That would be enjoyable.'

'It is a promise, is it?'

'Of course.'

He kissed me lightly on the cheek and I went in. Dorabella was waiting up for me. She looked expectant.

'Well?'

'Well what?'

'How did it go?'

'The play was not very memorable; there was an air raid warning during it, and we had supper afterwards.'

'And Richard . . . how was he?'

'Very nice indeed.'

'And?'

'Isn't that enough?'

'In the circumstances, no.'

'What circumstances?'

'He's very attractive.'

'Oh, goodnight, Dorabella.'

'Nothing to report, then?'

'Nothing.'

'You disappoint me.'

'There have been occasions when I felt the same about you.'

Banter, I thought. What did she expect? She was like my mother. They were both hoping that I should give up grieving for Jowan. They could not believe I would never forget.

The Dark Secret

Mary Grace had talked a great deal about her work at the Ministry and the people she met there, and she thought I might be interested to meet her special friends.

'Don't get the idea,' she said, 'that we are doing very vital war work – involved in top secrets and suchlike. This is the Ministry of Labour and our work has a great deal to do with putting papers in alphabetical order and finding jobs for the people who are registered with us which will be most suitable for their abilities. Those who work with me are rather like myself – inexperienced. Some have never been out to work before and what we have to do is simply the sort that anyone could do.'

I said I thought she was being modest.

'No, no,' she answered. 'That is not so. You will see I am right when you meet my special colleagues. We all sit together at a table, sorting out our papers, making notes of information, watched over by our supervisor. The supervisor is, of course, a bona fide civil servant.'

I realized what she meant when I met the girls. They often lunched together in a Lyons or ABC teashop. There were four of them including Mary Grace. She was what was called a 'part-timer' on account of certain responsibilities concerning her mother. The others worked full-time – nine until five.

The Ministry was in Acton, not so very far from the centre of town; and I was to meet them in the Lyons teashop at twelve-thirty.

No sooner had I entered the restaurant than Mary Grace

rose to greet me. Seated with her were the three I was to meet. They all surveyed me with interest.

'Mrs Marian Owen, Mrs Peggy Dunn, and Miss Florette Fields,' said Mary Grace with dignity. 'And this is Miss Violetta Denver.'

'Oh, that's a classy name,' said Miss Florette Fields. 'I like that. I was Flora but I changed it to Florette. Professional reasons, you understand?'

'Florette,' I said. 'That's charming.'

She flashed her rather toothy smile in my direction. There was something very friendly about her.

'We're ordering the Home Pie,' said Mary Grace. 'The ingredients may be a little mysterious, but it's tasty.'

Everybody laughed. I was to discover that they laughed easily and in this they reminded me of the soldiers in the theatre.

'You are staying in London for a while, then?' said Marian. She was different from the others and I realized that she was eager for me to know this.

'Yes,' I told her. 'I shall be going back to my parents' home at the end of the week.'

'Lucky you,' said Florette.

They were all a little stiff at first but it was not long before conversation was flowing easily. It was mainly about the Ministry. There was a Mrs Crimp, who was called 'Curly', and a Mr Bunter, who was known as 'Billy' for obvious reasons. They giggled a great deal.

Florette and Peggy Dunn were quite revealing about themselves; Marian Owen was more reticent.

Mary Grace, I discovered, had a hitherto unsuspected gift for making people talk. I think she was very eager for her friends to reveal themselves and over Home Pie, which was indeed surprisingly tasty, and coffee, I glimpsed something of the background of Peggy and Florette.

They were quite different and both had the gift of being

able to laugh at themselves. Florette was a girl with dreams. Within fifteen minutes of our acquaintance, I knew of her ambitions. She was without guile or pretence. She was going to be what she called a 'star'. Peggy admired her as someone she herself could never be. She listened avidly, watching her as she talked, with wondering eyes full of admiration.

'Florette won a competition once,' Peggy told me. 'Came first, didn't you, Florette?'

Florette smiled broadly.

'Tell Violetta about it,' said Peggy. We were on Christian name terms by that time.

'Well,' said Florette, 'there was this talent-spotting competition, wasn't there?'

I was reminded of Charley and Bert. She was not asking me to recall the occasion. It was just a form of speech.

'There were big posters outside the Music Hall. The Empire, wasn't it? "Try your luck," it said. "This might be your road to fame." Everyone was saying, "Go on, Flor, you can sing with the best of 'em."'

'She's got a lovely voice,' put in Peggy.

'Well,' said Florette modestly, 'it's not bad. You should have seen me. Practising for weeks, I was.'

'And she won it,' cried Peggy, impatient for the climax.

'Well, I got up there, didn't I? Was my knees shaking? You can bet your life. I was like a lump of jelly. I thought: I'll open me mouth, and there'll be nothing but a squawk. Well, there I was. "Blue skies over the white cliffs of Dover." You can always get away with that one, and then an old-fashioned one. "After the Ball was Over." My mum always wanted me to go on the Halls and she used to sing that one to me. Well, I got in the first six . . . and then we did it all again.'

'And she was the first,' cried Peggy again.

'Five pounds I got. First prize. Thought it was a fortune.

It was a start. Well, I reckon I'd be on my way if it wasn't for this old war. Where can you get in times like these? Still, I made my start. I've always got that. Gave me a certificate, they did, to say I'd won this first prize.'

'It must have been wonderful,' I said.

'You wait. You'll see me in lights. My mum used to talk about Marie Lloyd. That's what I'll be. You wait until this war's over.'

While this conversation was going on, I was listening with earnest attention. Peggy was as excited as Florette herself and Mary Grace was watching me, to see if I was enjoying meeting her friends. Marian Owen was sitting quietly by, with a faint smile on her face. Every now and then she caught my eye, as though to say, 'We must be lenient with these people. They are not as we are. They have not had our advantages of education.' At least, that was the construction I put on it. I would share the impression with Mary Grace in due course.

'Then I changed my name to Florette,' went on the owner of that name. 'Well, Flora . . . mind you, it's a nice enough name. I'm not saying anything against it. But it's not quite show business.'

'Florette will look better up in lights,' said Peggy.

'It is all very interesting,' I said. 'I hope you succeed. I am sure you will.'

Florette nodded agreement and Mary Grace said: 'Violetta wanted to meet you all. She thought you sounded so interesting.'

'You won't find me very interesting,' said Peggy. 'Poor old me.'

'I am sure you have had an interesting life,' I said, and I meant it. Peggy was small, thin and I guessed her to be in her mid-forties. Her face was prematurely wrinkled; her hair had been dyed – not very expertly – and was deep black. Her face gave me the impression of one who had lived through much – mostly tribulation. One had only to look at Peggy to see that life had not been easy for her.

It came out – if not all at that first meeting, soon after. She had married young – not very satisfactorily – and had had two children. One had emigrated to Australia five years before the war; the other had married and gone 'up North'. Her husband had drunk away his wages every Friday night; and there was nothing to do but keep the house going. She had some odd jobs cleaning other people's houses and so it had gone on. And now, here she was – husband dead, children far away and not really taking much trouble to come and see her; and she admitted that it was a great pleasure to her to have this 'cushy little job in the Ministry'. I admired her. She was irrepressible. Her wizened little face would light up with a smile and find something amusing in most situations. I supposed life had been so hard to her that she had learned to appreciate what she now had. Florette was her ideal, and she was as certain of her eventual success as Florette herself.

'What I'll do,' she said, 'is stand outside that theatre and look up at her name and say, "I used to know her at that Ministry."'

She smiled at Florette blissfully, who said: 'Get away with you! I'll have you backstage and you shall have free tickets for the orchestra stalls. Who knows, I might even introduce you to someone who is looking for a pet.'

This was a well-worn joke, I realized. Peggy had once said she had watched the dogs in the Park, and all the fuss that was made of them. Little pekes with fancy haircuts, diamond collars . . . and she had thought: 'What a good time these dogs have . . . nothing to do but be a pet. I wouldn't mind being a dog like that. I wish somebody would make a pet of me. Do you know anyone looking for a pet?'

That had amused Florette and it had become a joke.

'Peggy's looking for someone who wants a pet,' she said to me. 'Do you know anyone?'

And everyone, including Peggy, laughed hilariously.

Peggy and Florette were easy to understand. It was not the same with Marian. She did not come from the same background as the others. She had made it clear to me from the start that she, Mary Grace and I were of a kind – and apart from the other two. Marian's hair was probably touched up, but discreetly so; she wore tailored suits and spoke with the utmost care.

She told me that her husband had been an army man; she had been a widow for fifteen years. She managed, but things were not as those she had been accustomed to. She had a small flat in Crouch Hill and had had to adjust her standards.

I saw at once that there was something rather secretive about her; she was faintly uneasy. I felt sure she was harbouring some secret.

When we emerged from the teashop, regaled by the mysterious but tasty Home Pie and two cups of hot coffee, I had been completely taken out of the past and been absorbingly entertained. This happened to me very rarely.

Mary Grace and I said goodbye to the others, who had to return to the Ministry as they were 'full-timers'; and Mary Grace and I went to the tube and back to Kensington.

'Well?' said Mary Grace when we were alone.

'Very interesting. Amusing, some of it.'

'I like them all very much. They were strangers to me a little while ago and I see them every day now – far more than I see my close friends. One really gets to know people well in such circumstances.'

'Florette is amusing,' I said. 'Poor girl, I wonder how far her dream will take her. And Peggy . . . well, one should be sorry for her. She must have had a hard life, and yet she is not really in the least downcast. As for Marian, she is something of an enigma.'

'Oh, poor Marian. Seen better days. I am always sorry for such people. They spend so much time regretting the past that they cannot enjoy the present. If only she could stop worrying whether we can see the difference between her and the others. They don't mind being as they are . . . nor does anyone else.'

'Well, thank you, Mary Grace. It really was a most interesting lunch.'

'I'm glad you enjoyed the Home Pie.'

'Enormously – but most of all the company.'

When we returned to Caddington, my mother wanted to hear about everything that had happened.

'There is no doubt in my mind that the holiday did you the world of good,' she commented.

When I considered it I supposed she was right. I did feel more remote from Cornwall where the constant murmur of the waves, and all the surrounding country reminded me of Jowan.

And the days were passing. What hope could there be of news?

Both Dorabella and I were helping our mother with the work she was doing with the Red Cross; but working at the convalescent home was different – a definite occupation which every able-bodied person should have in wartime.

I supposed I should have to go back there.

When I suggested this, Dorabella protested. Mrs Canter and Mrs Pardell were doing our work very satisfactorily. She did not want to go back, of course; but we could not stay away indefinitely. She could not plead immunity because Nanny Crabtree was looking after her child. Moreover, Captain Brent had suggested that she might work in one of the offices connected with his unit. It would be a part-time job, not very significant office work, but she would have to be in London, though she might get down to Caddington for weekends.

'And what of Violetta?' asked my mother.

'Perhaps Mary Grace could suggest something,' I said. 'I gather her job is to find suitable places for people to work.'

I spoke half jocularly. I realized I did not want to go back to Cornwall. They were right when they said it was better for me to get away. I supposed I could stay at Caddington and help my mother, but I did feel I should be doing something more.

We were in this state of uncertainty when Mary Grace came down to Caddington for the weekend. We talked about it and she immediately said that she was sure it would be possible for her to get me into the Ministry.

'I know they are short of staff in my department,' she added.

I had a sudden picture of sitting at a table, filing papers with those I had met at lunch. I thought of going to the restaurant with them for lunch – Home Pie, coffee and talk; and my dear Mary Grace would be there. I felt a tremor of pleasure at the thought.

Mary Grace noticed my interest and went on: 'I could try, if you'd like me to.'

We talked and my mother, sensing a certain enthusiasm in me, came down in favour of the idea.

'I'll make enquiries,' said Mary Grace. 'It would be wonderful to have you there.'

It was not until the New Year that I joined the Ministry. I had spent the intervening time between London, with Gretchen, and my parents at Caddington.

Dorabella had a part-time job in London which pleased her very well. Most weekends we spent at Caddington and we were with Tristan for a great deal of that time. It seemed a very satisfactory arrangement and Dorabella was very happy with life.

Richard Dorrington and I met fairly frequently – whenever he could get away – and I found our encounters very pleasant. He seemed quite content to let our friendship drift along. It was different from the way he had been when he was courting me with marriage in view. He was more restrained and never referred to the past or suggested a resumption of our previous relationship. Indeed, there were times when I thought he was on the point of sharing some confidence. This undemanding friendship suited me perfectly.

As we came into that year of 1944 there was an air of hope throughout the country. Germany was losing the war on the Russian front; we heard stories of the hardship their armies were facing, not only from the Russians but from the weather, which was more severe than they had been prepared for. For the first time since he had made his bid for power, it really seemed as though defeat would be Hitler's reward.

The chance of an invasion of Britain seemed remote. There were still raids from the air and some of our cities had been severely devastated, but hope was everywhere. The Americans were now our allies and we no longer stood alone.

In the middle of January, I joined the Ministry. I received a warm welcome from the friends I had already met during the preceding months, for I had on several occasions lunched with Mary Grace, Florette, Peggy and Marian.

It was fortunate that there was room at their table and, as I was a friend of theirs, I was given a place there.

We were in a large room with windows on either side

taking up almost the whole of the wall space, which made the room very light but was something of a hazard if bombs were dropped in the vicinity. It was actually a table for six at which we sat, and, as there were only five of us working, we had some space to spread out our papers and work with ease.

Seated at his desk in the centre of the room was Mr Bunter – known as Billy – supervising the arrangements and instructing us in our work.

It was all very easy and I picked up what I had to do in a few days. I fell quickly into the routine, sharing the jokes, laughing often, joining in on the treats, when anyone had 'a bit of luck'. Marian Owen, surprisingly, had what she called her one vice, which was backing horses.

'Just a shilling or two here and there, you know, to liven the days – and sometimes it comes off.'

When it 'came off' we were all invited to have a drink at the Café Royal or some such place, and there was a great deal of bantering talk about the 'racing millionaire'. Unfortunately, the wins were not very frequent but that made them all the more exciting when they came.

Florette brought her book of cuttings to show us; they contained pictures of actresses and were arranged to indicate their rise to fame.

On the first page of this book was a cutting from a paper which informed the reader that Miss Florette Fields had won the singing competition at the Empire Music Hall with her outstanding rendering of 'The White Cliffs of Dover' and 'After the Ball was Over'. She had been awarded the first prize of five pounds. Good luck, Florette.

We all admired it, and I told her not to fill up the book with cuttings about others, for she must save it for those about herself.

That delighted her. She said she kept the book by her bedside in case there was an air raid. I think the most precious thing in Florette's life was that newspaper cutting announcing her triumph.

And we never failed to laugh when Peggy, overcome by some momentary annoyance, would cry: 'Wouldn't anyone like to take me as a pet?'

Little things amused us then.

It was March and I had been two months at the Ministry. My mother said it was the best thing I could have done. Dorabella agreed with her; and I was inclined to think that they were right. I very much enjoyed the company during working hours. Mary Grace was greatly admired for her ability to draw, and if any little incident occurred she would make a cartoon of it, depicting the people concerned in caricature. These used to be passed round the department and were greatly appreciated. When one of them fell into the hands of Billy Bunter, he smiled benignly and tried to look stern, but he could not repress a smile and ever after referred to Mary Grace as 'our artist'.

We never knew when we should hear the air raid warning. They came fairly frequently and were given in the first place if enemy aircraft were detected crossing the Channel. We were then supposed to leave our room with the many windows and descend to the basement, but very often these aircraft were prevented from getting very far and so much time was wasted trooping up and down to shelters that what was called an 'Imminent' was instituted, which meant that we should only be warned when the enemy aircraft were almost upon us. Then we should make all haste to take cover.

How quickly those days passed! The working week, the weekends at Caddington, meetings with Richard when he could get away, lunches at the teashop. Life was pleasant as it had not been since Jowan had failed to be among the survivors of Dunkirk.

It was the end of March when I noticed Dorabella was brimming over with excitement.

'Something has happened,' I said.

She shook her head from side to side in a maddening fashion.

'I shall tell you with the others this time. I shall make an announcement – at supper, I think – when both parents are there.'

She pursed her lips together, as though fearing to betray her news.

We were never sure at what time we should arrive at Caddington, so my mother always had a cold supper awaiting us and my father made a point of always being there, so there were just the four of us – unless Mary Grace happened to be with us for the weekend.

We would sit in the darkness, so that we did not have to draw the blackout curtains, and we would talk about the week's adventures. They knew of Florette's secret ambitions, the dark secret which we believed Marian was guarding and Peggy's desire to be adopted as a pet.

As we sat down, I could see that Dorabella was finding it hard to restrain her excitement, and as soon as we were seated she said: 'I have an announcement to make. James and I are going to be married.'

There was a brief silence. Then my mother went to her and kissed her.

'Oh, my darling, I hope . . .'

'It's all right this time,' said Dorabella. '*I* am sure. *James* is sure. And so, it must be right.'

She was clearly so happy that we had to share in it. It was only because we had seen that other disaster that we hesitated.

'You'll love James,' said Dorabella. 'Everybody likes him. He is the most wonderful man in the world. Don't look at me like that, Violetta. It's right this time. I'm experienced now. I know what love means. Stop worrying.'

My mother said: 'Well, you have known him for a little time.'

'For ages!' cried Dorabella. 'It's perfect. I want Tristan to love him.'

'That is very important,' said my mother solemnly.

'Oh, come on!' cried Dorabella. 'This is supposed to be a matter for rejoicing. Daddy, why don't you suggest champagne?'

'I think there are a few bottles left,' he said. 'Yes . . . we must drink to this. I am sure you will be very happy, my darling.'

'And I,' said Dorabella firmly, 'know I shall.'

I knew my mother would come to my room that night when I retired. It was a habit of hers when she was worried about Dorabella.

'What do you think?' she said.

'One never knows with Dorabella.'

'You're thinking of Dermot?'

'Of course. She gets these wild enthusiasms, and in wartime people can do rash things.'

'Dorabella can do rash things at any time.'

I laughed and nodded.

'This young man . . .'

'He has an important job with the Army, as we found out when Tristan was kidnapped. He is very charming and Dorabella has been fond of him for some time.'

'And he cares for her, I suppose?'

'He must, to suggest marrying her.'

'Your father and I feel a little uneasy about her after what happened before. There was that jaunt to France . . . and all she did . . .'

'She may have learned some lessons. She was very upset about Tristan and ever since she has been absolutely devoted to him. She is very happy now . . .'

The door opened suddenly and Dorabella came in.

'I have been listening to you two putting your heads together,' she said. 'I can tell you, it's all right. I'm happier than I've ever been before. I adore James and he adores me. So stop acting like a couple of old witches prophesying gloom, and rejoice with me.'

We could not help it. My mother felt as I did. It must be all right this time. She was so happy now and she carried us along with her.

We decided that if Dorabella was happy, that was all that mattered. We would take care of the future when the time came.

The following weekend James Brent came to Caddington. My parents had not met him before and they were favourably impressed. Captain Brent was urbane, much travelled, an expert in many matters. He knew something about estates as his family owned one on the West Riding of Yorkshire, and before the war he had helped to run it.

My father obviously liked him and there was some interesting talk about the war, though guarded on the Captain's side, which made it the more exciting.

He said that there would have to be a landing on the Continent, and that now the enemy were in a weakened state, in his opinion it would not be long delayed.

They discussed the wedding. There was no reason for delay. I gathered that he expected, when the invasion of the Continent began, that he would go overseas.

There was a feeling of urgency in the air and we understood that, before the great battle started, he wanted to be sure of a little happiness with Dorabella.

Before the weekend was over, my parents' doubts were diminished and they were caught up in the excitement of the preparations for the wedding. It would be a quiet affair and take place within the next few weeks.

Tristan liked Captain Brent from the start, and it seemed that everything was working out in the best possible way.

They were married in a registry office at the end of April; several others were married on the same day – men in uniform with their smiling brides.

Naturally I thought of Jowan and could not help the pangs of envy which beset me.

There was a small reception afterwards in a hotel in Kensington and I asked the girls from the Ministry to join us.

My mother was eager to meet the people of whom she had heard so much. Florette was rather flamboyantly attired, as became the great star; Peggy looked like a mournful puppy watchful for a home; and Marian was at her most graciously refined and was very impressed to converse with Sir Robert and Lady Denver.

Afterwards my mother said: 'They were perfect. Just as you described them. It was lovely to meet them in the flesh.'

And then a radiant Dorabella and her very attractive husband went off to spend a brief honeymoon at Torquay.

Richard had two days' leave. I met him as usual and he was rather excited because a friend of his, who had a little service flat just off Victoria, had offered it to him to use at any time he cared to. The friend had been sent off to the North of England so the flat would be vacant and Richard might find it useful during his occasional leaves.

'Of course,' said Richard, 'I could always go to the

family, but I think that puts a burden on Mary Grace, without much help in the house.'

'I am sure she is always delighted to have you there – your mother, too.'

'There are times when one has a fancy to be on one's own. It's a pleasant little place, and easier to get to than going out to Kensington. In any case, I've accepted. I wonder if you would like to come along and look at it.'

I said I would and we went.

It was certainly an attractive little flat. There was one bedroom, a small box-room, a sitting-room and kitchen, which was large for the size of the flat, and, being at the top of the building, it was light and airy. The kitchen cupboard was stocked with tins of soup and food – wartime variety, of course.

'I'm to take what I want and of course I can replace it when I go.'

Richard was enthusiastic. Often he had only one day off and he liked me to go there with him. I would select something from the array of tins and we would enjoy preparing a meal together. Richard said it was more comfortable than going to a restaurant.

The girls were aware off this and I guessed they talked about it when I was not there. I think they had decided that I was going to marry Richard, and of course my going to the flat would give rise to more speculation.

They were all dreamers, especially Florette, of course, who lived in a world of spectacular theatrical success, whereas Peggy, who had very little hope of achieving her ambition, was ready to dream for others. As for Marian, I was convinced that she lived in an atmosphere of perpetual apprehension that some fatal secret from her past would be discovered. Mary Grace, I knew, would be delighted if I married into the family.

I was not in the least discomfited by any significance they

might assume in my going to Richard's flat and cooking meals for him. I talked freely of Jowan to Richard and he understood my feeling. He was practical, full of good sense, and I think he had decided long ago, when we drifted apart after I had declined his offer of marriage, that we were not completely suited to each other. But that was no reason why we should not be good friends, and that was what we were.

So I looked forward to those days when I was able to experiment in the kitchen of the little flat, and how triumphant we both were when I made a good meal from the material at my disposal.

Spring was on the way. In September it would be five years since the war had started. Everyone was saying: 'It won't be long now.'

Richard was cautious. He thought the landing would not be successfully accomplished in a few weeks. There was a good deal of fighting power left in the Germans and they were a formidable race.

Dorabella returned from her honeymoon deliriously happy. She had the gift of being able to live entirely in the present. Impressive events were about to burst upon us, but she paid no heed to that. And so the days went by.

Marian had a win on one of her horses and we went to the Café Royal to celebrate. The nights were light now, which was a blessing, for travelling through the blackout was a tedious business.

We sat with our glasses of sherry before us and were very merry.

'This is lovely,' said Florette. 'This is where they always came in the old days. All the old stars. Marie Lloyd, Vesta Tilley . . . and the mashers would meet them here.'

'What's mashers?' asked Peggy.

'Come on, Peg. Don't show your ignorance! You know

the mashers . . . the stage-door Johnnies. Always hanging round after the actresses. They'd be in the theatre every night, picking out their favourites. Those were the days. No war then.'

'There was one in 1914,' I reminded her.

'Oh, that! That was nothing compared with this.'

'I expect it was rather awful while it lasted,' said Mary Grace.

'It wasn't the same. Won't it be fun when it's over? I reckon there won't half be some goings-on.'

'People don't take things as they used to,' commented Marian. 'In the old days . . .' She sighed. 'There was the Queen's Golden Jubilee. There was a day's holiday from school. There she was . . . a little old lady in a carriage. She was a queen, though. Anyone could see that.'

Suddenly she stopped and a look of panic came into her eyes.

'Do you feel all right, Marian?' asked Mary Grace.

'Oh yes . . . yes, I'm all right. Just felt a bit strange for a moment.'

'It's the sherry,' said Peggy.

'I don't know. It just came over me.' Her hands were shaking.

'You were telling us about Queen Victoria's Golden Jubilee.'

'Oh no . . . no. I didn't mean the Golden Jubilee . . . it was the Diamond.'

'Sit quiet for a bit,' said Florette. 'Then you'll feel better.'

Marian did so and closed her eyes. We all watched her in consternation, but after a few minutes she opened her eyes and smiled at us.

'It's all right,' she said. 'Just a bit of a turn.' Then she started to talk about some horses she fancied for a coming race.

'It's all a matter of form,' she said. 'That's what you have to study.'

We understood. She did not want to talk about the 'bit of a turn'.

Mary Grace and I discussed the incident afterwards.

'Something upset her,' I said. 'It was when she was talking about the past.'

'I think something must have happened. Some tragedy that she was reminded of, and it was connected with the Golden Jubilee.'

'That was years ago. I should have thought she wasn't born then. She said the Golden Jubilee . . . and then seemed anxious to tell us that it was the Diamond one. It must have been the Diamond. If she had been at school, which she rather implied, she would be over sixty and they don't have people in the Ministry over that age. I wonder what it was that happened?'

Marian became a cause for speculation at that time because both Florette and Peggy had been very much aware of the shock she had had in the Café Royal.

Whenever Marian was absent we talked about it. They fantasized about her. Peggy thought she had been 'crossed in love'. She had met a young man who was above her station.

'You know how she is about station and that sort of thing? He promised her a grand future; she thought she'd have a beautiful home where she would be petted and made a fuss of for the rest of her life. Then, right at the altar, he jilted her. Then she married Mr Owen.'

Florette said: 'He was a good husband, but he was not her true love and she never forgot. She had this rich lover. He was a great Music Hall star and all the women were crazy about him. He saw Marian and she was different from all the rest. Those actors fall in and out of love very easily. He seduced her and there was a child. She gave the child away and then one day at this Jubilee thing she saw her child, grown up into a beautiful young woman.'

'She couldn't have been more than five years old at the time of the Diamond Jubilee,' I protested.

'Oh, it wouldn't have been that, then. It was some other procession. There was the coronation of Edward VII, wasn't there? I reckon it would have been that.'

'Well, whatever it was,' said Mary Grace, 'it was undoubtedly there and we must not try to probe. She might tell us in time. Let us be especially gentle with her until she does.'

So we were. I wondered whether Marian realized this. There was certainly something stricken about her and it had become more apparent since that outburst at the Café Royal.

It was about three weeks later when we discovered Marian's secret. It happened in an unexpected way.

We came in one morning to hear that an inspector had arrived at the Ministry. There was a good deal of gossip about this.

'He's come to investigate,' said one of the women.

'Do you think there is a spy here?' asked another, looking round suspiciously.

'Something like that,' said the first speaker. 'Well, it's ever so exciting and there's a war on anyway.'

As the morning progressed, I noticed that Marian was in a state of increasing uneasiness. Mary Grace noticed it too.

'I am sure she is worried,' she said to me. 'I wonder what it is she has done . . . or is doing?'

'I could not imagine Marian as a spy, or involved in anything dramatic,' I said.

'You never can tell,' said Mary Grace. 'I could not

imagine it either, but sometimes the most unlikely people do these things.'

Two or three days passed. We heard that the Inspector was to be at the Ministry until Thursday. No one had any idea what he was doing. Billy Bunter was now and then called to his office and came back looking more important than ever.

Poor Marian was in a nervous state, I could see. Every time the door opened and someone came into the department there would be panic in her eyes. I tried to think of what misdemeanours she could have committed, and came to the conclusion that they must be serious to have this effect on her.

Thursday came. The Inspector was leaving that day. She was safe. I could sense her relief. But then, during that morning, Billy Bunter came to our table.

He said: 'Mrs Owen, the Inspector would like a word with you.'

I saw the colour rush into her face, and then she turned so pale that I thought she was going to faint. I wanted to run to her but restrained myself. Billy Bunter was smiling his urbane smile. We watched her as she followed him through the door, then we looked at one another in dismay, too shocked to speak.

We just sat there, pretending to work, shifting our papers round and seeing nothing but Marian's stricken face.

And then, at last, she returned.

We stared at her. We had not expected to see her. We had imagined her handcuffed and taken away to prison. Spying for the enemy. Or perhaps she had murdered someone years ago and it had just been discovered.

She was smiling as I had never seen her smile, and she looked at least ten years younger.

We waited breathlessly. There was a new air of confidence about her.

'It's all right,' she said. 'I've been worrying about nothing.'

'What was it?' demanded Florette.

Marian looked round the table.

'I shall not tell you now,' she said. 'I want you all to come as my guests to the Café Royal this evening. Is that all right? Free, are you?'

'Oh, you are mean, making us wait to know,' cried Florette. 'We're dying to hear.'

'You must be patient,' said Marian.

She picked up her papers with a happy smile on her face and began sorting them.

Florette was right when she said we were all eager to know. We all sat at our favourite table and Marian ordered sherries and then she started.

'You see, I was very worried. I'll tell you frankly, I needed this job badly. I had my little pension, but I just could not make ends meet. Then the war came and they wanted people for work. This was the kind of job I fancied. I didn't want anything menial. This was a nice office job where you met nice people.'

'All right,' said Florette. 'You wanted the job. What else?'

'They didn't want people over sixty. Well, I have a confession to make. I lied about my age.'

'Is that all?' demanded Florette.

'It's lying,' said Marian. 'It's a terrible thing to do in wartime, and when this Inspector came, I thought, he's going to find out. He's vetting us all and you know how thorough they are? I thought he'd turn me out and then what would I do?'

'And what happened?' I asked.

'Well, I went along and Billy left me with him. He was

a nice man. He had a ledger open on his desk and he said, "Sit down, Mrs Owen." I was shaking all over like a leaf. Then he said: "It's this matter of age." Then I knew it had come. He was going to send me away, I thought, and I just wondered what I would do. It's made such a difference. It was just what I wanted.'

'Yes, yes,' said Florette impatiently.

'"According to your records," he said, "you are sixty-two."'

She looked at us searchingly, to see what effect this information was having on us.

'You see, I'd let them believe I was ten years younger. Nobody had doubted it. You didn't, did you?'

'I never thought of it,' said Peggy.

'None of us did,' I said.

'I never think about people's ages,' added Mary Grace.

'Then he laughed,' went on Marian, 'and I burst out, "I wanted the job. I needed the job. If they had known my real age, they wouldn't have had me." "Well, Mrs Owen," he said, "it's always best to tell the truth. But I suppose you're right. There would have been some question about employing you at that age. Well, you're here now and Mr Bunter tells me you are as good a worker as the rest. I don't think Mr Hitler is going to care very much whether you are too old for the job, do you?" He laughed. That seemed very funny, so I laughed with him. I thought I'd burst into tears if I didn't. "Let's say no more about this, Mrs Owen," he said. "I don't blame you for knocking off those years. Nobody would guess." Then I came away.'

'Is that all you've been worrying about all this time?' demanded Florette.

The four of us looked at each other and smiled, remembering what we had imagined.

'How did you know I was worrying? Was it so obvious?'

'Poor old Marian,' said Florette. 'People in show business always knock off a few years. It's all part of the game.'

We all laughed. That was a very merry evening at the Café Royal.

The End of a Dream

May had come and there was a feeling of anticipation everywhere. Great events were about to burst upon us and people were saying that the end of the war was not far off.

Richard was reticent about his activities and I guessed that he was involved in some secret operation. His leaves were less frequent and when they did come we made the most of them.

He very much enjoyed those evenings we spent in the Victoria flat. He would send a message to me and I would be there, going through the cupboard so that I could make supper by the time he arrived, for it was always uncertain how long he would stay or even if he would be called back almost immediately. There was a telephone in the flat and on one occasion he was called back when we were in the middle of a meal.

It was a beautiful day and I had had a message during the previous one. He could get away. Could I be there? I think we all felt at that time that we must be free when a soldier friend wanted to see us. There was always a possibility that it might be the last opportunity for a long time.

I went to the flat and let myself in, for Richard had acquired a key for me. I went into the kitchen and prepared the meal. It was almost ready by the time he arrived. He looked a little strained, I thought.

'Has life been hectic?' I asked.

'I should say so! Hardly a minute when one isn't rushing

somewhere. I think these little respites are going to become fewer in the weeks to come.'

'Let me wait on you,' I said, and I poured a drink for him.

'It's good to be here,' he said. 'I've grown fond of this little flat. Have you, Violetta?'

'Yes, I have.'

'I have never experienced coming across an oasis in the desert, but I imagine it is like this.'

'I have the supper all ready.'

'That sounds like bliss.'

'So you think something is about to break?'

He lifted his shoulders.

I went on: 'All very hush-hush, I suppose.'

'Top secret.'

'I see. I hope you are going to like your supper. I've had to improvise a bit.'

'It will taste delicious, I am sure.'

'Don't be too sure. Just hope.'

I sat down with him while he finished his drink. I thought he looked a little uneasy. I tried to amuse him with gossip about the Ministry and made much of Marian's drama.

Suddenly he said: 'Violetta, I want to talk to you seriously. This may be my last visit to the flat for some time to come.'

I was alert. There was something different in his attitude.

'I can't tell you how much our meetings have meant to me. You remember how it was in the past.'

'I remember,' I said.

'I asked you to marry me then. If only you had . . .'

'We both felt it wasn't quite right, didn't we?'

'There were misunderstandings. We could have cleared those up . . . and then there was this Cornish man.'

'There really always was,' I said.

'Do you think he will ever come back?'

'I have to think that he will. I have to hope.'

'There is only one hope. If he is a prisoner and Europe is liberated, he might be able to get back.'

'I feel sure he is alive.'

'That's because you want to believe it. It's highly improbable, Violetta.'

'Lots of highly improbable things happen.'

'I think you must know that I love you.'

'I know we are very good friends. We always were.'

'One can love one's good friends, can't one? All these days we have been together, I've had to stop myself from telling you everything.'

'Everything?'

'Yes. I have a great deal to tell.'

'Do you want to tell me?'

'I must.'

'Well, I am listening.'

'It isn't easy, Violetta. When the war is over and it is absolutely certain that Jowan will never come back, would you marry me?'

'Oh, Richard!' I cried. 'I can't let myself think of his not coming back. I don't think I shall ever want to marry anyone but Jowan.'

'You can't spend the whole of your life mourning for someone who will never return.'

'I suppose some people have done that. In any case, I can't believe that he is dead. His grandmother feels the same. We understand each other absolutely.'

'It could be that you are deluding yourselves. Perhaps, when the war is over and he has not come back . . .'

'He will come back. I know he will.'

There was silence for a while, then he said: 'I dare say you have wondered how things could have been so different between us . . . different from the way they were,

I mean. You remember how in the past I urged you to marry me?'

'Yes, but it didn't happen.'

'I had reason for not asking you again . . . not, as they say, pressing my suit.'

'I just thought we were good friends and all that was over.'

'It is not over for me. But I will tell you why I could not ask you to marry me. It is because, Violetta, I have done a very foolish thing. I am married already.'

I stared at him in amazement. 'Then where . . . ?'

'Where is my wife? I have no idea. I have not heard of her for more than a year. It was a disastrous mistake. The war had just started. I had made friends in the Army. One of them had a sister. She was a very accomplished young lady. Lady Anne Tarragon-Lee was her name. She was sophisticated, clever, somewhat haughty, and I was rather flattered, I think, that she should show me some attention. I don't know how I could have been so foolish, but those were the first days of the war when everything seemed exciting. We were all waiting for the battle to start, and you know there was the long wait. It seemed like an unreal war. For me, army life was like being at school again. I felt irresponsible, I suppose, and I can't quite explain how it happened. It seemed wonderful at the time.'

I was so amazed that I remained silent. Richard, whom I had always thought to be so practical, so full of common sense, to have married rashly! It was hard for me to believe.

He understood my feelings, for he said: 'I see it is difficult for you to understand. It was the times, I suppose. We were all a little bemused then.'

'And you are no longer bemused?'

He nodded. 'I soon realized the folly of what I had done.'

He paused and, as he did so, I heard the air raid warning, faint at first but growing louder.

He disregarded it. After all, we were accustomed to hearing its frequent wail.

I said: 'And now . . . where is your wife?'

'I have no idea.'

'Do you not see each other?'

We started as the crunch of a falling bomb hit the air.

'Not far off,' commented Richard. Then: 'I hope they are not coming this way.' He went on: 'I think she is as eager to be free as I am.'

'There will be a divorce?'

'I expect so. There are many like us. We rush into these wartime marriages and then have to concern ourselves with getting out of them.'

'Well, if you both feel that way, it will be easier, I suppose.'

We heard another bomb fall, nearer this time; and we sat listening to the sound of falling masonry.

Richard said: 'That was very close. I think we had better get out of here.'

I rose, prepared to go down to the basement which was used as a shelter for the flat-dwellers. I picked up my coat and handbag and we went to the door, but we did not reach it, for suddenly the earth seemed to open and I was falling. Richard was not there. My eyes were full of dust; so was my mouth. I was lying down and then the darkness descended.

I awoke in a bed in an unfamiliar room. I noticed other beds. I was in a hospital.

I saw a girl in a nurse's uniform; then I vaguely remembered being in the flat and hearing the falling bombs.

Richard, I thought. Where was Richard? We had been

together on our way to the basement . . . and then this had happened.

The nurse came and stood by my bed.

'Hello,' she said. 'Feel all right?'

'Where am I?'

'St Thomas's.'

'Hospital?' I said.

'That's it. Nasty shock, was it?'

'We were bombed, of course.'

'That's it . . . along with others. It was a bad night.'

'My friend?'

'Oh yes, he's all right. I mean he's here. He came off worse than you did.'

'Can I see him?'

'Not now dear. See if you can drop off. A sleep will do you the world of good.'

'What time is it?' I asked.

She looked at the watch pinned on her apron.

'Just on two.'

'In the morning?'

'In the afternoon, dear.'

'So all this time . . .'

'Now, you get some rest.'

'But I must know.'

'You're all right. You've been lucky.' I could see she was not prepared to give me any more information.

I felt tired and dazed, unable to remember in detail what had actually happened.

I must have slept and when I awoke it was to see my parents at my bedside. My mother was watching me anxiously.

'Oh, she's come round,' I heard her say. 'Violetta darling, it's all right. We're here, your father and I and Dorabella. We came as soon as we heard.'

'It was a bomb,' I said.

She sat there, holding my hand; my father was on the other side of the bed. I saw Dorabella and the concern in all their faces.

I felt too tired to think, but I was certainly comforted to know they were there.

The next day I felt a great deal better. My mother said I had been in shock. Apparently the bomb had demolished a house nearby and what we had felt was the force of the explosion. It had damaged the block of flats considerably; the roof had fallen in and the windows were all shattered. We were lucky not to have been nearer to the bombed house. Two people had been killed and a number injured.

I was told I could leave the hospital the next day.

I was able to see Richard before I went. Although he had suffered more than I had, I was relieved to see that he was not seriously hurt.

His face was grazed and he had lost a certain amount of blood through a wound in his leg, but nothing was broken and the doctors said that in a week or so he could leave the hospital, though the leg would undoubtedly need further attention.

My mother said that when he was well enough he must come down to Caddington. She was taking me off at once.

It was wonderful to be at home. I was greeted rapturously by Tristan and by Nanny Crabtree with a mixture of tenderness towards me and fury against 'that Hitler'. She declared that if she could get her hands on him she would know what to do. There were tears in her eyes as she surveyed me.

'I never did hold with that going off to work in Ministries. Well, you're home now. We'll soon have you fattened up.'

Nanny's cure for all things was 'fattening up'.

They were lazy days. After my ordeal I needed a rest. I did have one or two dreams when I would be back in the flat, when I heard the crunch of the bombs and felt myself slipping down into darkness. I suppose the memory of that sort of experience stays with one for ever.

I thought a great deal about Richard's revelation. It was difficult to imagine his making a disastrous marriage. I should have thought he would have considered such a step very carefully before he undertook it. He had always seemed to me to be so prosaic, and practical in the extreme.

I supposed she had been very attractive. Lady Anne! He might have liked the title. Beautiful . . . seductive . . . poor Richard, he seemed to be unlucky in love. It occurred to me that one could never really know people. They so often stepped out of character and did the unexpected.

And now he was married to her. He must have been contemplating divorce seriously as he had suggested marrying me. I was sorry for him. He had obviously not wanted it known that he had married unsuccessfully. Richard was the sort of man who would hate to be thought unsuccessful in any way. So he had kept that marriage a secret.

He must have thought he owed it to me to make his confession. He had to explain why he had not asked me to marry him. Those visits to the flat, I supposed, had been a little unconventional and he wanted me to know that he still cared for me. He was really hinting that, when he was free and I was sure that Jowan was not coming back, marriage between us might be possible.

It all seemed very sensible, put like that. Yes, 'sensible' was the word I had always applied to Richard.

Dorabella was back at Caddington for the weekend. She was glad that I was home for a while. We had a pleasant weekend and when she went back I knew that my parents were uneasy. They did not like one of their precious daughters going into danger, and what had happened to me had enhanced their fears. One could be in danger, of course, anywhere in the country, but the capital was particularly vulnerable.

Dorabella was ready to face any danger to continue to live her exciting life; she took great pleasure in hinting that her fascinating husband was a man of great importance and guarding the nation's secrets.

Richard was released from hospital and had a week's leave before rejoining his regiment; he was spending half of it with us, the other half with his family in London.

I remember that June day well. It was the 6th – a day never to be forgotten. There was expectancy in the air, and most people must have been aware that great events were pending. We all gathered round the wireless for news and listened eagerly.

And there it was.

'*Under the command of General Eisenhower, Allied naval forces, supported from the air, began landing Allied armies on the Northern coast of France . . .*'

We all looked at each other, emotional, tense. The necessary invasion of the Continent had begun.

People could talk of nothing else. At the end of his leave Richard rejoined his regiment, though he was not considered fit yet to go abroad; and the following week I went back to London to resume my work in the Ministry.

There was an air of euphoria everywhere. People talked constantly about the landings. It was the beginning of the end, they said. We were coming out of the darkness which had enveloped us for the last five years and soon everything would be normal again.

This mood persisted, although the Prime Minister warned

us against too much optimism. We had made an excellent start, but there was a great deal to be done. We eagerly waited for any news we could get. Several of the Channel ports were now in Allied hands. Nothing could convince us that the news was not good and we were on the road to victory.

Although I had been glad to be home for a period when I might recover, I was looking forward to seeing the girls again.

Mary Grace had kept me informed and it seemed that nothing had changed except that Marian was like a different person and was quite merry. It amazed me that her life could have been so overshadowed by such a trivial matter; but, of course, what are trivialities depends on their importance to the people concerned.

I was due to return to London on the Sunday evening and it was on the preceding Friday that we heard the news of a new weapon which was being used against us. It was called 'Hitler's Secret Weapon' by the Germans; we called it his last desperate throw.

On the night of the 15th there had appeared for the first time over Britain a pilotless aircraft – a kind of flying bomb – which crossed the Channel and, when the engine stopped, fell to earth and exploded. This did little harm, we were told, and would in no way halt the progress of the war.

They were officially called Flying Bombs, but the people soon had a name for them. In those early days, they became known as Buzz-Bombs because one could distinctly hear them as they approached. If the engine was very loud, it meant that the thing was overhead and if it stopped suddenly, you were in danger because it was about to fall. We soon became familiar with them. This was a new hazard, but the mood stayed euphoric and we were all sure that victory was in sight.

I was given a vociferous welcome by them all when I

returned to the Ministry. Everyone came to congratulate me on my lucky escape. Billy Bunter referred to me as 'our heroine', which was too much praise, I thought, for having done nothing heroic.

Marian thought my return should be celebrated, and there we were, in the Café Royal, drinking our sherries.

It was strange to see Marian almost jolly, her dark secret revealed to be of no great importance. For as long as the war lasted, she need no longer conceal the dreadful truth that she was sixty-two years of age. Apart from that, little had changed.

I was leaving the office one day when a young woman approached me.

'You are Miss Violetta Denver, I believe,' she said.

I admitted that I was, and she went on: 'I am Anne Tarragon-Lee. I wonder if I might have a word with you?'

I felt shocked. Richard's wife! I could not understand why she wanted to talk to me.

'What do you want to say?' I asked.

She looked round. 'We can't talk here. Let's go and sit somewhere. Could we have a drink or a coffee somewhere?'

Bewildered still, I looked round. The only place was the teashop where we had our lunches.

I said: 'We could go in there.'

She wrinkled her nose slightly and said: 'There seems no alternative.'

She was very elegant. Her suit was of a pale grey fine material; her toque shaped with smooth grey feathers; it came down on one side to her eyebrows and accentuated the fineness of her large grey eyes. She was tall and slender and her features were finely chiselled, as though cut out of stone. There was something very cool and unruffled about her.

We sat and ordered cups of coffee.

'I expect you are wondering why I am here,' she said.

'Yes, I am. I have no idea why you should want to see me.'

'You know who I am. I can see that. I suppose Richard has talked to you of me.'

'He did mention you,' I said.

'And he has told you all, I suppose?'

'I do not think so. Really, he has told me very little. He mentioned you only just before we were caught in an air raid.'

'Yes, I know about that raid. You were in a flat together when it happened, weren't you? It must have been a great shock.'

'Naturally, that sort of thing is.'

'And how is Richard?'

'Do you not know? He is out of hospital and has rejoined his regiment.'

'But I believe he has not gone overseas.'

'It may well be some time before he is well enough for that.'

'Our marriage was a mistake,' she said, looking rueful. 'We didn't fit. It's strange how one thinks one does and quickly discovers one is wrong.'

'It happens to many people.'

'You know Richard well?'

'He is a friend of my family. I knew him some years ago.'

'He had this flat . . .'

'Yes, it belonged to a friend who lent it to him. He found it useful for his leaves, although his family have a house in Kensington.'

She smiled a little slyly. 'I know. The mother and the sister are there. The flat must have been very convenient for you.'

She was an enigma. It seemed odd that I should be sitting here, drinking coffee as though we were old acquaintances.

She was looking beyond me into the distance, almost speculatively. She was a strange woman, and I could not understand what this meeting was about, but I sensed there was something important behind it. Surely it was not idle curiosity to inspect one of Richard's friends?

'I think he will be all right,' I said. 'He is not really badly hurt.'

'No.' She put down her cup and said: 'It has been most interesting meeting you.'

'How did you know . . . who I was?'

'Well, I heard about the bombing, of course, and that you were there with him when it happened. He had mentioned your family to me once or twice. So . . . I thought I'd come and see you. I wanted to know how badly hurt he was.'

'As his wife, I should have thought you would have been told,' I said.

'Oh, I haven't seen him for some time. We were not together for long, you know. I took my maiden name again. It was like that.'

'I see. I don't think you need worry about him. He'll be quite fit again soon, I am sure.'

'Thank you for giving me your time.'

She stood up. Several eyes were upon her. Elegant creatures such as she was were not seen in the teashop every day.

We came out into the street.

'Goodbye,' she said in that cold way of hers.

I was still a little bewildered. I could not understand why she had contrived this meeting, yet I was sure it was not without some purpose.

* * *

Richard did not go overseas immediately but was posted down to the coast before I could tell him that his wife had been to see me.

I could not tell Dorabella or my parents that I had met Richard's wife because I did not know whether he wished his marriage to remain a secret, and I felt it was not for me to divulge it.

I tried to put the thought of that meeting from my mind. It was not easy. There was something about Lady Anne which repelled me, something a little sinister. I laughed at myself. I was building up some drama.

She was his wife, and as Richard had implied and she had confirmed, the marriage was not a success. It would probably be dissolved when the war was over.

Life slipped back to normal. There were the same jokes, the same lunches at the teashop, but now, whenever I entered the place, I thought of that cool slender figure in grey.

We had the additional menace of the Flying Bombs which were coming over in large numbers. Many of them were disabled at the coast, which was not much use, as the damaged objects just went on their way, dropped and exploded, so they were as lethal as the sound ones.

They were just an added trial. People said their unmistakable 'hum-hum' as they went along meant 'you, you', because, if you heard the noise, you were in danger and the thing might be intended for you.

But the cheerful mood continued. The Flying Bombs could not affect the people's morale while there were successes on the Continent.

I remember the day well. Indeed, it was one which I shall never forget. June had passed and it was a sultry July afternoon. We sat at our tables working, now and then gossiping in quiet voices, for while Billy Bunter knew it was impossible to stop the whispers he did not want our voices to become too audible.

Florette was very happy that afternoon. A week ago she had met a young man who was 'in the business'; he was a conjuror and had appeared in Blackpool for a few weeks. Not exactly top of the bill, but at least halfway down. He was working on munitions because he was not quite fit for the Army; but he had great hopes for the future.

So she had found a soulmate with whom she could share her dreams and learn a great deal about theatrical rules.

Peggy was looking forward to Florette's future as such as she could never have for herself; and, with a guilt-free Marian and Mary Grace her usual steady self, fitting in with everyone's mood, that began as a very happy afternoon.

Terry Travers, the conjuror, had given Florette some cuttings about his show in Blackpool; she had stuck them in her book and brought it along to show us. There was no room for it on the table, so she had left it in the cloakroom.

Halfway through the afternoon the sirens wailed forth their warning. As usual, no one took much notice of this. Then suddenly a shrill whistle was heard throughout the building. It was the Imminent. That meant that whatever was coming our way was very close indeed.

We stood up, and, as we did so, we saw the object come into view. I had never before seen a Flying Bomb at such close quarters. It was almost on a level with the window and moved in a lopsided way which indicated that it had been damaged.

We stared in horror. It was too late to take cover now. The thing was upon us.

Florette cried: 'I've left my cuttings book in the cloakroom,' which ought to have made us laugh because she could think of such a thing at a moment when death was staring us in the face. But this was no laughing matter.

'You, you,' said the thing very loudly. We scrambled under the table. Any moment now. It would drop and that would be the end of us and everyone in the building. 'You, you.' I was aware of Mary Grace beside me. She gripped my hand. I started to think of the past; the miniatures she had painted of Dorabella and me; the day I had given mine to Dorabella; the time when we had thought my sister was drowned; waiting for news of Jowan after Dunkirk . . .

Time slowed down. There was no sound in the room except that of the relentless engine which must stop at any second . . . and that would be the end.

'You, you.' It was slightly fainter. Billy Bunter was standing up.

He cried: 'It's gone past, but keep under cover.'

He himself did not. He went to the window.

Florette said: 'I'm going to get my book. I thought I'd lose it. I shall always keep it with me now.'

'Wait!' I said: but she was off.

Then Billy Bunter, who was at the window, called out: 'Hey, I do believe . . . Good God! It's coming back!'

There was silence.

'You, you, you.' It was louder.

Billy was right. The thing had turned and was limping its way back, which meant it was immediately outside the building.

'Get under cover!' shouted Billy, and we darted once more for the tables. Slowly, deliberately, the sound was increasing; the damaged bomb was coming our way.

Nearer, nearer and then . . . the dreaded silence.

It was like that other occasion. The explosion, the crump, crump, and then the rumbling that continued. Something was falling on to the table under which we were crouching. It must have been part of the ceiling. The table stayed firm, so it could only have been fragments that fell.

Had the building been hit? It was not exceptionally tall but a long and rather sprawling one. I felt dazed. This was the second time this had happened to me within a few weeks. I felt doomed, that fate was pursuing me.

I heard people shouting. There was Billy Bunter, taking charge, as he had always done. Mary Grace was beside me. I saw that Peggy was trembling. Marian looked shaken. But they were all alive . . . under the table with me. That strong table had saved us from being hurt by those pieces of falling masonry.

The sound of sirens and fire-engines filled the air. It was like a nightmare. I am not sure how long it lasted. These were familiar sounds in our war-torn city. So many times we had heard them. This was different. This was us.

It is difficult to remember exactly what happened. I just know that there was tremendous activity. We were numbed, bemused . . . and amazed to find that we seemed to be unhurt.

Then I heard Peggy crying: 'Where's Florette? She wasn't with us. She'd gone to get her cuttings book.'

Billy Bunter started to speak. We would leave the building as soon as possible . . . just in case it collapsed. The bomb had apparently not hit the building but had fallen close beside it. There was considerable damage and it would be better for us to get out. There was nothing we could do but wait for instructions.

'You'll be looked after, and as soon as possible. There'll be a bus to take you home. You'll have to report to the hospital for a check-up, but the main thing is to attend to the injured. You won't leave the usual way. You'll have to be shown. Go quietly, please. That's the best way you can help.'

We stood huddled together. Peggy was very anxious.

She kept saying: 'Florette. Where's Florette? Why did she go off? Why didn't she stay with us?'

'She'll be there in the cloakroom,' said Mary Grace.

'I hope she got her cuttings book all right,' said Marian.

It seemed a very long time before we were led out of the building. The bus was there and we filed in.

I looked back at the familiar building as we drove away. It was not the same; it would never be. One end had gone completely and there was a jagged gap. I saw part of a room with filing cabinets standing in it – open to the sky.

There were people everywhere. I saw the ambulances and a stretcher being carried into one of them.

Then we were off. I was glad. I did not want to look any more at the scene of devastation.

It was two days before we heard the news about Florette. The cloakroom was at that end of the building which had suffered most from the blast of the bomb and Florette had died, clutching the book of cuttings in her hand.

The news shocked us all terribly, but Peggy I think most of all. She looked shrivelled and bewildered.

We all met again afterwards. Mary Grace took us to her house. We could not have met in the Café Royal; that would have been too heartrending. We should have pictured Florette there all the time. It was sad enough in the Dorrington house.

All the gaiety had gone. We were all so unhappy thinking of bright Florette with her dreams of a future which now would never be. We tried to talk normally but it was impossible.

Marian should have been happy because both she and Peggy were being transferred to another branch of the Ministry. It was very near home for Peggy and not so very far for Marian, and they had both dreaded losing their jobs; but there was no happiness for either of them, particularly Peggy.

I told them that I was going back to my parents for a while and then I would plan what I should do. Mary Grace would not be returning to the Ministry.

It was no use trying not to talk about Florette. It was almost as though she was there with us.

'If only she hadn't gone back for that book,' said Peggy, 'she'd have been with us under the table. Why did she want to go?'

'We none of us knew the thing would turn back,' I said.

'Oh, why did she?' wailed Peggy. 'If only . . .'

Her poor face looked older and more tired than usual, even more wistful than when she was yearning to be someone's pet. She had lost her friend, it seemed to her, unnecessarily. It never would have happened if Florette had not gone back for the book.

'That's life,' said Marian. 'It all works on chance.'

And we sat there in silence, thinking of Florette, who had had such dreams and had died so cruelly before she could try to make them come true.

A Hint of Scandal

I had visited the hospital. No bones had been broken, but a rest was suggested, particularly as I had recently suffered a similar experience.

My parents were delighted to have me home.

'I only wish Dorabella was not up there,' said my mother. 'Those wretched bombs are worse than the other kind, it seems to me.'

I spent a lot of time with Tristan. Nanny Crabtree was inclined to treat me like an invalid and attempted the 'fattening-up' process; but there was no doubt of her joy in having me back in the fold.

I did not want to be idle and so helped my mother in her work with the various organizations in which she was involved.

There was a great deal of discussion about the progress of the war, which seemed to be going well in spite of certain setbacks; but clearly the end was not going to come as quickly as we had hoped.

I thought that, if Jowan were a prisoner of war and the Allies were advancing, it might be that they would come to where he was held, when I supposed all prisoners would be freed. Every day I waited for news with mounting hope. It would go first to Mrs Jermyn, of course, but she would inform me immediately.

My mother knew this and was afraid for me. I guessed that in her heart she did not share my optimism.

She said to me one day: 'Violetta, you still believe that Jowan will come back, don't you? It is four years now.'

It was one of those days – they came now and then – when my hopes seemed to fade. It *was* a long time. Sometimes I wondered if he would be the same man when he came back. People change. Had his love been as strong for me as mine had for him?

I hesitated and she was aware of this.

'Time is passing,' she went on. I knew what was in her mind. I should be twenty-five in October. I was no longer very young. She was wondering whether I was going to spend my life mourning a lost lover. She had known a friend who had been engaged to be married to a young man who was killed on the Somme during the last war. My mother had spoken of her occasionally. It was not only that she had missed marriage and family, but she had spent her life mourning for a man she had lost when she was eighteen. She did not want a similar fate for me.

She said: 'I am sure you are better here than in Cornwall. I wonder if Richard will have to go overseas? Gordon is lucky. Not that he isn't doing an excellent job. They couldn't have done without him on the estate. Oh, I do hope this wretched war will be over before Richard has to go out there.'

I could read her well. She was thinking: Here were two good men, both of whom, with a little encouragement, would be ready to marry me, and I must go on mourning for someone who might never come back.

There was a telephone call from Richard. My mother took it and when she came to me she was very excited.

'Who do you think has just telephoned? Richard. He's got a little leave and wants to come for the weekend.'

'And you said you would be delighted to see him, I am sure.'

'I did.'

'Is this leave because he is going overseas?'

'I asked him that. He said no, they can't make any

decision about that. He said the wound is playing up a bit and they won't let him go while he is in that state.'

She looked pleased and excited. I knew she was hoping.

Richard arrived. My father was delighted to see him and my mother was more pleased than she had been for a long time because my brother Robert had leave too, though I feared that might mean that he would soon be going with his regiment to the Continent.

Richard arrived in the evening of Friday and would have to leave on Sunday afternoon to be sure of being back in barracks by the appointed time.

He looked a little strained, I thought.

We sat round the dining-room table and talked about the progress of the war, and I was not alone with Richard until the following morning.

He suggested we take a ride and we went off together in mid-morning, telling my mother that we would have lunch out at some inn on the road.

Richard was able to ride with ease, in spite of his leg injury, but as we rode through the roads which I had known all my childhood, I sensed a certain restraint about him.

We found an inn, the White Stallion, with a sign depicting a splendid-looking horse over the door.

Over the food, Richard blurted out what was on his mind.

He said: 'Anne is going to divorce me.'

'That is what you both wanted, isn't it?'

'She is determined to do it her way.'

'She came to see me.'

'What!'

'Yes. It was when I was at the Ministry. I came out of the building and there she was, waiting for me.'

He stared at me in astonished dismay.

'I couldn't understand it,' I went on. 'There didn't seem to be any point. She talked about my friendship with you. She asked about the flat.'

'The flat!'

'She said I would know it well.'

He closed his eyes and muttered something under his breath which I could not hear.

'I'd better tell you right away. She is going to divorce me on the grounds of adultery.'

'Oh,' I said faintly, 'I see.'

'My adultery . . . with you.'

I stared at him. 'How can she possibly? It isn't true.'

'That won't concern her. I think she has been having the flat watched. It is known that we were there together. Then, of course, there was the raid. It was late in the evening and we were there alone together. It may be that will be considered evidence enough.'

'Oh, but it can't be.'

'She's tenacious. When she wants something she goes out and gets it. She had put off acting because she thought I might be at the Front and the chances of survival not great. That would have been a smooth and easy way to end the marriage. But I'm here and she believes the war will be over before I am sent out, that I shall stay on in comparative safety and her nice easy way of being rid of me will be denied her.'

'Do you really believe she is as calculating as that?'

'Calculation is second nature to her. I know her well. This is amusing her. She used to laugh at me . . . the virtuous barrister, she called me. So it will amuse her to see me caught up in an unsavoury divorce.'

'Oh no!'

'It is what she has in mind. This is the quickest way to end the marriage and that is her aim; she is tired of it and she wants it ended and to come out of it in the best possible way herself. The bored wife who wanted to divorce her husband who was serving his country would not be viewed with sympathy. But if he is unfaithful to her, she has every reason, of course.'

'But it is so false. We were just good friends. It was only natural that I should go there and cook something for you.'

'Not to her. She knew we were friends in the past. She knew how I felt about you. She will stress that.'

'What can we do?'

'Nothing. Just wait.'

'When . . . when will it start?'

'I don't know. Anne will have been working on it for some time. It was the air raid which made her see she had a good case. These things take time, you know.'

'I must tell my parents.'

'Would you like me to be with you?'

'No . . . no. I will tell them when you have gone. I think that would be best.'

My hand was lying on the table and he leaned forward and pressed it firmly.

'I am so sorry that you have been brought into all this,' he said. 'It is wretched for you.'

'For you, too.'

'Me? Oh yes. But I have brought it on myself. One must pay for one's acts of folly. But that I should bring it on you . . . that worries me. I would have done anything to have avoided that. You see, Anne is well-known in some circles. Her exploits are recorded. When we were married it was reported in certain newspapers. There may be some publicity over the divorce, and it is possible that your name will be mentioned.'

'I see. I would be branded as a loose woman, I suppose. That is what you mean?'

'It would be expected that we should marry when I am free.'

'Richard, you know –'

' – that you are waiting for Jowan's return. But when, Violetta, when? Soon you will have to decide. When Europe is liberated . . . suppose he does not come back?'

I was silent and he went on: 'I shall be waiting. And, Violetta, don't worry unduly about the divorce. These things are a nine days' wonder.'

'Perhaps Anne is just threatening.'

'I do not think so. She wants a divorce quickly and she sees this as the easiest way to get it. It may well be that she wants to marry again and is eager to be free to do so. That might be very likely. It is clear that she is regretting our marriage as much as I am.'

'I can see I've been very foolish,' I said. 'I should never have come to the flat as I did.'

'Don't say that. Those little suppers were wonderful. I can't tell you what they meant to me. I looked forward to them so much. Well, whatever happens, in time I shall be free. And when . . .'

He meant when I was sure Jowan would not come back. But I could not contemplate that. Since the Normandy landings, my hopes had been high.

I said: 'I think we should go now.'

He called for the bill and we left.

It was difficult to get through the rest of that weekend. Fortunately my parents were preoccupied with Robert, who was eager to talk about life in the Army and the prospects of going overseas shortly, which seemed to excite him but naturally had the opposite effect on my parents.

We all went to the station to see him off. He left in the

late morning of Sunday. Richard stayed until the early evening.

When he had gone I felt exhausted. I kept thinking about Anne as she had been when I had met her – so elegant, so cool, so sure of what she wanted. She would be formidable. I could see how she had attracted Richard. That cool acceptance of superiority, just the wife to be an asset to a rising barrister; he no doubt had visualized her at the head of his table entertaining the Lord Chancellor. I was sure she would have done so in perfect style. So Richard had been lured into committing that act which he now called folly.

Somehow it endeared him to me a little. I had thought him so sensible; and to find him vulnerable made him more human.

I did not blame him as he blamed himself. I just wished that I had not become involved.

My mother had guessed something had happened and that night, just as I was about to retire, she came to my room.

She sat on the bed and surveyed me.

'Well,' she said. 'What is bothering you?'

It was no use trying to keep anything from her. I had decided to tell her in any case.

I said: 'Richard is married.'

The shocked expression on her face turned to dismay. She had decided that Richard was the man for me and eligible in every way.

'Has he just told you?' she asked.

I shook my head.

'He told me in London. It was the night of the air raid. It was a disaster. She is going to divorce him on the grounds of adultery . . . with me.'

Her expression changed to one of horror.

'It is quite false,' I said quickly. 'There has never been

adultery . . . I think not with anyone, certainly not with me.'

I explained about the flat and the suppers and how he had always known I was waiting for Jowan. I missed out nothing; I told her about his wife's visit to the teashop, which had puzzled me at the time but now I knew why she had come.

'Good Heavens!' my mother cried. 'I don't believe this of Richard. He is the last person . . .'

'People often do unexpected things.'

'I should not have thought Richard would. But . . . er . . . when it is over, Richard will be free and . . .'

'He has asked me to marry him then.'

'It would be best,' she said. 'Mind you, there wouldn't be much talk about this. In wartime these things are trivial.'

'Richard says she is a socialite and that her actions are reported in the gossip columns so there could be some publicity.'

'I see. And you might be mentioned. Well, these things happen. If you marry him it would not seem so important.'

'I wouldn't want to marry him just because – '

'No, of course not. Well, we shall have to wait and see. I shall tell your father. He would know more about these things than we do. I saw that Richard was very upset.'

'He is, of course – mainly because he has involved me.'

'How do you feel about him, Violetta? You like him, don't you?'

'Yes. Very much.'

'And if it were not for Jowan . . .'

'I can't think of that. I still feel he will come back.'

She sighed, then smiled suddenly.

'Half the things one worries about never happen,' she said. 'This divorce, it might pass quietly. People are not as interested in that sort of thing as they used to be. There's a war on and we are not living in the Victorian age when everyone was so prim and prudish. Don't worry. You've been through enough lately. I think this may be like a storm in a teacup. I am sure your father will agree with me. I'm glad you came home for a while. It will all come right, I am sure. So try and get a good night's rest.'

'I certainly feel better now that I have told you,' I said.

She kissed me tenderly and waited until I was in bed. Then she tucked me in, as she used to when I was very young.

My parents were wonderful during those days. Dorabella came for weekends which was helpful. There had been no news of Richard's divorce and Dorabella said: 'That sort of thing is happening all the time. I doubt we shall hear any more of it.'

Richard was still declared unfit for active service and the war was progressing satisfactorily for the Allies.

Paris had been liberated and General de Gaulle was now there. General Montgomery, speaking to the men in North-West France, said the end was in sight and we must finish it off in record time.

It was August and we had had almost five years of war. Surely, I thought, if Jowan were alive I should have heard something by now?

I knew my mother was most concerned about my future and I guessed it was the main topic between her and my father. They had both been dismayed to hear that Richard had made a hasty wartime marriage which was in the process of being dissolved. It was out of character for him, but they had both decided that he was the best husband for me, though they had considered Gordon. Gordon was an honest, upright man, but he had a mad mother; also he was something of an enigma. So they had set their hearts on Richard, for I was sure they had long made up their minds that it was unlikely that Jowan would come back.

Even I was beginning to wonder. The time was passing. The invasion of France had begun in June and it was now nearly September. Hope was beginning to fade. Should I be one of those sad women who lose their lover during the war and spend the rest of their lives grieving?

It was 3 September – the fifth anniversary of the war. Everywhere the Allies were triumphant and this was a day of prayer throughout the country.

Dorabella was with us and would return to London that evening and we were dining early because of that.

My father was saying: 'It cannot last much longer. Our forces are only forty miles from Brussels and the French and Americans are in Lyons. This is great progress.'

Then the telephone rang. Dorabella was on her feet first. 'I'll get it,' she said.

In a few seconds she came back.

'It's Mrs Jermyn from Cornwall. She wants to speak to Violetta.'

My heart was pounding. Could it be news at last?

My mother glanced at me anxiously, fearful that I should be disappointed.

I dashed to the telephone.

'Violetta – ' Mrs Jermyn's voice was breathless – 'I've had news.'

'Jowan . . .'

'Yes, dear. He's in this country. I've just had a call. They told me he was here . . . and he was on the telephone. I've spoken to him. He's coming home!'

I could not speak. I was too overcome with emotion.

At last I stammered: 'I shall come . . . right away.'

'Yes, yes,' she said.

I went back to the dining-room. They were all looking at me expectantly.

I said: 'It . . . it's happened. Jowan is coming home.'

Reunion

My father would have driven me to Cornwall, but we decided it would be quicker by train. My mother wanted to come with me, but I said I should prefer to be alone. At least they could drive me to London and I could get the train from there to Cornwall.

I was overcome with joy. This was the day I had been waiting for.

My parents stood on the platform at Paddington waving to the train as it went out and the long journey to the West Country began. How slowly the train seemed to travel! It was impossible to sleep. I could only think of seeing Jowan again. He would have changed. Had I changed? I was four years older. So much had happened since we last met. I could not imagine what had happened to him, but I should learn. I should talk to him again, be with him, make plans for the future.

Then suddenly into my mind came the thought of Richard's divorce. It was such an unpleasant subject that I thrust it aside. Nothing was going to spoil this wonderful time.

It was seven o'clock when the train pulled into the station. To my surprise I saw Gordon on the platform. He seized both my hands and kissed me lightly on the cheek.

'I've come to collect you,' he said. 'Mrs Jermyn told me the news.'

'Is Jowan there?'

'Yes. He came in late last night.'

'You . . . you have seen him?'

'No. Mrs Jermyn just telephoned, told me and asked me if I would meet the train. I wasn't sure whether it would be this one.'

'I came immediately I heard.'

'I guessed you would.'

'Oh Gordon . . . it's such wonderful news!'

'Mrs Jermyn could scarcely speak for excitement.'

'It was good of you to come, Gordon.'

'It was nothing . . . the least I could do. I suppose you may be staying at the Priory, but if you want your old room at Tregarland's it is ready for you.'

'Thank you, Gordon. I hadn't thought of that.'

When we reached the Priory it was nearly eight o'clock.

Gordon stopped the car and said: 'I'll leave you now. If you want transport at any time, let me know.'

'Oh thank you, Gordon. You are good.'

'Good luck,' he said.

They were waiting for me in the Priory great hall.

Mrs Jermyn cried: 'It's Violetta.' And beside her stood a tall figure. Jowan himself . . . and yet different. He was very thin, a little haggard and he had lost his healthy colour. He was subtly different from the man who had gone away . . . and yet he was Jowan.

We looked at each other in wonderment for a few seconds, then I ran to him and he held me tightly in his arms.

'Violetta,' he said. 'After all this time . . .'

'The waiting is over now. It has been so long. So very long . . .'

I sounded muffled, incoherent. 'I've often dreamed . . .'

'I too. I can't believe it. I'm afraid I'll wake up and find I'm dreaming still.'

Such banal words after all those years of waiting. But our emotions were too strong to let us say all that was in our hearts.

Mrs Jermyn broke in.

'You two will have such a lot to say to each other. And, Violetta, you must be hungry. There's nothing much in trains these days. Now I am going to have something sent to you. Come into the little sitting-room. Then you can talk . . . I think you two would like to be alone.'

There were tears in her eyes and I saw that she was desperately trying to control her feelings and be practical.

'Thank you, Grandmother,' said Jowan. 'That would be good.'

He was holding my hand tightly, as though he would never let it go.

I was happy. I had never been so happy in my life – if only I could rid myself of the terrible fear that I was dreaming and this might not be true.

There was so much to tell. He insisted that I start first, so I related what had happened since that tragic day when I had been forced to admit to myself that he was not one of the survivors from Dunkirk. I explained how I had worked for a while in the Priory, which had been turned into a convalescent home for soldiers, and afterwards in London in the Ministry. I told him about the air raids in which I had been involved – not an uncommon occurrence for people who lived in London – and how I had been recuperating at Caddington when his grandmother had telephoned to tell me he was back.

He listened intently.

'We heard little scraps of information – exaggerated often to make it really bad. We were told that London was in ruins, together with the airfields and the docks. We didn't believe it, of course.'

'I want to hear about you, Jowan. I want to know everything.'

'I want to tell you everything, Violetta . . . every little detail.'

'We have a long, long time to talk.'

'First I will give you the bare bones,' he said. Then he told me how his company had been trying to get to the coast. They knew the Germans were in control and there was no help for it but to get back home, build up new strength and be ready for the enemy when they came to attack Britain.

'There was not much chance of getting to Dunkirk,' he said. 'The enemy were too numerous. Our company was surrounded. We were somewhere near Amiens when we were all taken prisoner. We knew what that meant. My corporal, Buster Brown, was with me. Bernard Brown, but always known as "Buster". He was sharp-witted, a wiry little Cockney. He was a good cook and could work all sorts of miracles with our meagre rations. He used to have a way of disappearing and returning with a couple of chickens. He'd concoct some dish with them, which was a luxury after tinned fish and meat of slightly mysterious origins. He admitted he raided farms for the chickens, and he used to say: "Well, what's a bit of nicking? Ain't we saving them from the Hun? Small price to pay for that, and you've got to feed the boys that lay the golden eggs."

'He was a great character and I never saw him disconcerted in any situation. He had always been my special servant and I often thought how different life would have been without Buster Brown.

'Well, we were surrounded and put in lorries. There was a great deal of confusion in the dash to the coast, and the gathering up of small groups of prisoners was left to young and inexperienced men newly arrived on the battle scene. We were close to a small deserted *château* which it was no doubt thought would serve for a temporary prison, but perhaps because we were not a large company and there were more pressing matters to occupy the German headquarters, we remained there. In most cases there would have been some notification that we were prisoners of war but there are occasions in such times as we were living through when these matters are overlooked.

'Life was not too bad in the beginning. We had periods of exercise, strict rules of course, not very adequate food, but most of our company were housed in the *château* and we were among our own people. The great adventure was to escape. We planned it continually. We knew there would be no early release. We were aware that the French were beaten and that we had lost much of our equipment and would concentrate on getting our men out. We did not know how fortunate we had been in that evacuation.

'Well, we started building our tunnel. It lent a spice of adventure to the days. We each had a turn at it. It was an arduous business – most would have said a hopeless task, but we lived on hope in those days. We had our little concert parties, and the Germans looked on at us in bewilderment. There was complete misunderstanding between us. They were amazed by our hilarious laughter at the jokes – usually jibes against them – and the amateur efforts of our "artistes". What amused us so much was that it was during these concert parties that the larger part of our tunnel digging was in progress.

'This went on slowly. Imagine our dismay when we thought we were near completion – that must have been over two years' work – to find that we had come out on the wrong side of the wall and were still inside the castle! But we were resilient. We kept going. We made plans for our final success. We arranged how people should escape. Not all at once, but two by two. We would have a rota. That was how it went.

'We kept a certain discipline among ourselves. We had to stay cheerful and hopeful. Someone had a pack of cards and we played some evenings; but the cards became dog-eared and having only one pack was constricting.

'It was the tunnel which was the great excitement. And then there came the Normandy landings. We were not sure what was happening, but everything had changed. The attitude of our guards was different. They were jumpy, nervous. There was less food. There would be occasions when the guards were almost lax and at others the opposite.

'We knew something was going on. Some of our men had a smattering of German and they picked up one or two things through listening to conversations. So we learned that the Allies were now in France. You might have thought that, after waiting four years, we could wait a little longer to be released. But it wasn't like that. The fervour to be free had increased. We had more opportunities to get on digging the tunnel and we seized them.

'Then . . . it was completed and this time it came outside the *château*. Several of the men escaped and we believed they had got safely away. We only went two at a time, but it was not long before absentees were noted, in spite of the slackness of control. A guard was set at the top of the tower to keep watch throughout the night. At any movement they would shoot immediately. Sometimes during the night we would hear shots and wonder if those who were attempting to escape had got away. We were never told, of course.

'And then it was my turn. I was to go with Buster Brown. He looked upon me as his protégé. He reminded me of a nanny I once had. He thought I needed looking after and there was no question of one of us going without the other.

'Violetta, I shall never forget that night. The watch was in position and there was a crescent moon – enough to show them any movement, I feared. We preferred the moonless nights, of course, and cloud was welcome; but on this night the sky was cloudless.

'We could take little with us and we had no money; but we did have a little food which we had been storing over the days and which was given to those who were attempting to escape.

'We got through the tunnel – not the easiest of feats, for it was very low and in some places too narrow for comfort; but we were agile and determined. Then there was that glorious moment when one emerged into the open – no longer prisoners, but, for the first time in more than four years, free men.

'The searchlight moved quickly over the expanse of grass outside the *château*. We must miss that and had to remain very still crouched on the ground when it came our way.

'It was not easy. I heard the shots ring out and I was aware of a sudden burning pain in my arm. I thought: I've had it. This is the end. Then I heard Buster whisper, "Keep still. Flat on the ground. Don't move a muscle." I obeyed and the searchlight passed over us and went on.

'"Now," whispered Buster, and, with a tremendous effort, for I was beginning to feel faint, I rose and ran. Buster was pulling me on. "Get a move on, sir," he whispered. "Want the Jerries to get us?"

'We were crouching in the bushes. I was aware of the searchlight and that we were beyond its range.

'"Cor blimey," said Buster. "That was a close 'un. Thought it was goodbye, home and beauty. Come on now, or we'll miss the boat. Got to get going."

'My sleeve was wet. I touched my arm and my hand came away red with blood.

'"You'd better go on, Buster," I said. "I think I might . . ."

'"Don't talk tripe, sir. Begging your pardon," said Buster. "'Course I'm not going on without you. Who'd look after you? We're going to make it. They've had their bit of fun. They won't come after us now. They're kidding themselves it was a fox they saw. Makes life easy that way."

'He was half dragging me along with him. I was beginning to feel rather vague. We were on a road and I saw the lights of a lorry in the distance. Buster dragged me into a hedge until it had passed. Then we went on. I hardly knew what was happening. I think I must have been delirious. Buster told me later that I kept asking where I was and saying, "Where is Jermyn's? Where's the Priory? I'm coming home." "You was saying your own name over and over again," he told me, "and talking to some bird called Violet . . . or something like that."

'I think he must have carried me, which would have been awkward as I am considerably taller than he is. He probably dragged me most of the way. We had great good luck because in a field he found a wheelbarrow. He was very good at improvising and I had seen him make good use of the oddest things. Now the wheelbarrow proved to be a carriage for me. It was easy just to push me along. I think that wheelbarrow probably saved our lives. He would never have gone on without me. He's a marvellous fellow, old Buster. He was as clever as he boasted he was. He used to say he could get round anyone, from commanding officers to the shyest bird. He saw himself as a powerful manipulator of everything, including women. I used to call him Casanova Brown. He had never heard of Casanova, but he was pleased when he realized the implication.

'I shall always believe I owe my life to Buster Brown.

'We came to a house, some way back from the road. Buster took a chance. He told me afterwards that he had to. He thought I would pass out if he did not get me somewhere quickly. I was losing a lot of blood and he couldn't push a wheelbarrow in daylight.

'The house had been a farmhouse and was set in the midst of several acres; there were some chickens pecking round, a pig in a sty and a donkey in a field. This I discovered later, of course, for I was not in a state to notice anything at this stage.

'When the door opened I was faintly aware of a woman speaking rapid French, of which I might have understood a little if I had been in a better state of health. Buster's knowledge of the language did not go beyond "*Oo-là-là*".

'However, he must have managed to convey to her that he had escaped from the *château*, that his friend was wounded and that he needed help.

'What good luck we had that night! Marianne, as we later discovered her to be, had an intense and abiding hatred of the German invader. They had shot her husband before her eyes and if she had an opportunity of harming them in any way she would eagerly take it.

'We also learned that she had helped others from our company to escape to freedom. She took in the situation at once – our clothes, our state, Buster's sign language, my blood-soaked sleeve . . . they all told the story.

'Briefly, she took us in. She attended to me first; she bandaged my arm, got me into a bed and gave Buster a hunk of rye bread and something which bore a resemblance to coffee.

'I think I was delirious. I was not sure where I was and most of the time thought I was in the Priory. Buster slept well – on the floor beside my bed.

'He said afterwards: "I knew that Marianne was a good 'un. Some might have took us in and then given the alarm. Not this one. She's going to get her own back on the Hun, and his enemies are her friends."

'Well, Marianne was indeed a "good 'un". She was so good to us and without her I could not have survived. Through everything she did, she showed her hatred of the enemy, otherwise she was a placid sort of woman, good-looking in a rather blowsy, dreamy way – except when she was giving vent to her hatred of Germans. Then she would look fierce and mutter what she would like to do to them.

'Buster and I smiled on these occasions. "All the better for us," was Buster's comment. I believed she would have taken any risk to work against them.

'But she was tender and sympathetic. When she dressed my arm she would murmur, "*Le pauvre petit garçon.*" It comforted me, for the pain could be great.

'We learned a little from Marianne of what had happened, how the great General de Gaulle was going to save France, of the Allied landings in Normandy, of that villain Pétain who had betrayed France and become a slave to the cruel conquerors. The English and the Americans were "*magnifique*" and here they were, back on French soil to rise against the conquerors and betrayers, to wipe away the country's shame and make her great again.

'It was her duty to help escaping prisoners, she said. She was doing it for France and she had liked so much the charming men who had come her way. There had been two airmen. They had dropped from their parachutes. She had kept them for two nights. There had been men from the *château*. She could tell them about the country . . . she could get clothes for them. She had some which had belonged to her husband who could no longer wear them because of the cursed Hun.

'I could see that I was a handicap for Buster and I said he should go on without me. We were too near the *château* for comfort. What if the guards discovered that we were in this house? Not only should we suffer, but Marianne herself would.

'Buster turned this aside, and so did Marianne. She would not allow me to go with such an arm, though she could do but little for it, alas. It needed a doctor. She could not call one, for how could she trust him? No, she would do what she could. At least it was something.

'Then we met Lisette. Lisette had been staying at her uncle's farm and had now come home to her mother. She was a younger version of Marianne – the same plump and shapely figure, the same hooded eyes and full lips and overwhelming femininity. She smiled warmly at us. She must have been accustomed to her mother's helping men to escape: she could speak a little English, which was helpful.

'She said: "Escape. You? From the *château*?"

'We told her we had and that her mother had been very helpful.

'"My mother like much English and Americans. I too."

'"Lucky for us," said Buster.

'We were at Marianne's for several weeks. Much of the time I was hardly aware of my surroundings. It seemed so unreal there. My arm began to fester, but Marianne was afraid to ask the doctor to come. She was wonderful to us. She kept us there and fed us; though we had no money with which to pay her.

'"She do for France," declared Lisette dramatically. Buster worked on the farm, which I am sure was a great help, but I was unable to do anything.

'There was a time in the beginning when I suffered from delirium. It was a sort of fever . . .'

He paused, as though looking back. I guessed he was seeing the old farmhouse, and recalling the strangeness and uncertainty of those days.

'The Allies were advancing,' he went on, 'and there seemed to be numbers of Germans everywhere. We had to be very careful not to be seen. Marianne had a big cupboard in which she proposed to hide us if they ever came to the house. It contained heavy farm implements and we were to cower behind some sacks if it was ever necessary. I was sure, if they ever came, we should be discovered at once. Fortunately, we did not have to hide.

'I was always urging Buster to get away. It would be easier for him if he did not have an invalid to look after. He would not go, of course. I think he was enjoying his stay at the farmhouse. It was clear that he liked Marianne and her daughter. He had mended and painted the wheelbarrow and it was placed on the farm. It was almost like a shrine.

'"Our saviour," he called it. "Do you know, sir, we couldn't have got by without that? Makes you think." He would go and look at it every day and, as he left, blow it a kiss. There was an unsuspected sentimental streak in Buster's nature.

'I think he was on rather special terms with Marianne. He told me once that Marianne was "a bit of all right". This was always accompanied by a wink. He was equally devoted to Lisette.

'There was something cosy about the atmosphere of the farmhouse, in spite of the danger which was lurking all through the days and nights.

'They used to get me to talk in the evenings when we sat in the dark. Buster was always alert for noises which might suggest the arrival of unwelcome visitors. I told them about the Priory, the old monks who used to live here. I described the wild Cornish coast. Lisette was enchanted. Her slight command of English made it possible for her to ask questions, and she would convey the answers to her mother. Buster would sit there listening, smiling on us all. He always regarded himself as the man of the house. I didn't qualify because of my wound. He was the one who would look after us all. It was a strange set-up. Perhaps because we all knew that it was transient and could disappear at any moment.

'Inevitably it came to an end. Marianne came in one day with the news that the British soldiers were only a few miles away. She took out a tattered Tricolore from one of the drawers, muttered fiercely over it and hung it from one of the windows.

'Lisette told us: "Her great-grandfather hung it there when the Germans came in 1870." It was fluttering from the window when we left. I said to Marianne: "I do not know how to thank you." She began to speak rapidly and Lisette translated: "She is happy to have you here. It is her duty to France . . . and she likes you."

'"We owe her our lives," I said. "We shall not forget."

'"When war is over, maybe you come back," she said.

'Violetta, you will come back with me? I want to show it to you.'

'We shall go together,' I said. 'And what about Buster?'

'He will want to see it again, I dare say.'

'The rest is predictable,' he continued. 'We joined the Army which was getting closer every day. Buster thought they'd want him to stay but they sent us both home. We had been all that time in a prison camp and they thought we should both be checked. They set in motion the necessary arrangements and we left. Before we did so, the army doctor had looked at my arm and did not much like what he saw. He said it had needed attention when it had happened. When we arrived in England, Buster went his way and I went mine. I am to report to Poldown Hospital without delay. So, here I am.'

'I still can't believe it.'

'Nor I. We'll go ahead with our plans, won't we?'

'Oh yes, Jowan.'

'And the war can't last much longer. We must be near the end. It will be as we planned it. We'll forget the years between.'

'We will.'

'You haven't thought of changing your mind?'

I laughed. 'No. I always believed you would come back. I could not have borne it otherwise. Others thought you never would, but your grandmother and I went on believing.'

'And I believed you would be waiting for me. That belief helped me through. I used to recall details of those meetings we had. Do you remember the first time at The Smithy's, all those years ago? And I thought of you, wondering . . . and there was no means of getting a word to you.'

'It's all over now. This wretched war has brought misery to millions. One man's mad dream and a deluded nation following him! Well, disaster is overtaking them now and we can only rejoice. But enough of that. Let's talk about ourselves.'

So we talked. He was not sure what his future would be. It might well be that he would rejoin his regiment.

'I wonder what happened to Buster?' he said. 'He must have been undernourished after those years in a prison camp, although his energy had not flagged in the least. They will soon discover.'

'You must ask him to our wedding,' I said.

'He would love that!' He looked blank and went on: 'Do you know, I haven't got his address. I could get in touch with him through the regiment, I suppose.'

'I should like to meet him.'

'He's a fine character. You'll be impressed.'

'He saved your life. That will be my main reason for liking him.'

And so we talked and planned.

Life was wonderful. When I went into the town, people rushed up to congratulate me. Gordon was very kind. I thought what a good man he was and remembered that, in the beginning, I had been suspicious of him. But in those days everything at Tregarland's had seemed uncanny.

Dorabella rang often. She said how happy she was for me. She knew what it was to be happy and she wanted the same for her twin sister. My parents were constantly in touch. They urged me to bring Jowan to Caddington, but they understood that that was not possible immediately. As soon as it was, we would come.

When Jowan reported to the hospital, they were a little grave about his arm. It needed special treatment and there might have to be an operation when he was considered fit to take it. In the meantime, there must be daily visits to the hospital and there would be no question of his rejoining his regiment just yet. I rejoiced in that.

Richard telephoned.

He had heard of Jowan's return.

He said: 'You were right. I never thought he would return. Are you happy now, Violetta?'

'Yes, Richard, I am.'

'Well, I must congratulate you.'

'Thank you.'

'I wish you great happiness and the best of luck. I hope everything goes well with you. If . . .' He paused for a few seconds. 'If, any time, you need me . . . if I can help . . . just let me know.'

'Thank you, Richard, I will,' I said.

That night I dreamed I was in the teashop near the Ministry and Richard's wife was sitting opposite me. She was smiling her cold smile, saying, "I want a divorce and I am citing you. You are very pleased with life, but what will this wonderful lover of yours have to say when he knows you are being cited in a divorce case?'

I awoke and sat up in bed. I felt a terrible foreboding.

Jowan would have to know. I had assured him I had waited for him and that never had I swerved in my fidelity to him. I had said that vehemently and he had assured me that it had been the same with him. And now it was very likely that Richard's wife would be granted a divorce because of her husband's alleged misconduct with Miss Violetta Denver.

I had recovered a little from the first shock of this revelation when Richard had told me what was happening. I had convinced myself that there would be no publicity which would affect me. Perhaps there would be a reference to it in some little-read gossipy publication – no more. I had been lulled into thinking this would be a trivial matter.

But it did not seem so now. All through the night I lay awake. What should I do? By the morning I had made my decision. There was only one way. I must tell Jowan.

He knew something was wrong. I could not stop thinking of that woman with her cold, calculating eyes.

I had driven Jowan into the hospital where they had examined and dressed his wound, and when I was taking him home, I went instead to that field where we had first met. I pulled up the car and we sat there.

'Tell me all about it,' he said. 'What's troubling you? Have you changed your mind? Are you going to tell me that you are having second thoughts about marrying the poor old invalid?'

I forced a laugh. 'I want to marry you more than anything. I have something to tell you, though.'

'I guessed that,' he said. 'Well, what is it?'

'It was when I was working at the Ministry with Mary Grace. Her brother is, of course, Richard Dorrington.'

I heard him take a deep breath and his manner changed slightly. He would remember the time when Richard had come to visit me in Cornwall and he knew that Richard had once asked me to marry him. That was before the war had started.

'I saw Richard now and then,' I went on quickly. 'He would have short leaves. Just a few hours sometimes. He knew that I was waiting for you. There was nothing but friendship between us. Someone lent him a flat and we used to go there, and usually I prepared a meal for him.'

'It sounds rather . . . intimate,' said Jowan.

'Richard always knew that there could be nothing but friendship between us.'

'I expect he hoped I wouldn't come back.'

'I want you to know that what I am telling you is the truth.'

'And what happened?'

'I was caught up in an air raid when we were in the flat together. Richard was hurt . . . not really badly, but badly enough to prevent his going to France for the landings which he would otherwise have done. Richard was married.'

'Married! But I thought . . .'

'So did we all. He had just kept it secret. She is a society girl and often mentioned in gossip columns. The marriage was a failure and they both wanted to be free of it. She was waiting because she thought he might go to France and not come back and that would be a way out of it for her. But when she heard he was not going, she decided to get her divorce in the quickest way possible. She is using the incident of the bombing to support the evidence that I was in the flat with him. You see, it was late in the evening. The fact is, she is divorcing him on a charge of adultery . . . and . . .'

'With you?' he said.

I felt a certain withdrawal and he murmured: 'Good Heavens!'

'It worried me,' I went on quickly. 'But Richard said it

would very likely go unnoticed. Before the war, the papers reported these cases in detail. It is different now.'

I was watching him closely and I could see a hint of doubt in his face.

I said vehemently: 'You must believe me. There was nothing. Nothing!'

He turned to me and kissed me fiercely. 'Violetta, my love . . . of course I believe you. And suppose there were . . . It was a long time, a long and weary time. I would have gone on loving you whatever you had done.'

My relief was intense. I had told him. It no longer seemed of any importance.

'Oh, Jowan!' I said. 'I love you so much! I could not bear it if anything went wrong now.'

'It can't if we won't let it.'

'But you believe me?'

'I believe you. Well, now that's over. You can smile again. We are here together, aren't we? We love each other too much to allow anything to upset that. We know what it means to have been separated and we will never allow that again.'

'Jowan, I am so thankful.'

He took my hands and kissed them. 'I don't think we should delay our wedding, do you?' he said. 'This wretched arm of mine will be cleared up soon, but we won't wait for that.'

'I don't want it cleared up until the war is finished,' I said.

We sat for a moment in silence; his arm was round me, holding me close to him.

Then he said: 'There was something that happened in France. As this is the time for confessions, I should tell you, I suppose. It is all rather vague, and I am not sure . . . but I'd like you to know.'

'You mean . . . ?'

'Let me explain. I told you about Marianne . . . I mean, the sort of woman she was. She had loved her husband dearly, but I doubt whether she had been entirely faithful to him. There was something earthy about her. She was motherly and deeply sensuous. I think Lisette would be the same. Marianne had a deep tenderness for men. She regarded them as little boys. There was a lot of the mother in her. I think the soldiers whom she had helped had comforted her in more ways than one. There was one night when my arm was particularly painful. I vaguely remember her dressing it for me; she settled me into bed, murmuring tender sympathy . . . and there she was, beside me, her arms round me, holding me tightly and kissing me to make the pain better, just as you hear mothers do with their children. It was a disturbed night. I was not sure whether I was dreaming. I kept thinking of you. I thought I was with you. I was only half aware. I thought that you were there beside me. I must have been delirious. Someone was there. I believed it was you . . . What happened during that night, I could not say. It may be that I was unfaithful to you . . . I was in that farmhouse . . . and there was this woman and, Violetta, I do not know . . .'

'Strange things can happen during wartime,' I heard myself say uncertainly.

'I cannot say,' he went on. 'I fancied she regarded me differently after that. I was never very sure about those nights of delirium. So often I thought you were there with me, and I remember the bitter disappointment when I awoke and found you were not. The longing was almost unbearable.'

We were both silent. It was difficult to find words. All I knew was that we must not look back. The war was going to be over. We would be happy. We were determined on that.

A Visitor from France

We were making preparations for our wedding. I had never seen Mrs Jermyn so pleased with life. She had seemed so much younger when she started the convalescent home and now, of course, her happiness was unbounded. Jowan was back and her dreams were coming true. I knew she was visualizing a wonderful life ahead with her great-grandchildren running round. She told me that, if she could have chosen a wife for her beloved grandson, I would have been that one.

We were a little emotional, still very much aware of our good fortune, and one day she said: 'I do believe that, if it had not been for this terrible war, I could not have been so happy as I am now, for it has all been brought home to me how precious life is, now that I realize how near I came to losing what I most cared for.'

Jowan's arm was getting better under treatment. There was still some way to go before it was completely well, but we were not going to delay our wedding for that.

Those were wonderful days. Each morning I awoke with a thrill of excitement. I was staying at Tregarland's in my old room, but I would be at the Priory every day. We still had a number of soldiers whom we were looking after, but there was an air of rejoicing everywhere, for the Germans were in retreat and the end could not be far off. The future looked dazzlingly bright to me.

It was late one afternoon. Jowan and I were in the solarium with Mrs Jermyn. She liked a cup of tea at this hour and for us to have it with her if possible. We were, of course, discussing the coming wedding when the maid came in to tell us that we had visitors.

'Who is it, Morwenna?' asked Mrs Jermyn.

'Well, ma'am, it's a Mr and Mrs Greenley seemingly. I've never seen 'em before. They's got a young girl with them. They do want to see Mr Jowan Jermyn, they said.'

'Well, you'd better bring them up. I don't know a Mr and Mrs Greenley, do you, Jowan?'

'Like Morwenna, I've never heard of them,' said Jowan.

'Well, let's see.'

When the trio were brought in, there was a cry of astonishment from Jowan.

He stood up and went towards them.

'Why . . . Lisette! What are you doing here?'

Lisette, her dark sloe-like eyes wide with pleasure and her thick black hair falling about her shoulders, cried: 'Jowan! Darleeng, I am here. I have come because . . .'

She hunched her shoulders and raised her eyes to the ceiling.

'And Mr and Mrs Greenley,' began Jowan.

'We've been living in France,' explained Mrs Greenley, 'since ten years or so before the war started. We couldn't get out until now. Lisette had to come, so we took her under our wing and promised her mother to bring her here.'

'And Lisette, why . . .' said Jowan. 'You . . . your mother . . . ?'

'She think it good I come. And Monsieur and Madame Greenley, they say we take. They are good.'

Jowan was clearly bewildered, and Mrs Jermyn said: 'You'd better sit down. Violetta, will you ring for more cups and perhaps some fresh tea?'

The Greenleys said they would not stay. They really had to get on.

'In the circumstances . . . we thought we should bring Lisette,' they said.

I had by this time noticed something about the girl. She was very young and there was that slight thickening of the figure. Could it really be that she was pregnant? If so, why had she come here? Perhaps her mother had thought it would not be good to have a child in present-day France, but why . . . ?

Lisette was explaining in her broken English. 'I am going to have a little baby.' She smiled dazzlingly at Jowan. 'Yours . . . and mine.'

There was silence in the room. Jowan was stricken with amazement. Mrs Jermyn had turned pale.

Then Mr Greenley said: 'Well, if you will excuse me, we'll be off. We promised Lisette's mother to bring her here and we have done so. Goodbye.'

I roused myself and said: 'I will show you down.'

Mrs Greenley turned to me when we had left the room and said: 'I think this is rather a shock to you. But, of course, the poor girl needs to be looked after, and it seems only right.'

'I think there must have been some mistake . . .'

'These things happen. Apparently the young man stayed at the farm. Marianne had been good to our men all through the war. She saved many of them from capture and imprisonment . . . death most likely. It is a poor reward to seduce the daughter. The girl is only sixteen. So it's only right that something should be done about it. Marianne was really distressed and, when Lisette said who was responsible, we thought the young man should be aware of it. So we promised to bring her with us . . . and, here she is.'

'This can't be true,' I insisted. 'It must be someone else.'

'She knew his name and where he lived. It seems it was so.'

I was glad when they had gone.

I went back to the solarium.

Jowan was saying: 'It's impossible, Lisette. You know it is. You know there was nothing . . .'

'Oh, but yes,' she insisted. 'You were ill and I come to comfort. And then I am in bed with you . . . all through the night. I am there . . . not one night only. I make you very 'appy. I did not think this would be, but it is . . .'

'It was *you*,' murmured Jowan disbelievingly.

'Yes . . . and we have the little baby. I say to my mother, "Jowan, 'e is rich man . . . good man. 'E will look after little baby." My mother say it not good to have a baby in France now. Not enough to eat . . . not good. There must be father for baby.'

Jowan was stricken, as we all were. Only a short while before we were thinking how happy we were. I could not believe it. And the girl was only sixteen. Yet he had been there. He had told me of that incident with the mother. It seemed it had not been the mother but the daughter.

And this was the result.

Our consternation and bewilderment were great. We could not believe this which had suddenly been thrust upon us. Jowan was astounded.

'It is not possible,' he kept saying. 'You cannot believe this.' But, remembering what he had told me, I thought it was just possible; and so did he.

Mrs Jermyn was practical about the matter.

She knew that Jowan had stayed at the farmhouse after his escape; she knew that this young girl had been there. Even she believed that it was possible.

She busied herself with details. The girl must be looked after. A room was made ready for her. If her story was true, we must do our duty by her, she said.

As for Lisette, she showed no great concern. It was clear that she was excited and was enjoying the situation in which she found herself. The house overlooking the sea was a delight to her. This was a great adventure.

'Thees beautiful 'ouse,' she said. 'This will be my baby's 'ome. Oh, darleeng Jowan, we will 'ave our little baby. He will be big and strong like you.'

She giggled a great deal and then I began to notice there was something strange in her attitude which mystified me. That frequent, high-pitched laugh – was it a little nervous? Once I found her laughing to herself and, when I looked closely, there were tears in her eyes.

I said: 'What are you laughing at, Lisette?'

'I laugh because I am 'appy. My baby will live in this *grande maison*. It is very good.'

'You are not really happy though, are you?' I insisted.

She looked scared for a moment.

'I very 'appy. It makes me 'appy to have my little baby who will live in this *grande maison*.' She added almost defiantly, 'That makes me 'appy.'

I wondered what was on her mind. She was too young to conceal her thoughts successfully. She was not yet seventeen. She would remember little of what it was like before the war, I guessed. It was now over five years since it had started. Children grew up quickly in such times. She would be wise in certain matters, though ignorant in other ways of life.

I felt sorry for her in spite of the trouble she was causing us. She alternated between moments of deep satisfaction and a certain desperation. At times she was like a sleek kitten, at others like a scared one – sophisticated in the extreme at times, and then childlike.

On more than one occasion I tried to probe her inner thoughts.

I said: 'You are not really happy, Lisette. You are worried about something.'

She opened those sloe-like eyes very wide and shook her head. Her protestations of her happiness were too vehement to ring entirely true.

Mrs Jermyn, deeply disturbed as she was, continued to make plans.

'What are we going to do about this child?' she said. 'It's a most extraordinary situation. The mother saved your life and the daughter is threatening to ruin it. But we won't let that happen. We shall look after her until the child is born and, if necessary, keep it. I think she has some idea of marrying you. Quite out of the question. We shall see that she is all right. Money, of course. She could go back to France and we will look after the child.'

I often thought how easy it was to settle other people's problems, and I am sure Mrs Jermyn knew that as well as anyone. As she spoke, she made it seem a simple matter. We would send Lisette back to France, compensated; and the child would remain and we would try to forget what Mrs Jermyn purposely called it, to give it less substance, 'this unfortunate matter'.

We were all miserable. Jowan could not bear to look at Lisette and every time he did so I could see the incredulity in his eyes. He must, however, accept the fact that it was just possible that, in a moment of oblivion, he might have become the father of Lisette's child; and yet he could not believe it. I could see that he must remind himself of those days and nights when he had lain in bed in that farmhouse and it was possible that Lisette had come to him . . . a shadowy figure . . . whom, when he had come out of his delirium, he had believed to be Marianne.

It could have happened as Lisette said, and there was to be a child. Nothing could alter that.

In the circumstances, we could not proceed with our wedding plans. We lived uneasily through those days.

It was difficult to know what steps had to be taken.

In the midst of all this, I heard from Richard. The divorce had gone through. It had all been accomplished speedily and unobtrusively as no objections had been raised and it was desired by both parties.

I need have no fear on that score.

It seemed of no great importance now.

•

One morning a letter from Buster Brown arrived. Jowan showed it to me. It was written in a large scrawl.

Dear Captain [it said],

Here I am and glad to get your letter at last. Must say, I'd like to see that home of yours. What a time we had, didn't we?

I'm at Lark Hill now. They're giving me duties at home for a while. I could come on Wednesday. Stay a couple of nights if that would be convenient to you. I expect you've got room for a little 'un.

It will be good to see you.

Your humble servant,

Buster Brown

Jowan was cheered at the thought of seeing him, though I could see he was thinking about the difficulty of explaining the situation regarding Lisette.

He drove to the station on the Wednesday morning and came back with Buster.

I ran down to meet them. Buster was exactly as Jowan had described him – of medium height, rather wiry, with dark hair and lively eyes, and a smile which made up for any other shortcomings. It appeared frequently and gave a comical look to his face which was endearing.

'You're Miss Violetta,' he said. 'Have to say I've heard about you.'

We took him into the hall. He gazed at the vaulted ceiling and his eyes ranged around. He stared in wonder at the tapestries on the walls.

'Blimey,' he said. 'Never seen nothing like that before.'

'They belonged to my ancestors,' said Jowan.

Buster was about to say something when Lisette appeared on the staircase. Buster stared at her and she at him. Buster opened his mouth, and I believe he controlled some expletive.

Lisette turned pale.

Then I heard her say in a somewhat stifled voice: 'Bustaire.'

She ran to him and flung herself at him.

'Here,' said Buster. 'Steady.'

'Oh, Bustaire . . . Bustaire,' she cried.

Buster held her tightly and gazed over her shoulder at Jowan.

'Lisette is staying here,' said Jowan.

Lisette was crying and laughing, clinging to Buster.

'You 'ave come,' she cried. 'I knew you come. You 'ave come for me.'

It was salvation.

Lisette had exhausted herself with emotion and we told her she must rest, for the sake of the child.

Buster explained to us what had happened.

'This is a real turn-up for the books,' he said. 'I come to see you, and find Lisette here.'

He went on: 'You know how it goes? We was there and she was young and the fruity sort. It was natural that we took to each other. We got up to tricks. Just human nature, after all. Then you and me went off. I often thought about her. Nice kid. Needs a bit of looking after, and I'm tickled pink about the little 'un.'

I realized that Buster had difficulty in taking life seriously.

'You see, sir,' he said to Jowan, 'this ain't none of your business.'

Jowan explained how Lisette had arrived with English people who had brought her from France with them.

'They were determined that justice should be done and she had told them I was the father of her child.'

'Cor, what a nerve! You wasn't never near her.'

'It was difficult. There were times when I had been unaware. There were times . . . Marianne . . .'

'She was a real one for coddling the boys. She had a way with her. Made you feel you was a little 'un again. She'd slip in beside you and give you a cuddle. True, she wouldn't be above a little bit of fun. But Lisette, no . . . she kept an eye on her. We had to pick our times, I can tell you. And we did.'

Buster looked rueful.

'I reckon that kid's mine,' he went on. 'Do you know, I rather fancy a nipper – half Lisette, half me. I reckon that's a mixture hard to beat. I've been thinking. It's time I tied myself up with a bit of trouble and strife and now, well, there would be this nipper . . .'

I found myself laughing spontaneously for the first time for weeks.

During Buster's two days' stay he made up his mind.

He was going to marry Lisette. He was fond of her. She was a 'dainty little piece', he said, and he'd look after her. Crafty little box of tricks, too.

'Coming over here like that and blaming you. Well, you can understand that. Just imagine how Marianne would have gone off when she heard. Frighten the life out of the kid. What'll the priest say, and all that. It's all right to have these little flings as long as there's no result. Poor kid! She knew a lot about you. Remember how you used to talk? Lapped it up, she did. She's told me she didn't know what to do. She never thought she could find me, so she hitched on to you. Well, I could do worse. I couldn't sleep at night if I let her down.'

We could not make enough of Buster. Mrs Jermyn took a great liking to him, apart from the fact that she regarded him as our saviour from a really very uncomfortable situation.

'You must come and see us when this wretched war is over,' she told him.

'I'll bring the wife and kid,' he said.

Mrs Jermyn made rapid plans. They should be married from the Priory. They could put up the banns and be married in three weeks.

'Then,' added Mrs Jermyn practically, 'Lisette's condition would not be so very noticeable.'

They could have their honeymoon at the Priory.

She was so grateful to Buster for appearing when he did – like the god out of the machine – that she wanted to shower him with blessings. She forgave Lisette for her deception because she knew what a desperate position she must have been in; she was only a child; and it was so fortunate that that nice Buster had come along and sorted the whole thing out.

It was an incongruous relationship between her and Buster, but they seemed to understand each other and she was immensely entertained by his method of expressing himself.

As for Jowan and me, life had become wonderful again.

There was a double wedding in February of that triumphant year of 1945. Jowan and I were to have a week's honeymoon in Devon while Lisette and Buster were guests of Mrs Jermyn.

It was all rather amusing, and to crown it all the papers were writing about the final defeat of Germany and our Prime Minister was going to meet President Roosevelt and Marshal Stalin at a conference in Yalta.

It was a wonderful honeymoon, more so because of the ordeals through which we had passed to reach it. The weather was somewhat wintry but we were together. There was a new hope in the world. No longer did we have to listen to the warning wails of the sirens. In his inimitable manner, Field Marshal Montgomery had told his men that we had our opponent where we wanted him and he would now receive the knock-out blow.

There was no doubt that the end of our tribulations, suffering and anxiety was coming.

In May of that year Lisette's baby was born. Buster was very proud and excited. He and Lisette were in London now where they had set up house. Buster was still in the Army, of course, but he was planning to resume his calling as an electrician as soon as he was free to do so.

They had a little flat and Buster was getting plenty of time off because he was a newly married man and no more men were being sent overseas. The war in Europe was over.

They were very proud of their baby, a little girl who had been named Victoria. She was born in victory and it seemed appropriate.

I cannot describe the feeling of contentment that was with me at that time. Only those who have lived through those six years could understand that.

I shall never forget that day in the May of 1945. People gathered in the streets and among them at Buckingham Palace we saw the King and Queen with the Princesses on the balcony. The Prime Minister, addressing the crowds in Whitehall, declared: '*In our long history, we have never seen a greater day than this.*'

Jowan and I walked back to our hotel together. The nightmare was over. The long days of waiting for Jowan were past. We were together and the future looked good.